# Haven't Stopped
# Dancing Yet

SCEPTRE

# Haven't Stopped Dancing Yet

## SHYAMA PERERA

SCEPTRE

Copyright © 1999 Shyama Perera

First published in 1999 by Hodder and Stoughton
A division of Hodder Headline PLC
A Sceptre Book

The right of Shyama Perera to be identified as the Author of
the Work has been asserted by her in accordance with the
Copyright, Designs and Patents Act 1988.

10 9 8 7 6 5 4 3 2 1

A CIP catalogue record is available from the British Library.

ISBN 0 340 72820 5

Typeset by Palimpsest Book Production Limited,
Polmont, Stirlingshire
Printed and bound in Great Britain by
Clays Ltd, St Ives plc, Bungay, Suffolk

Hodder and Stoughton
A division of Hodder Headline PLC
338 Euston Road
London NW1 3BH

For my mother, Mallika,
with love and gratitude.

# PERMISSIONS ∫

*1*

My mother has two hundred hankies, neatly ironed, in one of her drawers; yet she sniffs, all the time. Sinus. Always, one is packed in her handbag – for my use, for her friends' use, perhaps even for your use – but never hers. And always it's the yellow or blue checked ones, the least attractive of her collection, as if the prettiest are on stand-by for some divine calling. Perhaps they're for waving in times of distress – but in that case, two hundred is barely enough.

Like marker flags, the pattern or embroidery on each little square represents a pivotal point in my mother's life: in our lives. So many memories tightly folded away, and one day I will take charge of them and shake them out. And dust away the cobwebs.

Four little girls in a Paddington playground. Four rounds of free dinners, four different social workers, four strains of problem family. It is 1966 and only one has a bag of sweets – and I wasn't going to be her friend unless she gave me one: Caroline.

It was just the usual mid-morning scrap. I'd guzzled my penny tea cake, Bethany's digestive was digested and Janice was looking on sullenly because her break money had gone in the Mitre the night before. In fact, her dad still wasn't home. Caroline was the only one with the goods; but like waiting for the communion wafer, you'd be down on your knees before she'd part with a fruit chew, and when it was finally, grudgingly, handed over, it was gone in moments.

Now we were having to squirm and wheedle our way into her favour: promising to pick her at games, offering to drink the remains of her curdling school milk, even to mind her mother's washing while she went off to play with the others. All this for a flying saucer!

'Oh go on, Caroline,' I whined. 'You can't eat them all your-self.'

'Yes I can, Mala, just not at this very minute.'

'Then share them,' Bethany said.

'Why should I?'

'Because we're your friends.'

'And I'll drink your milk for you,' I reminded her.

We were standing in a circle under the dragon mural on the playground wall – last year's art project already smudged from endless games of two-balls.

Somewhere outside on a tinny transistor the Kinks were singing 'Sunny Afternoon' above the descant of the juniors' latest clapping game: Under the bramble, under the tree, true love for you, my darling, true love for me.

But love was never enough to swing an argument with Caroline, and while she made a point of thinking carefully, Janice said to nobody in particular: 'Of course, I'll be doing *our* laundry today anyway, so I could easily mind a couple of extra machines.'

'What about you, Bethany?' Caroline snapped. 'Promise to pick me first for the rounders team?'

'I said I would, didn't I?'

'All right, then.'

As usual, the bag was passed round as the bell went, and we hastily stuffed our mouths, anxious to swallow before our swollen cheeks brought upon us the humiliation of spitting out into scraps of sugar paper.

'Why does she make us beg?' Bethany muttered as we filed in.

'They're her sweets.'

'We always share what we've got, Mala. She should too.'

'We've had them now: what does it matter?'

'I'll have to choose her for rounders, that's what, and she's useless.'

I nodded sympathetically, and gave thanks in my head that I was milk monitor that morning and could tip the remains of Caroline's rancid half-pint down the sink.

\*　　\*　　\*

Other people grew up to a Beatles soundtrack – or the Monkees, depending on their level of sophistication. But we grew up to a cheap-sweet chant: 'Fruit-salads-black-jacks-sherbert-dabs-flying - saucers - chocolate - tools - love - hearts - parma - violets-TWIZZLERS.' While little boys sat on walls marvelling at BOAC jets leaving trace-lines in the ether, we carved up fudge bars in worshipful wonder and argued over whose turn it was to suck the gobstopper. Bethany and Janice even came to blows over a Lucky Bag the morning the blue salt twist in Caroline's crisps burst in her mouth. 'Why are you laughing, Mala?' she asked crossly.

'Because I'm happy.'

'Happy that I've got a mouthful of salt?'

'No. Happy because this is the best year I've ever had. I'm eight. I've got a Sindy. And I'm going away during the holidays.'

'You're really going?' Janice sounded envious.

'Yep. My mum's got the fifteen bob.'

The head had signed me up for a Children's Country Holiday with a host family, but first my mum had to pay something towards it. She'd made the finishing line just in time.

'You'll both enjoy the rest, Mrs Fonseka,' the official said as I queued to be checked for lice, TB and other unpleasantnesses at the fund's medical centre. 'At least you'll know she's safe for two weeks of the summer. I don't suppose you have baby-sitters?'

But of course she did. She had Janice Connors, Bethany Stephens and Caroline Chong – although she disapproved of the lot.

'They're a rascally crew of ragamuffins,' my mother said. 'Why do you have to go loafing with them?'

'What else could I do?'

'Come home and read.'

'But I'd be lonely on my own.'

Anyway, by the time she returned from work, exhausted from hours on her feet folding fresh linen in the bowels of the Grosvenor House Hotel, I was back in our room – curled up on the double bed listening to *The Clitheroe Kid* or *Round the Horne* on the Home Service.

Sometimes I walked down to Lancaster Gate Tube station and waited for her to emerge from the crowded lifts – small, fair-skinned, hidden under yards of sari and a black cardigan, even on the hottest day. 'You shouldn't cross big roads on your own,' she'd scold, but she was smiling as we walked back arm in arm.

Fresh from the Commonwealth, we'd arrived in London full of ambition and purpose just four years previously, but my mother was still cranking up the dream machine when my father decided to die, leaving us alone, alienated and paying four guineas a week to live in one room in Craven Hill Gardens.

There one day, gone the next. All trace of him removed as if he'd packed for heaven: clothes, photographs, shaving brush, Brylcreem. This great brown hope, making a new life for us, and all that remained of him was an old Grundig tape with 'The Banana Boat Song', 'Volare', and a recording of me crying. It was worthless: we had nothing to play it on.

The high points of our new life, so vividly outlined by my mother on the P&O *Chusan*, had been dashed for ever by a man I had then not seen for nearly two years. Even as we disembarked at Tilbury that dismal November day, he'd been less than enthusiastic: 'I don't know why you've come – I told you. This is not a country for families.'

As we came into London and passed the imposing houses and hotels on Lancaster Gate, our hopes rose. Close to cobbled mewses full of sports cars, we drew up outside the handsome but peeling four-storey home he'd rented in Craven Hill Gardens. My mother squeezed my hand. But inside it was a rooming house like the rest, and our room on the top floor measured twelve by eight. Within weeks we had frozen pipes and unusable toilets. Disaster. 'How the mighty fall,' my mother muttered behind his back.

Much later I realised he was already ill when he met us: what else could explain his sudden demise? How rotten he must have felt, I thought, leaving us unprepared, inexperienced and broken-hearted in a cold country where the winter smog confused our eyes. A country for which my mum's colonial education had not equipped her: 'I learned Wordsworth, Mala, not domestic science.' A country where we knew nobody and became nobodies.

'It doesn't matter,' my mother said. 'These things are only temporary. One day our karma will change.'

But I didn't mind – as I told our social worker.

'Everything's brilliant, Mrs Brown. I'm very happy. I've even stopped wetting the bed.'

'That's very good news, Mala.'

'So it must mean I don't miss him any more.'

'Well, you'll always miss him, but you're being adult about it.' She looked at my mother. 'That must be a relief.'

My mother, who said as little as possible to Mrs Brown, nodded; but I'd heard her discussing it much more openly with my Aunty Mina, who was a nurse and had given us some old linen with 'Hammersmith Hospital' stamped on it.

'It's getting better,' my mother said, 'now only once a night.'

'What does the doctor say?'

'Always the same – that the child is unsettled. It's been very difficult, Mina. We have only one set of sheets. Before your help I was using towels – even saris. Sometimes it was three times a night. All that washing – see how the flesh of my hands is swollen and cracked.'

'Can't you run her to the toilet when she starts?'

'Mina, the toilet is two floors down.'

And we shared the toilet and bath with the occupants of thirteen other cramped rooms. My mother had enough problems without starting the battle of the bedpan!

But the spare sheets weren't needed any more, and Mrs Brown duly noted the good news on her standard form.

Afterwards I quizzed my mother: 'Mum, because you didn't wet the bed after Daddy died, does it mean you didn't care?'

'Of course I cared.'

'But you didn't show it.'

'Adults have different ways of expressing themselves.'

'Like what?'

'Like feeling sad.'

'But I felt sad too, and I still wet the bed.'

'Well . . . adults have mature functions.'

'What does that mean?'

'It means that we have better bladder control.'

'What's bladder control?'

A pained look crossed my mother's face. 'It means that, unlike children and animals, adults don't need to spray to mark important points along the route.'

Sometimes, I just couldn't understand my mum – for example, her objections to Bethany, especially since they shared a love of hankies. The Stephens's basement home was next to the old linen shop on Craven Terrace, and Bethany and I spent ages choosing between the embroidered sixpenny specials in the window before clattering down the stairs to the gloom of her flat and the smell of the 4711 Mrs Stephens was always dabbing at her temples.

There was a bathroom mysteriously hung with drying girdles and a kitchenette behind louvre doors where a large tin of lemon puffs was lodged in silent welcome for small visitors. Of all the mums, Bethany's was the most generous.

Now we filled our hands to overflowing and sat down on the vinyl sofa in a vapour of crumbs. Beyond the plain tile fireplace the faded sheet that partitioned off Mrs Stephens's bed from prying eyes was open. 'My mum's sleeping in my room,' Bethany whispered.

Bethany's room was like a cupboard, but Mrs Stephens liked it for daytime naps, leaving us free to sit at her kidney-shaped dressing table, admiring our profiles in the three-way mirror and talking like grown-ups about cocktail parties, cigarettes and Harold Wilson. But today there were more pressing interests.

'You'll be going soon, Mala.'

'Four weeks tomorrow.'

'Are you excited?'

'Of course. I'm going on a mainline train from Paddington.'

'That's how my mum came here from the seaside.'

'Did she?' I wondered if it was the sea which called to Mrs Stephens: an invisible shell swishing in her ear. She was often distracted – like the woman in the new Beatles song: Look at her waiting, holding the face that she keeps in a jar by the door.

'They're sending me to a farm.'

'With real animals and everything?'

'I think so. What else do they have on farms?'

'Tractors?' She shrugged. 'You'll miss us, Mala.'

I took another biscuit. 'I know, but my mum says it's better that I'm off the streets, even if it's only for a little bit.'

'But you're not on the streets. You can come here.'

'She hates me coming here, Bethany, you know that.'

'Why?'

'I've told you – because your mum doesn't have any books.'

'Why should she?'

'Because she's a teacher.'

Bethany's mother had a card up in the newsagent's window offering French lessons from home. But it was true that they didn't have books, I'd never come across any of Mrs Stephens's pupils either, which was strange – because they formed the second part of my mother's objections.

Only Caroline's home, where the golden triangle of Paddington, Bayswater and Queensway merged in a haze of chip fat and pee on the communal balconies of the Hallfield estate, met with motherly approval. Mr and Mrs Chong worked in a Chinese restaurant near the ice rink and were considered respectable. This was probably why, I often thought, they guarded their sparely furnished flat so zealously – muttering angrily in Cantonese if we talked too loudly or stayed too long. But today we had no choice. We were rained in by a summer storm and Janice was squirming under scrutiny. 'Do they think we're going to nick something?'

'They don't want you to break anything,' Caroline said.

As Mrs Chong exited, Janice sulked around the room. 'All you've got is calendars from the Peking Inn restaurant and a couple of Jesuses – how could we break those?'

'The word, Janice Connors, is not Jesuses, but crucifixes.' The informed voice from behind the curtain made us all jump. 'It's a term you ought to know, given your background.'

Josh Chong emerged from the thin cotton furls at the window like Dr Who. Fourteen years old and effortlessly superior, he'd again caught us in a net of clever words. Now, as he grinned, I felt hot around the neck, but Janice sensed an insult and challenged: 'What d'you mean?'

'I mean that most Irish Catholics can recognise a crucifix.'

She looked confused. My heart sank on her behalf. The Connors weren't exactly God-fearing in the way Mr Day, the local curate, described the righteous at weekly assembly. Or, indeed, in the way of the Chongs, who went to church on Sunday mornings and always sent a loaf for the school harvest festival. Misery: Josh, as usual, had managed to take us right off track.

Now he turned to me. 'I hear you're off on holiday, Mala.' I stared at the ground, waiting. 'Where are you going?'

'To the countryside.'

'Where in the countryside?'

Where? Wasn't it all one place? I made a face.

He laughed. 'One doesn't know where she's from and the other doesn't know where she's going. I hope you're better informed than that little sister?'

But before Caroline could answer, Mrs Chong called them to the kitchen for dinner.

'He's such a bighead,' Janice said, 'just because he's clever. When I'm his age I'll know lots of things too.' She picked up Josh's grammar school photo. 'Aren't they funny in long trousers?' But I thought Josh, in his navy blazer and slacks, thick black beatnik hair and devil-may-care grin, was the most handsome boy in the photo. I traced round his face with a stubby finger.

'Handsome fellow, eh, Mala?'

Again he'd arrived silently, this time from behind us. Startled, I dropped the picture on to the lino and a corner of the cardboard frame bent. Josh picked it up. 'You see, this is why she watches you all the time.' Putting his face within an inch of mine he put on his mother's voice and said something horrid in Chinese: 'Fu Manchu.' Janice and I ran for our lives.

We could still hear his laughter as we clattered across the puddled balcony and down the stairs, heading for the Connors midden on Westbourne Terrace.

As we entered, the maisonette throbbed with a life of its own. In the lounge Mr Connors was watching the telly with his greyhounds. We found Mrs Connors in the noisy nicotine fug of the kitchen, bristling in her nylon housecoat: 'I'm sick of the lot of you.' She yanked the dishcloth from the baby's neck and turned the radio up as he started crying. Janice and I grinned at each other, creeping upstairs to escape Sean's wails and Marie's continuous whine. A dog had been sick on the landing.

Sometimes, before he became a teddy boy and got sent to Borstal for his part in the big knife fight outside the Great Western Hotel, Janice's big brother Eamonn had let us pace the dogs with him along the terraces of Paddington, down Spring Street and across Sussex Gardens, where he leered at the old pros. Sometimes we ran them alongside the Serpentine, part of a family in perpetual motion. Now Mrs Connors was shouting: 'What's the bloody point of these dogs? They never win.'

My mum said they never would: 'Animals take after their masters, Mala. The industrious farmer has an industrious herd; the lazy farmer has to wake his cows in the morning.'

My mum and I met Mr Connors every now and then when he was coming back from the pub in Craven Terrace. Sometimes he'd stop and tell us a story. Like his joke about the little boy who was walking down the street singing 'The blacks have got the houses'.

God stops him: 'That's not a very nice thing to sing, little boy. Don't you know about Jesus?'

'Yes,' says the boy.

'And where was Jesus born?'

'In a stable.'

'Why?'

'Because the blacks have got the houses.'

I'd thought this very funny, but my mother's mouth was like a bulldog clip as she walked away without comment. I told Janice the joke now and we giggled in the crowded bedroom: 'He's always telling jokes like that. He doesn't like immigrants.'

'Immigrants?'

'Black people. Asian people: like your mum.'

'What's wrong with her?'

'There's nothing wrong with her, he just doesn't like them – he doesn't much like anyone, come to think of it.' She shook off her wet shirt and pulled on a grubby cardigan lying on the corridor of floor between the bunks and Allie's carefully arranged single bed. 'I don't even think he likes us, some-times.'

Janice's window looked out on to a wall. It was always cold, whatever the weather. I shivered. 'I'm starving.'

'Me too. There's nothing downstairs. Shall we go to yours?'

I shook my head. My mother complained that Janice ate more with us than with her own family. She needed a break. I prayed for a miracle and my prayer was answered by Allie, creeping in in a white raincoat and brightly patterned headscarf, a pair of stilettos in her hand. Seeing us, she put a finger to her lips and, shutting the door, whispered: 'I don't want the old bat to know I'm here or I'll get lumbered minding Sean.'

'Where are you going, Allie?'

'Up Church Street.'

'Can we come?'

'If you like. It's stopped raining.'

We watched as she shook out her beautiful white hair and brushed it so the little dark bits near the scalp were hidden under cascading candy-floss strands. She ran her hands down the side of her body, as if to check it felt as good as it looked.

'You're just like Diana Dors,' I said admiringly, and she chuckled: 'Come on, if you're coming.'

We walked past houses being demolished for the new fly-over, and crossed Paddington Green to Church Street market, haloed by a rainbow, and busy busy busy as we burrowed past gesticulating greengrocers and gossiping women, past the blaring cart selling cut-price records – 'Summer In The City', the Lovin' Spoonful – to the stall where Allie's boyfriend sold car-cleaning kits. Janice whispered: 'Stick close and we'll get some money,' but I already knew the form and was limpet-like around Allie's endless legs.

'Hey, kids, here's half a crown – go off and enjoy yourselves.'

'Thanks, Barry.'

We took the money, leaving them to prod, poke and tease each other, and bought apple fritters from the van at the corner of Lisson Street: sweet, hot, floury. Sheltering in the entrance to Tesco's, I gave thanks for the laws of gravity and brevity which together had provided such unexpected delights.

*     *     *

I loved Allie and I said so. Caroline sniffed. 'You must be a lesbian, then.'

'What's a lesbian?'

'It's a woman who likes other women.'

'Then you must be a lesbian, Caroline,' Bethany retorted, 'because you like us.'

We were sitting by the fountains in the Italian Gardens in Hyde Park, letting the spray cool our faces, overheated from vigorous after-school games of hide-and-seek amongst the giant weeping willows. It was the last day of term, and next year we'd have a new teacher – Miss Ampley – who was young and wobbled inside her twinsets, especially when the music master walked by. I said: 'I bet Miss Ampley isn't a lesbian.'

Caroline didn't respond. Instead she jumped up and ran into the trees. 'Last person up is "it"!'

Bethany and I were still panting on the walk home. 'Where d'you think Caroline learns all that lesbian stuff?' I asked.

She frowned. 'Josh, I suppose.'

'It must be great to have a brother or sister.'

'I had a sister. My mum found her in the cot one morning, all stiff. She wouldn't stop screaming.'

'The baby?'

'No, my mum. She'd been out all night, working.'

'That's horrible!' She nodded. 'Don't you miss her?'

'I don't think so. I was only four.'

'That must be why your mother's so sad.'

'She said she'd been punished by God.'

'For what?'

'For trying her best.'

'Why would she be punished for trying her best?'

'Because her best wasn't good enough.'

'Like you.'

'Yes, like me.'

We both laughed and I went on my way. At school, Bethany's written work was atrocious but she always claimed she was doing her best and Mrs Frinton always replied: 'In your case, Bethany Stephens, best is not good enough.'

The next night, my mum had a little party for me. My aunties

Mina and Prisky grabbed the chairs; Anu and Seeli sat on our bed, and Uncle Oliver, who arrived with chocolates, lounged on the floor alongside, where he was teased about his haircut and news from home that his parents were vetting potential wives: 'So London's most eligible bachelor is to lose his liberty?'

'What nonsense you women talk!' But he was smiling.

'I hear your mother is having the reception at the Galle Face Hotel – no expense spared.'

'Have you nothing better to think about?'

'Is it true, Uncle Oliver?'

'It's absolute rubbish, Mala – I hope you'll find better ways of employing your mind when you're an adult.'

The women sniggered.

In the corner by the window, my mother was heating curries on the two-ring electric stove and the smell of cooking deliciously permeated every inch of space. Most of my aunties were primary school teachers in central London, and now they turned their attentions to me: what was I reading, what arithmetic could I do, was the class project on the Bayeux Tapestry completed?

Anu picked up my globe from the mantelpiece: 'Show me France,' but thankfully, at that moment, the peach wine came out. 'Trying to get me drunk, Oliver?'

'No, Anu, trying to distract your mouth.'

Mum poured me half an inch of the rich, sweet liquid. 'Here's to you, Mala – happy holiday.' Everyone raised their glasses.

In our home all adults were aunties or uncles.

'Are they really relations?' Caroline asked.

'No, but they're just like family.'

'So they're not all your granny's children?'

'I don't think so, Janice.'

Oliver often took me to the cartoon cinema in Baker Street and Mina, Nita and Mum were going to see *Dr Zhivago* in my absence.

'I could happily marry Omar Sharif.'

'But could he happily marry you, Mina?'

Dinner arrived on rose-patterned plates. 'That child has a good appetite.'

'You must exercise while you're away, Mala.'

'It's healthy that she eats.'

'Ranji's child doesn't eat a thing. She looks like a Biafran.'

'Have you heard the latest from there?'

And then, thankfully, the spotlight was off me and on to more important matters until Prisky announced she wanted coffee. In the winter we kept milk cold on the windowsill, but now I was despatched to the Milko machine in the humid ten o'clock twilight.

On the way back, I passed Bethany's. I could see shadows dancing behind the curtain: a man and a woman. Curious, I stopped, and heard the faint strains of an old song: Perry Como, 'Catch A Falling Star' and put it in your pocket. In my hand the half-pint carton was getting squashed out of shape. I ran home, climbing the four flights two steps at a time. The grown-ups were spooning ice cream and tinned peaches into glass bowls.

'Ah, there you are, Mala, just in time.'

And then it was morning, and my bag was packed and my mother was in tears, and we walked together to the meeting point at Paddington Station where a little badge saying CCHF Worcester and with my name printed on it was fixed to my cardigan. A taxi driver, coming out of the traffic tunnel into the mainline station, stopped to give the officials a fiver because 'I was one of them once, and it done me a power of good'.

Our little group of twenty said our goodbyes and were marched off in pairs to the platform entrance by smart ladies who spoke kindly in posh voices. I was mute with excitement: my heart was beating so hard I could feel it through my shirt. Then I heard my name being shouted by familiar voices.

Bethany: 'Mala! Turn round. We've come to say goodbye.'

Janice: 'Bye, Mala! You're so lucky . . . don't forget us.'

Caroline: 'We'll see you when you come back – if you're not too grand for us after your country holiday.'

Bethany again: 'She couldn't get any grander than you, Caroline Chong, so leave off!'

And as they jostled and argued, my heart sank, and where, a few minutes earlier, I'd been all set for my new adventure, I now felt great sadness that I'd be stuck in a field of sheep while my wonderful friends loafed around Hyde Park and Bayswater, sharing sweets and secrets in the sunshine for a large chunk of the summer.

2 ∫

On my return, only my mother was there. 'You're looking so well, little one – so brown and healthy. I've missed you.'

'And I've missed you.' But not very much.

'Your letters were so full of adventures.'

And all were true: picnics and paddling in the Wye Valley; games of hide-and-seek in the biggest house I'd ever seen; flapjacks in the kitchen; lemonade mixing in the garden; and for those lucky enough to early-rise, a chance to milk the cows in the shed and carry the jugs warm and creamy to the breakfast table. Sitting in the sunshine in a stubbly field, watching the men harvesting, I'd been in another world. I felt flat to be home again – and not one of my friends had come to meet me.

That afternoon I found Bethany sitting on the wall outside the estate agent's in Craven Terrace. 'You've come back, then?' She sucked on a strand of curly blond hair. 'I thought you'd try and stay longer. So did your mum.'

'Is that what she said?'

'It's what you said, isn't it? She showed me one of your letters.' I sat next to her in deep gloom, not chipper enough to fight my way out of her accusation. 'Did you miss us at all?'

'Of course I did: I wish you'd have come too.'

'You'll have some explaining to do: Caroline's really mad. She thinks you've gone all lah-di-dah.'

'I've only been away two weeks.'

'Grace Kelly became a princess in an afternoon.'

But I couldn't be Grace Kelly because, I realised as I grew older, there were no princes in Paddington, and by the next summer

I was prepared for the ribbing I'd get on my return from Enid Blyton country.

Instead of being drawn into exposing myself for ridicule, I poured my energy into loafing and scoffing. Caroline still managed to turn Janice and Bethany against me a few times, but before we knew it, school was upon us again. Anyway, Caroline had enough problems of her own: Josh Chong, who'd taken O-levels a year early, was learning the hard way that success does not confer celebrity.

'They call him the "Chinky swot",' she said. 'They make silly jokes about *The Teahouse at the August Moon*.'

'The restaurant on Lancaster Gate?'

She picked up a conker. 'No – the stage show.'

We were in Hyde Park. The flat acres of green had turned almost overnight into a shimmering slither of golds and browns. Our anorak pockets laden with nature's collectables, Caroline and I walked up Rotten Row because it was less slippery, jumping off the dirt track when riders reared up behind us. There was a smoky bonfire residue in the air, intensified by a fine shower that descended as we crossed the Serpentine Bridge and headed for the Albert Memorial. We pulled up our hoods, defying the elements from the cosy warmth of our nylon helmets.

'I love the spring rolls at the August Moon, but I wish the manager didn't make us wait outside.'

'This isn't about food, Mala.'

'No. Have you any glacier mints left?'

She pulled a fluff-covered sweet from her pocket. 'He's locking himself in his room for hours. He just stares out of the window.'

We came to the statue and started up the steps as a young couple stopped to kiss with open mouths. 'Disgusting!' Probably European tourists, I thought, they're always fiddling with each other on buses and things. Why travel if you never look up?

'These Westerners and their "free love",' my mother said. 'Don't be fooled by it, Mala. Free love, heavy price.'

'But I'm only nine and a half, Mum.'

'Where has it got Mrs Stephens?'

'Does she believe in free love?'

A hesitation. 'Well, yes, but you have to pay.'

'So she's not free, she's expensive?'

From the top of the memorial, we looked down on to the midweek traffic of Kensington Gore. Immediately in front of us, the Royal Albert Hall sat in squat spherical splendour, dull yellow lights winking at its windows. Outside were posters of a girl in a swimsuit: Eric and Julia Morley proudly present the 1967 Miss World Contest!

'My Uncle Oliver's going to that next month, sitting in a box.'

'Can't he afford a seat?'

'He's got a seat, Caroline, but the seat's in a box.'

'I don't see the point.'

'The point is a box costs more. That's what.'

She shrugged. 'I don't know what we're going to do with him.'

'You don't even know him!'

'Not your uncle: Josh. He's driving us all bonkers.'

'He's not doing anything wrong.'

'But he's not doing anything right, either.'

The shorter afternoons had that sort of effect. My mother was boiling saucepans of disgusting herbal brews sent from home to help fight flu and bronchitis; and in Westbourne Terrace, war was finally declared.

We were playing jacks on the pavement, so we couldn't miss it when the window opened and the black smoke belched out. 'You stupid bitch, you'll kill us all!'

'Don't speak to me like that, Con.'

'The dogs are *choking*.' The sound of a scuffle. 'Don't even try it, Stell.'

'Try and stop me.'

A bowl of meat marked 'Pooch' came flying out of the window followed seconds later by Mrs Connors' Blue Grass perfume, which shattered aromatically on the concrete. 'Swine!' Fierce barking and shouting followed. Hastily we gathered up our game but were stopped from leaving by Allie, who ran outside and thrust the babies at us. 'It's a bloody madhouse. The old cow's burnt the chips. *Again.* One day they'll kill each other. I'll try and calm things down.'

Now three voices were raised:

'Bitch.'

'Swine.'

'Please, Mum, please, Dad, the whole bloody neighbourhood can hear you – don't embarrass us.'

'Don't you use that language in this house, Allie Connors.'

'I only said bloody.'

'See how you're dragging them up – you fat cow.'

'Get out of here.' Mrs Connors started screaming. 'Get out of here: you miserable BASTARD.' Outside we gasped and I clapped my hands around Marie's ears. 'My mother was right, Con Connors – you're no use to anyone! If it wasn't for me this bloody house would fall apart.'

'It already has, you stupid mare.'

A pouch of Old Holborn emerged through the smoke in a final act of defiance. Mr Connors bellowed, Allie cried out and someone got slapped. A man walked by, whistling: 'Silence Is Golden'.

Inside, there was pandemonium. Seconds later Mr Connors came striding down the steps, his florid face steamed purple by the acrid kitchen heat. Stopping only to take in our little tableau and shout: 'Bloody women, bloody kids, bloody blacks,' he strode off into an orange sunset, the dogs forming an orderly line of trotting boniness behind him.

Janice looked across at me, blue eyes misted, and I smiled; but I slunk silently home, almost grateful to drink the coriander water my mother had made in her zealous attempt at mucus control; at least she didn't show me up in front of my mates. As I went to sleep that night, I wondered how Janice could bear it.

The Connors were the only parents who rowed. Well, apart from the Chongs, they were the only full set we knew.

'Where's your dad, Bethany?'

'I don't know.'

'What does he do?'

'You've asked this before, Mala.' She waited as I sprinkled vinegar on my chips. 'I haven't really got a dad.'

We left Micky's fish bar and joined Caroline and Janice against the railings of the Hallfield estate. My Aunty Anu's flat was further up the same road, Inverness Terrace, and I'd be returning later to bow and scrape round some visiting elderly dignitary who was sleeping on the put-you-up and demanded fresh meat for every meal. But right now the day stretched unpromisingly before us. 'You must have a dad, Bethany, ladies only get babies from lying next to a man.'

Bethany shrugged and the others perked up at the prospect of some personal embarrassment. 'My mum'd rather not remember him.' She crumpled up the empty chip paper. 'It really doesn't matter as he's not here.'

'Of course it matters – your father is a part of you.'

'Well, I'll never know which part, will I, Caroline?'

'I think it's your legs,' I said. That morning Bethany had entered the dancing competition at Saturday morning pictures, strutting crazily to 'Even The Bad Times Are Good'. 'You're a great dancer. I bet your dad had long bendy legs.'

'For running away on,' Caroline leered.

Janice blew on cold fingers. 'I hope I haven't got my dad's legs, all hairy and knotted with veins.'

We all laughed, and, inside, I gave silent thanks that I had the best of both worlds: a known but absent father.

When angry with me, my mother often said: 'If only your father were here to control you, Mala. You wouldn't dare treat him as you treat me.' It seemed to me that fathers generally were like Captain Von Trapp. And there was only one Maria.

I said as much to Caroline as we left the others and went back to her flat, but she just said: 'You don't have to do what they tell you, you just have to pretend you will.'

Inside she got out pencils and paper: part of a hopeful weekly ritual initiated since I'd won ten bob for having a letter printed in *Diana*. Thinking of possible subject matter, I scratched my ear with one of the wooden toothpicks that were always lying around.

'Where d'you get all these?'

'From the restaurant where my parents work.'

'But you've got hundreds – doesn't the boss notice?'

'They're only bits of wood.'

'From China?'

'I suppose so.'

'Imagine spending your life making little bits of wood.'

Josh, wandering into the lounge crumpled and distracted from continued exile in his bedroom, jumped at this: 'How does it happen, do you suppose, Mala, that the world's third-oldest civilisation now supplies the West with waiters, toothpicks and transistor radios? Is that what we call progress?' He circled, laughing wildly at our blank faces. I shivered with happiness. Bending down, he pinched my cheek playfully. 'Think of it, Mala – your ancestors and mine were reading and writing and building palaces when the people of this country were still wearing animal skins – yet look at us now.'

'Ignore him,' Caroline whispered, but I was too busy feeling the heat of my cheek where he had touched it, and wondering how many dogs it would take to make a trouser suit.

Later I returned to Queensway with Mum, stopping at Mac-Fisheries, where live eels wriggled in white tubs on the pavement outside and peppermint Matchmakers were on special offer. We bought airmails at the Post Office and, in Woolworths, the Stanley Gibbons facsimile stamps I'd been promised all week. On the pavement the blind accordion player was squeezing out a churchy tune. We put a coin in his hat and headed round the corner into Westbourne Grove. 'A penny is enough, Mala. Charity begins at home.'

At Pataks, the only local source of fresh garlic and ginger, I waited outside with the shopping trolley. An elderly lady came up to me. 'Where are you from, little girl?'

'Paddington.'

'I mean which country do you come from?'

'Ceylon.'

'Ceylon! Such a lovely place. Why don't you go back there?'

Mum was furious: 'This is why I tell you never to talk to strangers. She was a Powellite.'

'She didn't say anything about black people.'

'No – she just told an innocent child to get out of her country.'

Then we were at Anu's flat in Inverness Terrace, carefully carrying our basket down the steps to the basement of the imposing balconied house – owned by an old Armenian and his flirtatious son, Armand: 'Ladies, I'm going to a ball at the Hilton tonight. How do I look?'

'Like Englebert Humperdinck.'

'Have the last waltz with me, Anu – I'm very nimble-footed.'

'You'd only stand on my toes, Armand.'

'Won't you just adjust my tie?'

'I'd be tempted to pull too hard.'

This evening we had good news: great news. 'I've passed the Civil Service exams,' my mother said. 'I got the letter this morning. I'm joining the General Post Office as a Clerical Officer in the new year.'

'Congratulations!' Anu pulled me to my feet, and started singing 'If I Were A Rich Man', twirling me round to the diddles and the dums.

My mother laughed. 'After all these years folding sheets in a hotel basement – thank God my parents never knew, it would have killed them.'

Anu got her purse. 'It's an auspicious day. Come, Mala, let's buy some wine and make the most of it.'

We left just as Aunty Prisky turned up to meet the old relation. 'What are we celebrating?'

'Deliverance.'

We walked to the off-licence by Moscow Road. Anu said: 'Your mother has sacrificed much for you, Mala – don't waste it by loafing around. Work hard – make something of yourself. See how, in the end, it was your mother's education that rescued her from the troughs of despair.'

I nodded: slowing wistfully outside the Indian newsagent where meat curry and samosas were dispensed from huge stainless-steel tureens on the counter. But today Anu had cooked a feast herself – stringhoppers with milk gravy, chicken, lamb and lentils; and my mum, in the bottom of her shopping trolley, had Pyrex bowls of sour fish and quick-fried spicy cabbage in honour of the old man, to whose ramblings they listened in respectful admiration.

Mum and I were always entertaining uncles or aunties flying around the world. They came to our room, arms heavy with gold, loaded with gifts of shrimp sambal, curry powder, milk toffee and love cake. We'd talk about mutual friends and relations, the black-market exchange rate and the service on Air Ceylon, but never once about the black mould around our sink or the little army of ants that my mother was constantly bleaching off the worktop.

'Mum, why don't they give us some money?'

'Back home we have both money and land, Mala – have you forgotten so quickly? My family has dominated the district for generations. Everyone comes to my father for help and advice. It would be wickedness to bring shame upon him.'

'How is it shameful to be a widow?'

She frowned. 'Mala, in life we can only go forward. I can't return. A woman alone is a target for gossip.'

I tried to imagine what sort of gossip my mum could provoke – after all, she didn't entertain men like Mrs Stephens, or drink or smoke or go to pop festivals. Perhaps, I thought, it was her extravagance – though only visitors benefited from it. Later that week we would take an ancient aunty and uncle, who'd flown in for a Harley Street consultation, to see *Swan Lake* at the Royal Opera House. Front row tickets £4 each: two weeks' pay just for the four of us to sit down, and they'd never know.

I yawned loudly as the familiar catalogue of questions about people, places and politics was placed before Anu's visitor: How is Amrita's family? Is the Lanka Oberoi open? What is Mrs Bandaranaike up to?

On the way home, my mum told me off: 'You should take more interest. He was a junior minister for several years; it's not just Anu, our family's connected to him as well, you know.'

'How?'

'Well, his first cousin married my mother's second cousin's stepdaughter. In fact,' she went on, 'his father's father was married to my grandmother's aunt's son-in-law's sister.'

'I don't understand how family works,' I said to Janice as we did measuring experiments with jugs in the class sink. 'I think everyone in Ceylon must be related to each other.'

She sniffed: 'At least they don't come to stay like my horrible cousins from Cork.'

'Allie said one of them was gorgeous.'

After leaving school in the summer, Allie had got a job in a boutique in Carnaby Street. She went round in frilly shirts and short A-line skirts like someone off *Jason King*. 'This is flower power,' she said; 'Sergeant Pepper and all that – "Lucy In The Sky With Diamonds" – you know.' But we didn't really, though we thought the Bee Gees were great.

'Do you believe in free love, Allie?'

'Of course I do.'

'Do you do it?'

'That's for me to know, cheeky.'

We filled in our chart and gave it to Miss Hicks for checking before moving on to air experiments, measuring our puff and filling in diagrams labelled 'The Breathing Process' and 'Cloud Formation'.

'Do you girls understand what's expected here?' We nodded. 'In that case, there'll be no need for constant discussion on the subject.'

Bethany and Caroline were looking at heat generation with two boys. 'I hate Nicholas Ford,' Janice whispered, 'he pinged my knickers at PE. I'm glad they've got him and not us.' Carefully, she copied my spelling of carbon dioxide. 'I wish she'd put us on earth study, there are no foreign words in that.'

After we'd hung up our rubber aprons, it was time to sit and listen to the next chapter of *The Hobbit* before the final bell. Then we caught up with each other at the dummy house in Leinster Terrace, where the painted façade hid an underground chimney spewing vapour clouds of hot air overhead. Normally we'd watch tourists from the row of hotels do a double-take; but today it was quiet so we wandered down to J. M. Barrie's house at the end, to read the blue plaque for the hundredth time.

The Beverly Sisters drove past in a Mini. 'Why don't they buy a bigger car?' Bethany said. 'They look so silly squashed up like that.'

Janice sighed. 'Perhaps their dad's got debts?'

Money: a constant barrier between us and our aspirations. As Janice noted one afternoon, sitting on the stairs outside my room, 'Why do social workers waste time checking our health and asking our parents things that make them angry? We don't need questions, we need money.'

I nodded. 'Then we could afford some Crunchies or something.'

It was a bad autumn: and all that I knew was, the hole in my shoe, it was letting in water. Unable to generate enough for hot chocolate from the machine in the launderette, we were reduced to eavesdropping on the phone calls made by downstairs tenants.

Christmas was in six weeks, and the way things were going, we'd be lucky to get a Tiny Tears between us.

Caroline was particularly cross because her parents had promised Josh a record player, which meant she'd only get something small. 'They say it'll chase out the sad spirit that's in him, but he won't work any harder – he'll just listen to music instead.'

'Can you do it like that – just play a record and it goes? My mum says you have to drink potions and things, and they put on devil masks and dance to drums to get it out.'

'Who cares, Mala: it's all rubbish.'

'It isn't, Caroline. Somebody stole a strand of my grandfather's hair and buried it with a curse in his garden. They had bad luck for years until the exorcist dug it up. My mum knows people who've died because of curses and wicked spirits.'

'Do you know any?'

'Of course not – it doesn't happen here.'

'There you are.'

Bethany said: 'What happens when the sad spirit goes?'

'I suppose Josh becomes a doctor or a lawyer or something.'

Caroline was suddenly furious: 'What about me: maybe I'll be the doctor. Where's my record player? It makes me so mad!'

Downstairs, the Jamaican woman in Room 3 was having a loud argument on the phone. I whispered the story of how she'd been knifed by her boyfriend: 'They took her to St Mary's but she came straight back.'

We shook our heads in wonder.

Janice returned crossly from the loo: 'There's no toilet paper – just strips of the *Daily Telegraph*.'

'You should have asked – I'd have given you our Bronco.'

Afterwards we made Christmas lists. Bethany wanted a Triang

bike and Mrs Stephens had said she'd get extra work hand-sewing sequins for a lady in Cleveland Square who made evening gowns.

'Are they for wearing or taking off?' Caroline said snidely.

Willem came up the stairs: a thankful distraction. Small, yellow-haired and generous, he was our immediate neighbour. On the evening Ray Charles sang live on telly he'd let half the house crowd into his room for the concert: 'Hit The Road Jack' – what a night! Now he was smiling, smoothing creamed hair with a leather-gloved hand: 'Have you girls nothing else to do?'

We shook our heads glumly.

'I have to pick up a parcel from the post office. Would you like to watch *Blue Peter* or something at my place?'

'Yes please!'

'Okay: half an hour and then you're out.'

We sat on his bed as he put sixpence into the meter of the small black-and-white set. 'Now don't make a mess.'

Willem was always nice to me. Occasionally he'd make eyes at my mother, who enjoyed, but resolutely ignored, his admiration. And he was great compared to the Arab amputee who rented the third room on our landing, climbing the stairs ape-like, his muscular arms and hands propelling his torso ever upward. Even now, after his artificial legs had been fitted, I was fearful of their monotonous thumping on the landing and, in the early morning, the quick climbing actions of his hands.

'Don't be silly, Mala,' my mother said. 'He's harmless.'

But he was also legless, and that was what filled me with fear.

'Mum, why do I only get a ten-bob book token for Christmas?'

'We're not Christians. You're lucky to get anything.'

'But I get the same for birthdays.'

'Because reading's good for you.'

'But can't you spend more?'

'We don't have it.'

'Will it be different when you're in the GPO?'

'Not really. I'll just be able to save at last.'

Finally the festivities were properly under way. Allie took us on the bus to see the Christmas lights in Regent Street, and the

Hamleys window display. In the neon Coca-Cola brightness of Piccadilly Circus and the Trocadero, we sat on the steps of Eros listening to carol singers and eating hot dogs with onions from a street-side stall. The tree above Swan and Edgar was a glittering mass of colour in the foreground, like the burning bush in the story of Moses. To left and right were the grand displays of Simpson's of Piccadilly and the Café Royal.

Barrow-boys wearing Father Christmas hats and selling cheap wrap called out from the station entrance, and a pavement artist who'd done the twelve days of Christmas outside the Criterion Theatre was making so much he emptied his box every five minutes to keep people giving.

'The winter of peace and love,' Allie sighed.

'Yeah, man,' said Caroline, and we got the giggles.

On the way back, Allie took us to meet her boss in the indoor market at the junction of Carnaby Street and Foubert Place. He gave each of us a little neck bell on a leather thong. 'Hi, kids – stay cool – merry Christmas.'

I was awestruck. 'These are seven and six in Indiacraft.'

For the next half-hour we followed Allie in and out of the open-fronted boutiques as she laughed, kissed and flirted with young men who wore embroidered Afghan coats and pale cravats against the cold. 'D'you fancy them, then, Al?' Janice asked.

'Of course not – they're out of their brains. I'm just being friendly – it *is* Christmas.'

Music blared from all directions, the layers of sound making it seem like the air itself was celebrating – the Beatles, Donovan, Georgie Fame, the Scaffold: 'Thank U Very Much'.

'This is the best bit of Christmas,' Janice said. 'It's always a let-down at home: burnt dinner, useless presents, a fight over my dad's drinking and nobody's speaking by the time the Queen comes on at three.'

'Does he stand up for the National Anthem?'

'Not since the time he fell over and cut his head on the telly.'

And then it was suddenly Christmas Eve and we'd all got money for the simulated sleigh ride at Whiteleys department store. As the electric doors closed behind us and the elf switched on the rocking mechanism, the scenery on the sides started moving, so it truly felt like we were going to the North Pole. Reindeer flew by and the snow was so thick I would have reached out and touched it if I hadn't thought Caroline would make some stinging remark. At the other end a man with bad breath was in the grotto, his padded Santa stomach divided in two so he had a centre parting under the red felt.

'And what would you like for Christmas, girls?'

Me: 'Something worth more than ten bob.'

Janice: 'Some peace and quiet.'

Caroline: 'I'd like equal treatment.'

Bethany: 'I'd like everyone to be happy.'

And we laughed delightedly at our own wit while Santa's lady helper pursed her mouth into a scarlet pustule of distaste and gracelessly presented us with our presents.

Outside, we opened them with pure pleasure – bead sets and little dolls with removable dresses – brilliant! We felt like millionaires. Mrs Stephens had sent a packet of chocolate buttons and a sherbert dip for each of us – deep and crisp and even. We ate them while keeping warm by the heating ducts outside the food hall, watching last-minute shoppers struggling past with overspilling carrier bags. Life could not be better. *Gloria in Excelsis Deo!*

As we broke up and headed home in readiness for the big day, a group of lads tumbled out of the Railway. 'Hello, girls!' one of them shouted. 'Can I walk you home?' And the others hooted and wolf-whistled, dragging him noisily away from us and into Westbourne Grove. 'Cradle-snatcher!'

Janice shuddered. 'Men.'

'You sound just like my mum,' I said.

Heading for Paddington, we could hear them swaggering in the distance, singing loudly: Long John Baldry, 'Let The Heartaches Begin'. Caroline, whose block was just yards from the main shopping area, stopped and looked at us regretfully. 'I won't see you for days.' But we were all smiling so she straightened up, black eyes glittering, and said defiantly: 'I don't care that Josh is getting a record player because it won't make him happy. Nothing does. But I am happy, and no matter how mean my parents are, I won't let them take that from me.'

# 3

*'Je suis, tu es, il est, elle est.'* Like Mrs Chong doing the rosary at times of trial, we recited in monotone: *'ils sont, elles sont, nous sommes, vous êtes.'*

'Come on, children: too much figgy pudding!'

Yet another Christmas gone in a blur and this time there'd been no complaints, not even from Caroline. We were too busy saving them up for the months ahead: *'J'ai, tu as, il a, elle a, ils ont, elles ont, nous avons, vous avez.'*

A loud groan: 'How will I ever get you through the Eleven Plus?' Mr Thompson's New Year resolution for 1969 was that we would all try harder. He'd introduced French for ten-year-olds, started a country dancing club which regularly visited Cecil Sharpe House to cross-hand gallop and doh-si-doh, and was entering us for everything from carol festivals to Keep Britain Tidy quizzes. The previous week I'd won a copy of *Born Free* in the Brooke Bond handwriting competition. Now lions were added to my two other enthusiasms: Tufty Club membership and Jack Wild. I stared blankly at the pictures of Jean and Colette on the slide screen.

'Mala: can you identify what's happening in the picture?'

*'Maman prépare le petit déjeuner. Colette mange le petit pain. Jean boît une tasse du chocolat.'*

'Good.' We followed the words in our textbooks: *croissant, petit pain, beurre, jambon, confiture, café, thé, chocolat.*

Bethany slid down in her chair. 'This is a waste of time.'

'You should know it all anyway.'

'How?'

'Your mum teaches French, doesn't she?'

*     *     *

'It's all right for clever clogses like you and Caroline,' Janice moaned, 'but I'll never pass the Eleven Plus, so why bother?'

'You certainly won't pass if that's your attitude.'

Caroline, already eleven, had taken on superior tones, muscling in on things that weren't really her business and constantly wanting to be top dog. 'How did you do in the spelling test, Mala?'

'I got them all right.'

'Every single one? Well, there you are, Janice – there's no excuse.'

Yet again Caroline had minimised one of my achievements, but if a slight had been intended it wasn't clear in her expression; and when the bell went for morning break, she put her arm through mine and shared her threepenny packet of chocolate digestives unasked. 'Of course, you and me, we'll go to grammar schools.'

'Why d'you say that?'

'Because we'll pass the Eleven Plus, Mala, no problem. You know my mum's already put my name down for Sion Manning and Greycoats?'

'Is that what you want?'

'Yes: it'll prove I'm as good as Josh.'

'Mum, I want to go to the same schools as my friends.'

'You'll make new friends.'

'I don't want new friends.'

But already my aunties were finding out about local grammar schools and testing me at weekends to see if I made the grade; and while it still felt far away, I had a sense of the walls closing in. Anu ruined a weekend by marching me round the Science Museum to see bits of ancient machinery: 'This, Mala, is the Spinning Jenny.'

Prisky bought me the 'classics': 'Too much Enid Blyton. This is real literature.' *Tom Sawyer, Kidnapped, Ivanhoe* – boys' books.

Bethany surveyed this activity with great amusement: 'You'll be Einstein by the end of the year.' We bought a bag of apples and wandered across to Bathurst Mews, to feed the horses. 'You won't get airs and graces at your new school, will you?'

'Who says it'll be me and not you?'

'Don't be silly.' She grabbed my hand to cross the busy road behind the Royal Lancaster Hotel. 'You know, Mala, you're my best friend out of all of them. Even Mum says we're like sisters. I can tell you things I'd never tell anyone else.'

'Like what?'

But neither of us could find an example, though I knew what she meant.

I was everybody's best friend that term; probably, I thought, because I moaned the least. I yearned for my own bed, and some wall space for my pop posters, but in the great scheme of things this was nothing compared to Janice, whose list of responsibilities was longer than Pinocchio's nose. She pushed round the Ewbank, cooked the tea, did the washing, ironed her dad's shirts; even changed the beds.

'Why can't your mum do it?'

'Bad back.'

'She should get tablets.'

'You don't get tablets for a trapped nerve, you just have to rest.'

'But it's not fair. Why don't you say something?'

'You try saying something in our house. All my dad does is shout about the mess and his missing conjugals.'

'What missing conjugals?'

'Don't ask me. I've looked all over the place but they're not to be had.'

And then it was not just his conjugals but Mr Connors himself who went missing. He came home one night in a terrible mood, picked a fight with his wife requiring police attendance, and was removed from his home in a flurry of f-words and fear. The next morning, he was taken in a Black Maria from Paddington Green police station to Marylebone Magistrates Court, where he was bound over in the sum of five pounds to keep the peace. After his appearance before the beak, he returned to the near-empty flat – Mrs Connors was sleeping off the shock – packed a couple of shirts into Allie's vanity case and went.

Allie said: 'He's been threatening to go for years. He's probably got another woman.' But Mr Connors was hardly an appetising prospect. The very thought of him even kissing someone with his furious furry tongue made us shudder. Bethany and I wept with laughter at the thought of the burly Irishman, drunk and damned, tripping off into the sunset with his drip-dry nylons crammed into the peach-striped overnight bag like Tony Curtis in *Some Like It Hot*.

His departure confused everyone because it had no logic. We heard he'd found digs in Kilburn, and local sightings were reported, but still he stayed clear of the marital home. Mrs Connors said 'the Judge' had frightened him off with threats. Eamonn wrote from Borstal claiming the police must have fitted him up. The man himself was incommunicado. The various permutations of the story were no more than an expression of the family need to blame anyone but themselves.

'At the end of the day,' Allie said, 'he went because he couldn't stand the sight of us. Good riddance.'

For people like my mother, it confirmed all their prejudices: 'No sense of responsibility. This is what they mean by permissive society – do what you like and let others shoulder the burden.'

Josh Chong stirred it up: 'He's gone because his wife is incompetent. She may claim she's the victim, but to trot out a favoured courtroom cliché: she would say that, wouldn't she?'

But Mrs Connors was no Mandy Rice-Davies. The nearest we had to her was Mrs Stephens, who refused to be drawn: 'Who knows what goes on behind closed doors? I shan't sit in judgment over Con Connors – he hasn't had the easiest of lives.'

Ob-la-di, ob-la-da, life goes on, rah! Despite the trapped nerve, Mrs Connors found the strength one morning to physically throw three greyhounds on to the street. Inside, Sean and Marie were learning to lie low. Janice was continually tense and miserable. 'Allie won't take time off and the kids are in a state. The welfare's been round. My mum says she can't cope. Even worse, we're behind with the rent – that man Suri's outside every night. I'm going to pieces.'

Mr Suri was rent collector for the Sikh conglomerate that owned the local tenements. A handsome man with green eyes and a trimmed white beard, he wore a red turban, a hound's-tooth jacket and dark slacks. When we were really poor, my mum and I lay silent in the dark, hardly daring to breathe, as he banged on the door. 'I have seen your light from the street, Mrs Fonseka – I know you are hiding. It is not your money, it is ours!'

Sometimes he would pretend to leave, but would wait by the stairs; and Mum, who was wise to every movement on the landing, put her finger to her lips to warn me that the danger remained, until, unable to bear the pantomime, Mr Suri would come back and bellow helplessly: 'Mrs Fonseka – I know you are taking up the residence forthwith! Open the door – I cannot give you any more understandings.'

But while the landlords gave us some leeway, they were less sympathetic to those whose circumstances were too reduced to rally. We were all inside the night he stood on Janice's top step shouting, 'Mrs Connors you must pay. You are not some hippie to take up squattings!'

In the end Allie found the money, but her interest and involvement in the day-to-day shambles of the Connors home was plainly diminishing. When Janice complained of tiredness, she just shrugged. 'I'm keeping Suri from the door. You'll have to battle it out with the old cow: I've done my time.' She ruffled our downcast heads affectionately and then, gathering her bits and pieces, went upstairs grinning. 'Now I don't want you two coming up and ogling while I'm getting ready – I've a hot date tonight.'

A hot date on a cold February night somewhere up near Marble Arch; walking home to Paddington, hands tucked in each other's pockets, for a kiss on the doorstep. As I lay in bed, forcing a little space between me and my mother, because the closeness didn't feel natural any more, I put myself in Allie's red shoes with the giant silver buckle and enjoyed the sensual pleasure my imaginings evoked.

Somehow, the unknown date always looked like Josh Chong, who, despite his constant distraction, still tied us in verbal knots. Now in the upper sixth, he'd grown his hair and wore granddad vests with tight black bell-bottoms, but nothing seemed to give him pleasure. When, in my dream sequence, I got close for a chaste forbidden kiss, he turned into a bean sprout – pale, thin and crunchy with a bitter aftertaste, like the detritus on Mrs Chong's chopping board.

I wondered in that uncomfortable darkness how far Allie went with her boyfriends: whether she had love-ins with men in bean-bagged rooms. Was she, secretly, one of those girls who whipped their tops off at pop concerts and let everyone see? Watching her in front of the mirror clipping platinum split ends with blunt nail scissors, a cigarette unattended in the overfull ashtray – she was so adult and unknown. She got up and put on a Supremes record, singing along while she curled and coloured her lashes with a clogged mascara brush: 'I'm Gonna Make You Love Me', oh yes I am, oh yes I am.

When she went down in her cream crochet mini-dress her mother nearly choked. 'You brassy tart!'

But Allie just laughed. 'Would you like a few tips, Ma? It might help you win back your husband.'

We knew Allie wasn't a tart: that sort of information soon came back on the school grapevine. Lisa Carroll's sister was a real slag – she'd had half the Blue Watch at Warwick Avenue fire station; Peter Metcalfe's sister was up the duff – and not yet sixteen; but Allie, despite leaving a crock-full of broken hearts in her wake, was okay. And now there was a new one who was obviously special because there weren't any jokes about invisible wallets or bad breath – and no matter how much we pried, she gave nothing away.

Neither did Josh, which was a real let-down for the giggling gaggles of girls who stopped to ask Caroline about him. 'Where does he hang out, then – not round here.'

'Discotheques.'

'Hark at her. Discotheques! Discos, you mean.'

'Call them what you like – you're not going to meet him at the Stowe Boys Club.'

'Where does he go really?' I asked Caroline.

'How should I know? He does what he wants when he wants. No one says a bloody word.'

'It's a shame Caroline hasn't got tits or she could burn her bra,' Bethany said. 'That's what it's all about.'

I mixed my chocolate pudding into the chocolate custard and

sucked it off the spoon. 'She only wants the same treatment. They always treat sons as if they're special. My mum's the same. She thinks I'll marry and go off, but a son would look after her.'

'My mum says the opposite.' Bethany pushed away her half-eaten semolina. 'Really they should look after themselves.'

We got up, put away our bowls and went into the playground. The nit nurse wandered past for the monthly comb-through.

I said: 'My mum's going back to Ceylon soon.'

'For ever?'

'Three weeks. Her sister's ill. She might die – like yours.'

'Fancy remembering that.'

Some of the younger girls were playing a skipping game – Bluebells-cockle-shells-evie-ivy-over. It was babyish but we joined in, knowing we'd be better than them.

'She's bought a white mourning sari. Did you wear mourning?'

'I don't remember. I can't even remember *her*. I know she had dark hair. She was called Ayesha, like the woman on *Lift Off*: funny name. Are you going too?'

'No. It's too expensive and I'd miss The Exam.'

'Where will you stay?'

We took our turn swinging the rope, shouting to each other past a bobbing pigtail and a long plait. 'With Aunty Anu.'

'That'll be fun.'

'Not really. She says I'm an urchin who hasn't a home.'

'But you do have a home.'

'Yeah. And she'll make sure I stay in it.'

It seemed to me that our mothers were forcing attention away from us and on to themselves. Mrs Connors, a month into her separation, was a miserable mass of oaths; my mother, who resented paying for a Mars bar, spent all her savings on Wilkinson Sword razor blades and Sta-prest pleated skirts for the family at home; and Mrs Stephens went out and got a proper job as a cleaner at Whites Hotel, clearing up after American soldiers on leave from NATO duty.

'She's up to something,' Caroline said.

Walking past the glass-fronted hotel on Lancaster Gate at

night, you could see the GIs, dark and handsome in their navy uniforms, drinking, laughing, shouting to each other across the bar. I always wanted to stop and watch, but my mum hurried me past: 'Let them not think we're loose women.'

Once, in a fog on Craven Road, a man stopped and asked my mum, who was in a sari and woolly coat: 'Would you like to join me for a cup of coffee?'

When she said no, he turned to me: 'What about your friend?'

Paddington was full of it, my mother said; but whatever 'it' was, Mrs Stephens had apparently opted out. Maybe she was too old or too tired; maybe she was doing it for Bethany. But if that was the case it was too late – because we all knew now, and although we didn't discuss it, Bethany knew we knew. It was a barrier: more than Janice's chaotic misery or me and Caroline's foreignness. Bethany walked in the shadow of shame.

'Mum, why is *Family Favourites* only for British Forces Posted Overseas? Why not Americans, like the ones in Whites Hotel?'

'They're just breaking flight before returning home to their families.'

'Like you?'

'Yes: except that I'm going with a heavy heart.'

'But Shreela's getting better.'

'Who knows what fate holds in its hand, Mala. As soon as I'm home I shall go to the shrine at Kataragama and make a vow for her.'

'Will that save her life?'

'I hope so. If not, it will give her a good start in the next.'

'How many lives do we have?'

'Too many.'

'I'll miss you, Mum.'

On the Home Service they were playing a special request for Corporal Michael Rose in BFPO something or other on the Rhine: 'Walkin' Back To Happiness', Helen Shapiro, with much love from your wife Susan and baby son David, who can't wait till you're home again to make the family complete.

'And I'll miss you, my little treasure, every single minute of every single day, but we'll be together again before you know it.'

\*     \*     \*

Aunty Anu didn't get back from her school in Barlby Road till five, so I could still loaf around before sitting down to the worksheets she'd prepared. 'This is an important time – all hands to the pump.' Afterwards, I slumped in front of the telly with a dull dinner. 'You're getting too plump, Mala. No sweets, no desserts, only fruit while you're here. We'll surprise Mummy.'

In the evenings, as at our home, stray callers popped in in the hope the pot was full. Mina, temporarily lodged in a women's hostel across the road, was constantly over, lounging on the bed and complaining about the weather or her shifts or, tonight, clothes going missing from the laundry room: 'They are only cheap knickers from Woolworths, why should anyone want them?'

Anu coiled her thick waist-length hair, pinning it up like Rita Faria. 'Perhaps they pay for Green Shield stamps on the black market.'

Amal and Shyam, postgraduates at London University, were regulars. When they turned up with a bottle of wine, the four of them would pull out the atlas and plan the overland journey home. By week two I could identify most countries in Europe; by week three, the northern plains of subcontinental Asia.

'Are you really going to do it, Anu?'

'Of course. If not this summer, then the next.'

'Will you come back?'

'We all come back, Mala; our hearts may be at home, but it's here that we've invested in the future.'

'I don't know about that,' Mina said. 'If something better comes up, I might stay.'

'Well, it would suit you certainly to live in Colombo 7, shopping all day, waited on hand and foot. You'd better make a play for Shyam – even his toilets are Carrara marble.'

'So is his mother: she won't budge from the place.' Mina went back into the kitchen. 'No sweets?'

'I've put Mala on a diet.'

'What nonsense.'

'You say that, Mina, because you're getting fat yourself – in all seriousness you better find a husband soon.'

Mina returned with a banana, elaborately peeling it and biting off big chunks. 'I'm perfectly happy on my own.'

'Now you sound like this child's mother.'

'She hasn't done so badly in the circumstances.'

'She would have done better with her husband at her side.'

The same was probably true of Mrs Connors, whose husband was both alive and in riotous health, but she was about to have the option removed. She found this out when Mr Connors arrived at Westbourne Terrace one afternoon in a generally foul mood, and demanded a divorce.

'You'll get a divorce over my dead body, Con Connors.'

'That's the way I'd best like it, you miserable sow.'

Janice and I stayed out of the way upstairs where we were helping Marie with her reading.

'I'll never give in. You'll have to wait the full five years.'

'You'll suffer for it, Stell.'

'I've suffered from the day I met you.'

I made a face at Janice. She shrugged: 'Some people are never happy – look at Caroline.'

'She's not unhappy, she's angry.'

'So's my mum – it's just that she's been angry all her life.'

Downstairs, the volume dropped. We crept on to the landing.

'I'll give you money.'

'That's mighty grand of you.'

'Regular money, Stell, don't turn your nose up at it.'

'You haven't managed regular money in twenty years.' Silence. Mrs Connors made an attempt at reconciliation: 'What about the children, Con?'

'What about them?'

Janice, laid low by his departure, turned and went back into her room. Dimly, I saw a scene from my own life: my mother in a grey coat with a little mouse brooch on the collar, looking in a mirror; and my father, controlled and angry, suddenly slapping her across her soft, silent face.

But there would be no slaps tonight: Mr Connors didn't have the enthusiasm for it. 'Look, Stell, I just want to get this over and done with as quickly as I can.'

'You can't just wipe out a lifetime.'

'What kind of a bloody life is this?'

When he'd left with threats about solicitors, Janice and I went downstairs. Her mother was standing white-faced at the window. We made jam sandwiches for the kids and Janice walked me down Craven Road.

'Why doesn't she just let him go?'

'How would we manage? Allie won't be here for ever.'

Allie had already embarked on her big adventure like the girl in the Peter Sarstedt record: 'Where Do You Go To My Lovely'. We certainly had no idea. We didn't even know if she was alone in her bed.


And then it was the morning of the exam and Mr Thompson, coming into the classroom to wish us luck, told one of his silly jokes: what's the difference between a stag, a thought, something sad, and a pig? Nobody knew.

'Well,' he said, 'a stag is A deer, a thought is I-dea and something sad is Oh dear.'

Caroline put up her hand. 'Sir, what about the pig?'

'The pig? Why, that's You dear!'

The whole class roared, but Caroline's mouth had an angry set. Ahead of me, her shoulders were tightly tensed and afterwards she cried tears of frustration. 'I couldn't concentrate! He showed me up so I couldn't concentrate!'


Across the white wall on the corner of Craven Terrace and Craven Hill, someone had painted in huge black letters: 'Hendrix is God'. My mother shook her head disapprovingly.

She'd come back darker and fatter, her sister recovering: 'The power of prayer, Mala: I went to the temple every day and by the end she was fit enough to see me off at the airport.' A sigh. 'I wish I could have taken you. I don't want them all to be strangers.'

In her suitcase were presents from the family – a beaten brass wall hanging of the Buddha; moonstone jewellery for me; batik sarongs; five pounds of Harrison's best foil-wrapped tea; and, of course, lots and lots of edibles: maldi fish, curry powder, seeni sambal, cinnamon, tamarind, jaggery, dried chillies, cokis biscuits, and every type of sweet – kaung, dodol, thalaguli, love cake, milk toffee. We had visitors every night for a month.

Janice was there too, her wavy brown hair scraped back off her face as if brushing it was too much bother. She'd been round most nights since news of her parents' impending divorce. Sometimes Bethany's mum fed the little ones. Mrs Connors meanwhile increased her intake of Mackeson and Senior Service. The flat constantly smelt of fire. 'I'm sick to the stomach with it,' Janice moaned.

My mum took our plates. 'More curry, girls?'

'No thank you, Mrs Fonseka.'

She washed the dishes in the corner sink as my Aunty Winnie, a stenographer at the high commission, started telling us a ghost story. We sat at the foot of her chair.

'Now, girls, this is really true, about a guardian angel called Kalu Kumar – Black Prince – who appeared one night as a shadow in my uncle's almirah mirror.

'His servant was asleep outside the door – no person could pass; but when my uncle awoke, the figure was there, clearly visible in reflection. My uncle cried out, but the man didn't answer. When his cries turned to screams, the servant came running. He put on the light. The room was empty.

'As my uncle insisted he had seen someone, a giant cobra slithered from his sheets, on to the pillow. Immediately the significance of the apparition was apparent. Without that warning, my uncle would still be sleeping – and have lost his life.'

I shuddered. Janice said: 'How can an angel be black?'

'Angels can be anything. They simply are spirits, Janice, that help and guide.'

'But they're not supposed to be scary.'

'Fear comes from inside. My uncle's terror was not because the spirit was frightening – after all, it did nothing. What he feared was the unknown – yet often it holds more promise than that which is familiar.'

My mother clapped her hands. 'Enough now: who wants some tinned mangoes and Nestlé's cream?'

Afterwards we listened to *Sing Something Simple* with the King Singers, and I walked Janice home.

'What we need is a guardian angel,' she said. 'To bring my dad back and make everything all right again.'

'Can't we talk about something else?'

'It's all right for you, Mala, your mum gets on with it. Mine's falling apart.'

'Janice, you're starting to sound like Eeyore.'

The next day our results came. Caroline had failed. While I'd sport the bottle-green skirt and jacket of the nearest grammar school, she'd be alongside the others in the navy tunic and white blouse of Sara Siddons secondary mod. The shadow of Josh Chong now blocked all the light at Caroline's window, and coloured every comment and action she made during our final term together.

And it did feel very final. We were aware of moving into different worlds. And while it didn't affect our friendship, it would change it. I was filled with anxiety: with a twenty-minute journey home, would the gang wait for me each day or seek new adventures alone?

Caroline, sensing my ambivalence, made mean comments. But one Sunday, walking up to Speaker's Corner, she apologised: 'I'm sorry, Mala, but I'm just as clever as you and I could kick Mr Thompson for messing it up.'

Bethany said: 'It's typical of you to blame someone else,' and they argued all the way.

My uniform came from Selfridges: sixty-eight pounds. My mother was proud and horrified. For economy, the gaberdine mac was three sizes too big. We spent two hours arguing over the height of the hem. I hated the sensible flat shoes she bought. 'This is what they wear in good schools, Mala – Princess Anne has them at Benenden.'

My belt had a zip purse. 'What's it for? We don't pay dinner money.'

'Never advertise poverty, Mala. If people know your weakness they'll exploit it. If anyone asks, say that I pay monthly by cheque.'

All these things I hid under the bed in case I got called a cissy or a toff; and I gave thanks that my embroidered name tags, which looked so red and so grand, were a secret between me and the washing instructions on my clothes.

\*      \*      \*

On the last day of term, Mr Thompson shook hands with each of us.

'Mala: we shall miss your smile, but we'll be following your progress with great interest.

'Caroline: don't be disheartened. Sara Siddons is a good school; with the right approach you'll get top marks all the way.

'Janice: you've suffered a lot of upheaval, but you're one of life's survivors. Whatever you do, you'll do it well.

'Bethany: you're a clever girl – have confidence and you'll surprise yourself.'

We had a late assembly. The music was detailed on the display board: Offenbach, *Orpheus in the Underworld*.

Marieca read the lesson, and we sang 'All Things Bright And Beautiful'. As we filed out of the hall for the last time, I looked at Bethany and saw that she, like me, was crying.

And then it was the holidays. The four of us were hanging out on Caroline's communal balcony one morning when we heard a strangled sound from inside the flat and Josh Chong ran out, waving his A-level results. He was gibbering as he held the paper for us to see: two Bs, a C and a D. Brilliant! We were all smiling as he threw the paper down in disgust and squared up to Caroline. 'It must be catching, little sister – we're both failures now!'

Smiles were replaced by fear as she stood her ground, meeting his eye unflinching until he pulled away and went inside. She picked up the notification and grinned: 'He needed three As for Cambridge – now he knows what it feels like.'

Below us, a young lad was fiddling with his car stereo – Simon and Garfunkel: 'The Boxer'. In my mind's eye I saw the bloodied fighter struggling to his feet after each successive pounding and thought, Yes, that's Caroline all right. In a strange way, it was each and every one of us.

# 4 ∫

By the fourth week of school, I'd got into a routine of walking to Maida Vale station with my classmate Margaret, who got the Tube to Baker Street. Already she'd invited me home, but I had too many fixtures. As I came up the escalator at Paddington, Bethany would be there, duffle bag thrown carelessly over her shoulder. 'Hello, brainbox, what did you do today – Latin?'

'Yes, if you must know. *Caecilius in horto sedet.*'

'What does that mean?'

'Caecilius is sitting in his garden.'

'That's *really* useful.'

We walked down Praed Street joking and sharing a bag of crisps, popping home to change before meeting up with the others or just going window-shopping. Later my mother would read the nightly Riot Act: 'You haven't taken out even one book! If you waste this chance, Mala, you'll be a poor immigrant all your life.'

It was a glorious autumn day. I ran upstairs, pulled on slacks and jumper and went back out to meet Beth. On Craven Road I ran into two old classmates and we had a moan about our various new regimes. I'd been reported for eating in uniform: 'One lolly on the way home!'

Marieca's St Christopher had been confiscated: 'How can that count as jewellery?'

Mr Cheatham, our old school caretaker, came round the corner and stopped admiringly: 'Goodness, you all look very grown up – you'll be getting married next.' Laughing, he went into the Express Dairy for his milk and pork pie.

I crossed the road and headed for the Stephens' home. The

old linen shop was being replaced by a boutique. I ran down the steps and rang the bell. 'Come on, Beth!'

There were voices. She opened the door looking cross and tearful. 'I'm not coming out, Mala.'

'What d'you mean, you're not coming?'

'My mum wants to talk to me.'

'What – right now this minute today?'

Mrs Stephens appeared in the opening, a little fatter these days – nice with some sun on her face. 'There's some family business to sort out, sweetheart. Maybe tomorrow, eh?'

She waited as I hovered uncertainly, then smiled and closed the door in my face.

'I don't know what's up,' Caroline said. 'They're both weird.'

'Not Beth.'

'Stop shortening names, Mala.'

'They all do it at my school.'

'What are you called: La? I'm glad I didn't go there.'

'The only family she's got is the uncle with the hearse.'

'Who cares? I've got enough problems of my own.'

'What problems have you got?'

'Maths homework and a demented brother.' She groaned. 'Look, Mala, I'm having a bad day. Why don't you go and find Janice – she's always glad for a break.'

Disgruntled, I arrived at Westbourne Terrace to find Sean and Marie watching telly and Jan watching them. 'My mum's seeing a solicitor – about my dad.'

'My mum says she should sue for everything he's got.'

'What's that? An account at Sid Kiki's, one pair of good trousers and angina?' She lifted Sean's feet off the settee. 'We'll be lucky to get a thing. She was three sheets to the wind when she went – hair like a meringue; a ladder as long as Jacob's in her tights.'

We made sugar sandwiches and watched *The Five o'Clock Club*. Then I went home and got my work out. Only later, as I closed my Nuffield biology textbook, did I wonder again what strange circumstances had caused Mrs Stephens's rudeness.

In drama we were being tightrope walkers. The blubberiest of us was wobbling dangerously as she tried to keep a steady pigeon-toed pace along a parquet slat in the main hall. I clapped a hand over my mouth to stifle the giggles.

'Your turn now, Mala.' Oh God, no. I got up reluctantly. 'Try and pretend there isn't a safety net: it might be easier.'

I took a deep breath, put on my most earnest expression and teetered. My hair kept falling in my face. The class bullies, Fiona and Jenny, started singing under their breaths in Peter Sellers accents: Hare krishna, hare krishna, hare krishna, hare hare. Ignoring them, I straightened and strutted and finished with a theatrical bow. The others laughed and clapped. As I joined the dinner queue, Fiona said: 'Flash cow.' Deep inside, I felt victorious.

Friday: greasy battered fish, soggy chips and revolting, salty, processed peas. Margaret rolled them with her knife. 'You could knock out a whole armada with these.'

'They're all right.'

'You called them hailstones last week.'

'Margaret, all I am saying is give peas a chance.'

'Give peas a chance?' She snorted. 'Did you know John and Yoko use the toilet together?'

Heading home hungry, I dragged Beth into the Wimpy on Norfolk Place for chips and enlightenment, but she looked away, fiddling with her Roger Daltrey curls as I strong-armed ketchup from the plastic tomato.

'Janice didn't come in till eleven today – she took Marie to have her verrucas burnt out.'

'Not when I'm eating, Beth.'

'Mrs Klein says if it happens again, she'll have to see the head.'

'What about *your* family business.'

She ate a chip, delicately licking her fingers clean. 'Oh, that.'

'Yes, that.'

'I've promised Mum not to say anything.' I met her gaze menacingly. She said: 'I really can't tell you, Mala.' I growled. 'Well, she wants us to move.'

'Move! Why? When? What for?'

'I won't go. Not even for Steve McQueen. I've told her.'

'What's brought all this on?'

'I wouldn't tell you that, even if she'd let me. It's a bloody joke.' She wrote a B with her finger in my pool of ketchup. 'It doesn't matter anyway – she's knocked the whole stupid idea on the head.' Suddenly she smiled. 'Have you heard who's opening the Christmas fair? Thora Hird. I love her, don't you?'

But I didn't care about Thora Hird – I wanted to know what mysteries had been laid out and rejected in the Stephens emporium. But though I badgered her about it from the Wimpy to Whiteleys and back again, Beth wouldn't add a word, so that, when I mentioned it to Caroline a few days later, I didn't really feel I was breaking a confidence as I hadn't been told anything in the first place.

Caroline said finally: 'If her mum had meant it, she'd have gone ahead no matter what Bethany felt.' The matter was relegated to the bottom of our list of great unknowns, alongside unresolved questions about body hair and Barbra Streisand's sexual allure.

Heading up to Bishop's Bridge, Caroline was in a great mood. She was top of the class; Josh, who'd got a last-minute place at Goldsmiths' College, was threatening to move across the river; and her dad had won a hundred pounds at an all-night card game in the basement of the Mandarin's Throne restaurant. 'I'll get those white wet-look boots at last.'

We went through the underpass to Warwick Avenue, and sat in the park, watching water traffic on the canal at Little Venice.

'If you could go anywhere in the world, Caroline, where would you go?'

'I don't know. America, maybe. Why?'

'We were talking in geography about the world becoming smaller – about air travel being affordable. Some of the girls in my class go to France and places like that every year, but they moan as much as the rest of us – more, even.'

'It's so unfair, isn't it – you or me, we'd never stop saying thank you, but it doesn't happen; they never stop moaning and get everything they want.'

We watched the last zoo boat of the day unload two very cold-looking passengers at Jason's Trip, and headed home.

My mother was back early after a bad day at work. 'Walking, walking – that's all you do – like shanty dwellers. People will get the wrong ideas, Mala – young girls idling on major thoroughfares. Why can't you find something useful to do with your time?'

'Like what? There's no room here for my friends, no money to go anywhere, and all the clubs are for teenagers.'

'Listen to the radio, read, broaden your mind. You must make something of yourself.'

'Tell me what, and I'll try it.'

And so I went off to Guides as my mother had once done, and inevitably the others joined too, and we had a brilliant time until enrolment loomed and Janice couldn't afford the uniform and Bethany just refused. 'It's a waste of money and it'll all be over in weeks.'

'It won't! There's fifteen-year-olds still going.'

'Not right now, Mala – just leave it.'

In the end only Caroline and I trekked up to St Peter's, the Guide Handbook under our arms, whistles and camping knives clipped to our belts, woggles polished bright and hats perched jauntily, to make our solemn promise to do our duty to God and the Queen and to honour the Guide Law; to practise darning, tie reef-knots and sing 'Ging Gang Goolie' around a candlelight campfire.

One Monday afternoon, at the very end of November, I came out of the station and Beth wasn't there. A detention? It was a miserable day, too dismal to look up the others, so I listened to *Storytime* and half-heartedly got on with my poetry. Halfway through *Twenty Questions*, Mum turned up with Uncle Oliver in tow. 'I found him in Elm Mews, kicking his heels and time-wasting.'

'I wasn't time-wasting, Vino, I'd stood in dog mess.'

'*Chi!* You didn't say.'

'You didn't ask. You just invited me for dinner if I had nothing to do – and I don't.'

Mum rustled up rotis, adding onions and herbs to the dough mix as Oliver described his intended bride: 'Her name's Sita. Her parents are airline people.'

'Have you met her?'

'I've known her since childhood. She's very bright.'

'And beautiful?'

'You'll have to judge for yourself. It'll be a good reason for you to visit your homeland. My uncle has asked me to update his teak-exporting business – his clerks still use the abacus for accounting.'

'I wish you would marry Anu.'

He laughed. 'Nobody is good enough for Anu, as you know. Anyway, I prefer a quieter, traditional type of girl.'

'What Oliver means,' my mother said, 'is a woman who'll let him do what he likes, when he likes.'

'Isn't that the dream of every man?' But sensing disapproval, he added quickly: 'But dreams and reality, of course, are quite different things.' He picked up my exercise book. 'May I see what you've been doing, Mala?'

'If you like.'

Turning to my rather lazy poem about friendship, he read aloud:

> 'Friends are always there for you
> They're there to share and care for you
> They listen to your daily news
> And cheer you when you've got the blues
> They turn a sigh into a smile
> And think about you all the while.'

My mother started laughing: 'Will you be thinking of Oliver?'

I nodded. 'We'll miss you, Uncle Oliver.'

'And I shall miss you all – though I hope we'll visit. I've enjoyed Anu's sharp tongue, and your wonderful hospitality, Vino; I shall even miss those ghastly cultural evenings at the Commonwealth Institute watching third-rate Kandyan dancers jiggling their bells.'

'Then don't go, Uncle Oliver. You can always refuse.'

'You don't understand, Mala: sometimes one has no choice.'

The next day Bethany was absent again.

There was no answer from their flat so I wandered across to

Westbourne Terrace. Mrs Connors, slumped in a chair with the *Daily Mirror* and a glass of Mackeson, said: 'Don't go dragging Janice out. I need her here to help with the kids.'

I found Jan in the kitchen. 'I don't know where Bethany is, Mala. She's probably got a cold – anything for a quick skive.' She sighed. 'Lucky devil – what I'd give for a few minutes' rest.' She pulled out a cornflakes box that was jammed down the side of the fridge. 'I've got to get milk and bread and stuff – we can try her again on the way back.' Fishing inside the packet, she pulled out a roll of money. 'My dad came round last week with sixty quid – God knows where that came from – said we wouldn't see him again before Christmas.' Taking a fiver, she put the rest back. 'I don't want her getting her thieving hands on it – she's down to her last five bob till next week's family allowance. If Allie goes off with Carl we'll be up shit creek without a paddle.'

'What's Carl like?'

'Peter Gordeno.'

'He's black? Good thing your dad's not around! What does he do?'

She looked embarrassed. 'It's sort of a secret.'

'Don't start having secrets, Jan: it's bad enough with Beth.'

'He takes his kit off in *Hair*.'

'What – "Let the Sunshine In", and all that?'

'Yeah.'

'And does he? Let the sun shine in, I mean?'

She started laughing. 'You won't tell anyone, will you, Mala?'

'Of course not. It can't be that rude anyway – half my aunties have seen it.'

Serious now: 'I mean, you won't say he's black.'

'Why not?'

'Because it could be awkward. You know what it's like here.'

The Age of Aquarius had yet to dawn over Westbourne Terrace.

At the Express Dairy, we ran into Mr Cheatham. 'Hello, girls, missing your pal?' We looked at him blankly. 'My Connie saw them up at the station. Poor mite was struggling with her case, she said.'

'Whose case?'

'Your little friend.'

'What little friend?'

'Bethany Stephens – who else is it that's moved house?'

'Bethany's moved house?'

'That's what I said, Mala Fonseka. Didn't you know?'

Putting his shopping on the counter, he fumbled in his trouser pocket for change. I said: 'Mr Cheatham, can you say all that again.'

He was bemused. 'Connie got off the train, they got on. The mother had two cases, the daughter had one. The mother said they were starting again.' He grinned. 'A clean sheet, so to speak. That's all. The doors closed, they were gone.' He patted my head. 'Like Tweedledum and Tweedledee – I thought you'd know. I suppose they'll do the place up now, get a higher rent.'

I pushed past him and ran across Craven Road. I ran past the restaurant, the gift shop, the off-licence, the newsagent, the chemist, and into Craven Terrace. I ran past the school, the sweet shop, the old synagogue, the YMCA, the butcher, the deli, the insurance office; past the black railings, each doorway so fixed and familiar, and down the concrete steps. I hammered on the door. 'It's me – it's Mala – come out!' And when nothing happened, I sat at the bottom and cried.

In my mind I kept searching Bethany's face for a clue: a twist of her mouth, an expression in her grey-green eyes, a deepening of the faint frown line. Nothing. She'd been quiet, but Beth blew hot and cold in the same way that Caroline was alternately full of fun or full of fight; the way Jan either dithered dementedly or rushed into decisions; the way Aunty Anu described me: 'When you're not rushing like the wind, you're sagging like a gunny bag.' She'd turned to my mother. 'I warn you, Vino – adolescence is knocking at the door.'

Had adolescence knocked on Bethany's door and lured her away? And not even the decency to hint at it! Nothing, not one thing that she'd said, had prepared me or any of us for this outcome. It was an idea that had been thrown up and chucked out over a plate of chips: 'She's knocked the whole stupid idea on the head.' I was filled with anger. It was as if she'd deceived and deserted her family, because that's what we were: the Little

Women. Not Jo, Meg, Amy and Beth, but Mala, Caroline, Janice and Beth, who, just five short months ago, had shared a promise on their last day at primary school: 'No matter where our futures lie, we'll all be friends until we die.'

Jan came down the steps. 'Come on, let's go back to mine.'

In the kitchen she put on the radio. Stevie Wonder: 'Yesterme Yesteryou Yesterday'. We sat in silence. The importance of what had happened was so enormous we didn't know where to start.

'People always let you down in the end,' said Janice, finally.

Every afternoon I rushed home praying for a letter in our pigeon-hole. It came the next Monday, neatly addressed: Mala Fonseka, Room 12, 92 Craven Hill Gardens, London W2. My heart was thumping so hard I wondered if I was having palpitations like Madame in the Mallory Towers books. I *knew* she'd write. Why shouldn't she: it wasn't as if she'd gone willingly. Now she was filling the gap – the chasm – left by her absence, with words. She was circumnavigating the obstacles like a modern Scarlet Pimpernel; a Nancy to Mrs Stephens's Bill Sykes.

I ran up the stairs savouring and delaying the moment – I wanted it to be perfect. Even before the envelope was opened, I had forgiven her. I threw my coat and satchel on to the bed, poured a glass of Tizer and curled up in the chair. Only then did I ease out the tightly folded sheets of pink paper: 'Dear Mala, How are you?'

But as I read on my heart grew heavy and my thoughts were bitter. No explanations here! It was a relief to get to the last line. I put the letter down and angrily pulled on my jeans and a jacket. What had I ever done to deserve this? I rinsed my glass and went out. The two scribbled pages fell to the floor. I picked them up, my lip curling again at the sight of the smiling Inuit girl in the photograph: 'Hold Hands across the Sea'.

Wasn't it just typical of life that in the same week you lose your dearest mate, you gain an Eskimo pen-friend. What kind of a deal was that?

Later, I made my daily pilgrimage to Beth's old flat and watched the workmen through the window. The walls, which had been papered with a peeling trace of green flower stalks, were now white and gleaming. I wondered if the bathroom was still blue. The old kidney dressing table was tinder in the stairwell and the back door, padlocked so long it had ceased to exist for us, now stood open. Please God, let Beth be all right.

A man in a smart suit turned to go down the stairs. 'You're here every day, aren't you?' I didn't answer. 'I'm the new landlord. Is there something you want to know? Why don't you just ask?'

There was nothing to ask. If you're running away, you don't leave signs along the route like a nature trail.

Over dinner my mother said: 'Mala, if the girl wants to contact you, she will. What's the point of standing by the railings like a sick calf? It's not a bad thing she's gone – it did you no good to associate with the daughter of a prostitute.'

'That's an awful thing to say.'

'But true. Back home women like that are treated as—'

'I'm not interested in what people do "back home". That's where you belong. I belong here.'

'These women are a degradation of any culture, Mala.' She shook her head. 'This is my fault for bringing you here. I can't look after you the way I should, but what choice did I have? I have to trust you.'

'What are you talking about, Mother?'

'The best life is a blameless life.'

'But you're always blaming people.'

'What matters is they can't blame me.'

I groaned, anticipating Part II of the lecture, and soon enough it came: 'This isn't the life I expected when I married – living on one meal a day so my child could grow healthily. But never did I stoop low: I can meet the highest in the land on equal terms.'

I could take no more. I shouted: 'I hate you, Mum! You're so mean, you're so snobby, you're so old fashioned – I just hate you,' and I stormed out. On a downstairs landing someone was playing records: Elvis. On a cold and grey Chicago morning another little baby child is born in the ghetto – and the mother cries.

In the weeks after Bethany's disappearance, the rest of us turned detective, exchanging notes in the Chong sitting room while Josh, zombie-like, watched *Crackerjack*. Now Caroline reported back: 'I asked Mrs Pym in the school office if there'd been any notification. She said a new address would be confidential anyway, but they don't have one.'

Jan sighed. 'We're not getting very far.'

I broke a Marathon into equalish pieces and gave them out. 'I asked Clive in the paper shop, but he said he didn't meddle in private business.'

'Since when?' Caroline snorted. 'Clive knows everything about everybody.'

'His wife's dying,' Janice said.

I continued: 'Mr Morris, the butcher, hasn't heard; Mr Wegener in the YMCA said he hadn't seen them in months; Mr Cheatham just laughs; the lady in the boutique—'

An angry bellow stopped me mid-sentence. 'Isn't it staring you in the bloody face?' Josh roared. 'Do you really need me to spell it out?' He leaned across, pointing to each of us in turn. 'She doesn't want you, you or you. Listen to yourselves. Night after night this endless drivel marking out the limitations of your silly little lives.'

'Have you taken your tablets today?' Caroline asked maliciously. 'Only you're sounding a bit mental.'

'Leave it, Caroline.'

Turning to us, she said loudly: 'Didn't I tell you? He's depressed – not half as much as those who *live* with him, of course. He's having a "minor nervous breakdown". You can see he isn't normal.'

Soundlessly Josh leapt across and pinned her in the chair. 'One day that mouth of yours will land you in serious trouble, little sister.'

Caroline pushed him away. 'Do me a favour, Loony Tunes – go take an overdose somewhere.'

Jan withdrew; I stayed, frozen and admiring – you could never ruffle Caroline. Josh tightened his grip. 'You may be bright within your puerile peer group, but you haven't enough intelligence to know when you've pushed it too far—'

'Schizo!' She gagged as he increased the pressure, her exquisite heart-shaped face beginning to colour.

Instinctively I grabbed one of his arms. A surge of electricity went through my body. 'Josh, leave her. She didn't mean it.'

'I bloody did,' she gasped.

'Shut up, Caroline. Please, Josh, let go.'

Without looking at me he loosened his grip and silently retired to the television twitterings of Leslie Crowther.

We resumed the meeting on the communal balcony. Jan said: 'Is he often like that?'

'He has good days and bad days.'

I said: 'You went too far, Caroline.'

'Give it a rest, Mala – you've no bloody idea what it's like. Some days he doesn't even wash. My mum and dad are begging him all the time – please go to lectures, please read your notes, please do some work. It's a joke.'

'Is he really sick?'

'If he was really sick, they'd put him in hospital.'

My heart went out to Josh Chong – beautiful, misunderstood and so unexpectedly and romantically mad. Had he felt that electricity too, or did it not work like that? Certainly there'd been no indication, no eye contact even, but it didn't matter: I wasn't yet twelve and he was eighteen, there was plenty of time. And if Bethany was back by then, she could be a bridesmaid. My chief bridesmaid.

Fitful fancies crowded my mind and kept it busy as I walked home alone in the sleet. It was a good thing Josh didn't have a girlfriend or he might be like Allie, threatening a trial marriage: what hope would I have then? Really, six years between a man and a woman was nothing at all once you got past sixteen. By then my brace would be off and, with luck, I'd have proper bosoms and long hair and Josh would see me bouncing along the walkways and be immediately smitten by my curves, my intelligence and my pulsating heart.

Home. I ran up the stairs full of excuses for my late return, but Mum wasn't there. I lay on the bed and thought about Bethany and Josh and secrecy and madness and then I put on the news and didn't think about anything. Mum arrived halfway through *The Archers*. 'I'm sorry, darling, I had an appointment to see somebody.' Darling? 'I'll make rice.'

'Is someone coming?'

'No, it's just the two of us: we're celebrating.' She smiled triumphantly. 'We have a new home.' Seeing my face fall, she laughed: 'It's round the corner only.'

'What's the point?'

'So you can have a bedroom. So we can have our own bath and toilet for the first time since coming here. For privacy; for health.'

My own bedroom and still in Paddington. Near to Caroline, near to Jan, to the park, my school, my aunties; to everyone and everything I held most dear. And close enough for Beth to find me, should she ever come back. I felt the excitement begin. 'That's fantastic. How did you find it?'

'You found it, Mala. When you mentioned the new landlord.'

Horror. 'You don't mean . . . You can't mean . . . Mum, we can't do that, it's not right.'

'It's been completely renovated – it's as nice as anything in Ambassador Court but half the price. There's even a little patio – I can grow plants. We'll be very happy there.'

I couldn't believe it, couldn't imagine living in a place scented with essence of Bethany. To enjoy good fortune born out of my best friend's unhappiness!

'You're worried it's bad karma? No need: I checked everything – Mrs Stephens already had a new place organised. There were no unlucky portents in their departure.'

'They left an address?'

'No address, he said. Who would write to someone like that?' She hugged me to her, resting her head on mine. 'You won't recognise the flat, it's beautiful.' I nodded into the damp coat that smelled faintly of curry and mothballs. 'And do you know the best news of all?' I shook my head. 'We'll be settled by New Year!'

# 5

New Year's Eve in Trafalgar Square. We are covered in the cold spray of the fountains and all around us people are laughing and shouting and singing. A sudden hush for the midnight chime of Big Ben, booming down Whitehall to the thousands massed in Nelson's moonlit water garden, and then an eruption of cheers as happy strangers grab hold of my mum and me and Anu and Prisky and, singing 'Auld Lang Syne', land kisses on our cheeks. Happy New Year! Welcome 1971! Crazed young men and women are bathing beneath the splendour of the National Gallery, St Martin-in-the-Fields and South Africa House. Fiona Richmond's bazooka bosoms fill billboards outside the Whitehall Theatre and raise a cheer from the crowds now flocking through Admiralty Arch and up towards Buckingham Palace. For that short, sweet hour, where all roads meet in the heart of London, we are part of a giant control centre: we are the control centre, sending good vibrations to fellow citizens of the world.

On New Year's Day the trail of friends popping in for milk rice and hot onion curry started at midday and carried on into late evening. Mum had made eighty creamy rice moulds with a teacup, and the meat and sambals were keeping warm in her new hostess trolley. Little diaries were wrapped and stacked in a drawer to give people as they left – to give and receive on the first of the year brings good luck *all* year. I'd received a shiny half-crown over breakfast and in return had given Mum a sixpence soaked clean in Coca-Cola.

'How times change, Mala. Just twelve months ago we moved

into this home. This time next year it'll be a new currency – no more half-crowns, only p's.'

I laughed, and the juice from my breakfast rum baba trickled on to my new baby-doll nightie.

'Dirty clothes for the whole year now.'

We cleared up – another series of omens put into action. Then it was quick showers with the rubber tap attachment and a wipe of Anna French before the doorbell started. 'Happy New Year! May all the blessings of the season be upon you.'

It was already full house by the time Caroline and Jan turned up. Four aunties were squashed on to the sofa bed and the men had taken the chairs. 'Sit on the floor, girls, it's good for your posture.' But we melted into my room where rationalised shelving along one wall and a fitted wardrobe in the end space had made it more accommodating. We sat on the bed, our feet against the opposite wall, balancing plates on our laps and sharing slivers of jaggery, the unrefined sugar which arrived in huge rocks from Ceylon. 'Eat it with the hot curry, it's just scrumptious.'

Afterwards Anu got everyone singing *baila*: songs about Surangani's fish and Babiachi's bicycle. Finally there were bowls of wood-apple cream and yoghurt with *pani*, the thick molasses treacle we kept in bottles.

'I'm blissed,' Jan said, and Caroline lay behind us on her tummy. 'I've eaten too much.'

I got the *Paddington Mercury* from under the bed and found the photo of Caroline, me and Jack Warner on page three: 'Dixon of Paddington Green! Local Guides whose sponsored swim at Porchester Baths raised over £100 for Paddington Green Children's Hospital presented their cheque to Dixon of Dock Green star Jack Warner on Christmas Eve. Mr Warner praised the girls' effort as "splendid and commendable".'

Jan grinned. 'You look a bit like François Pascal, Mala, and Caroline's like Wei Wei Wong, but with a Cilla haircut.'

'Because Wei Wei Wong is the only Chinese person you can think of, Janice.'

'What about Chairman Mao?'

'Very funny, Mala.'

Jan rolled her eyes. 'What do the stars say?'

I turned to the horoscopes. 'Capricorn: "The hardy goat has been put upon recently but hard work and effort should reap rewards this week."'

'Maybe I'll get those Inega jeans for my birthday.'

'They're twenty quid, Caroline.'

'So? It's my first teen year.'

'Pisces: "As always, the fish are being pulled in different emotional directions. Stick to one path for future happiness."'

'Great,' Janice said, straightening. 'I'll choose the path to Jack Tappett's door, as I don't have a choice.' She got up and stretched. 'The old cow's buying a white suit in the sales. Lord help us. My dad says no more money if she sees it through. What money? Twenty quid to see us through six weeks! But I can't tell her because she doesn't know he gives us anything.'

Soon it would be two years since Mr and Mrs Connors had separated, and the divorce was going through. In the meantime she'd announced her engagement to a Jimmy Tarbuck look-alike – Jack Tappett, the cellarman from the Railway Tap. 'Can't resist his cut-price booze,' Jan said.

'Cancer: "The home-loving crab never likes being unsettled. Seek solace in quiet contemplation."' I looked up. 'Perhaps I should do a Josh, and find God?'

Caroline rolled on to her back. 'I think the story's that God found him – popped into his head, just like that, for a quick chat.'

'Aries: "You've been digging in your heels for too long – give an inch and gain a mile."'

'Why Bethany?'

'I like to know how she's doing.'

'Rubbish.'

'It's a connection, Caroline – nothing more, nothing less.'

Seeking solace in new plimsolls, I was in Whiteleys when I spotted the familiar yellow-white hair and pink polka-dot mac in the perfume department: Allie. She was at the Elizabeth Arden counter under the main staircase. I crept up unnoticed, gave her a bear hug, and died of embarrassment. On the other side of the narrow waist was a hard and distinctly noticeable bump.

She turned round in surprise. 'Hello, sunshine.' Her stomach, now facing me, seemed to throb with life like something in *Tales from the Crypt*. Putting down a small puff bottle of scent, she grinned. 'Come on, I'll buy you a coffee. I could do with a rest.'

We went to the patisserie opposite. Immediately, two Arabs approached. 'May we sit with you ladies?'

'I'm afraid not – my friend and I are discussing women's matters that would only upset you,' Allie said sweetly.

'I love it when you sock it to me, baby.'

'Another time, buster.' Allie laughed. 'Men! So how's tricks, Mala: you're getting very pretty.'

'Not as pretty as you.'

'Even like this? I'm an old lady now – almost twenty.' She looked down and stroked her forbidden protruberance. I noticed her left hand was bare of rings. 'As you see, I'll be a mum in the summer. Don't be embarrassed, Mala – this won't be the first child born out of wedlock. Everyone's doing it.'

But nobody I knew was doing it apart from Marsha Hunt and Joanna Lumley, and they weren't real people.

'Wouldn't you like to know about the father? He's called Guy Johnson. He's got a furniture business on Lots Road: reproduction antiques – very posh, not like me. He'll be running G Plan before we know it.' She dropped her voice. 'He's gorgeous, Mala, and crazy about me. I've even met his mum and dad; God forbid he ever meets mine.' I tensed as she reached across and put her hand on mine. 'You don't need a piece of paper to prove that you love each other, you know.'

Even if it was true, I thought, what about her family and friends? We weren't all hippies or trendies, but normal people getting on with life.

'Spit it out – you've obviously got something to say.'

'I think it must be a big shock to your mum.'

'My mum? The only thing that'd shock her is eighty volts.'

I gazed hungrily at my chocolate éclair but pushed it aside for a moment. 'You'll be the first girl round here that *chose* to have an illegitimate baby.'

'What does illegitimate mean? Just that we're not married. It counts for nothing.'

But we both knew that wasn't true. That illegitimacy was a lot worse than the other options like separation or divorce. That the baby would always be a little bastard to Mrs Connors and, if Guy ever left her, she'd be unsaleable goods to the lads round our way, who were full of brag and bravado but had the good manners to marry any unfortunate who fell pregnant by them.

I ate my éclair and told her about the woman aviator Sheila Scott coming to our school prize-giving, and Caroline starting her periods; about Jan's crush on her English teacher, Mr Warren, and my mum's sister finally dying. 'We've been going to the temple every month to give a *danae* so her merits build up.'

'What does that mean? No, go on, tell me. Guy's very interested in it – his brother's hanging out with the Maharishi, he's even met George Harrison – "My Sweet Lord" and all that. You know, meditating, omming, reaching higher planes.'

I tried. 'Well, with Buddhism there's a reincarnation system. What goes around comes around. If you're good in this life you come back as a higher form of human, and if not you're returned as a cat or something. You improve each time till you reach nirvana and then you don't come back because you've made it.'

'Is your aunty a cat or a higher being?'

'I don't know. But at the *danae* we offer food to the monks and anyone who wants it, and we chant and pour water into a tower of different-sized glasses to help the dead person build up merits for their next life – it's like giving them a leg-up.'

She burst out laughing. 'I wonder what merits this precious little thing has got – am I the reward or the punishment?'

I laughed too, though given the circumstances I suspected the latter. And I didn't let on that when my mum told me off for 'demanding too many Western freedoms' I often wondered if I'd come back as me because I'd done something terrible in a previous life – like killing too many spiders or giving in to desire. What other possible explanation could there be for my being the only girl in the class denied a Ben Sherman?

'You're turning out like Bethany, Jan.'
　'I don't know why you're going on about it.'
　'I'm your best friend. You should have told me.'
　'You can't tell me what to do, Mala.'
　'But if I don't tell you, who will?'

*　　*　　*

Caroline said: 'It's typical – they don't come more common than the Connors.'

'That's not fair.'

'Not fair? I haven't got an older brother sewing mailbags in Pentonville, or a sister up the duff. I don't sleep at my desk because I've been up all night while my mother carouses with a cellarman. They are *common*.'

'You make me sick with all that stuff, Caroline. You're not so grand yourself.'

'I'm better than them. So are you. Our parents work and we're going to be somebodies. You want everyone to be the same, Mala, but we're not.'

'I just don't look for the worst in everything.'

'Because you're naïve.'

'Naïve? You don't even know how to spell that word, Caroline, let alone what it means.' I picked up my things angrily. 'I'm not wasting my time here.' She said nothing as I marched out.

On the stairs I met Josh, thin and pale, bowed under a raffia shoulder bag of textbooks. 'Mala: you look flushed.'

'I'm angry with Caroline.'

'She's an expert at upsetting people.'

'Like you?' I said, meaning that he too was her victim, but he misunderstood. 'It's a family failing. Too much passion, too few outlets.' He smiled sadly: unJoshly.

I said: 'It gets a bit much when she turns on her friends.'

'What are friends for?' he replied, and pushed past me.

'What's the matter, Mala, sitting silently like the old *dobi*?'

'Oh, that's typical, isn't it? If I go out, I'm a streetwalker; if I stay in, I'm a washerwoman.'

I went crossly into my bedroom and got out my book of logarithms. Turning up the radio to muffle my mother humming 'Bridge Over Troubled Water' in a martyred manner, I struggled with sine and node until my inability to concentrate through bad temper triumphed over visions of Mrs Kessler's wrath at half-finished homework. I settled down to read *Mirabelle* and *Valentine* while Tony Prince read the love requests on 208: 'And this one's for Tina Neave in South Shields from Keith, who says you are the coolest, grooviest chick in town – dig those hot pants, baby. The Partridge Family – "I Think I Love You": smoochy coochy . . .'

French kissing: this is kissing with your mouth open. The boy puts his tongue inside your mouth and you move yours around in his. This technique is one where only practice makes perfect. Gross.

I'd practised normal kissing on the wooden bust of Winston Churchill at Aunty Mina's place; it had been of little help. What could I use to practise this new phenomenon? Caroline had read *Portnoy's Complaint* in which a teenage boy did something very rude with offal from the family fridge, but the thought of putting my tongue into the grizzled ox liver my mother stocked was revolting. I sighed and put the magazines back under my bed. I could smell dinner.

'Something must be wrong, Mala.'

I gazed silently into my stuffed marrow.

'Why aren't you seeing your friends?'

I shrugged. 'We're not getting on.'

'Then invite Margaret – always you're talking about her. Isn't her father a doctor? It's very useful to know professional people.'

'Why? Will he give me Clearasil on prescription?'

'You are so bad-tempered these days, Mala. Just ask the girl to play.'

'Girls my age don't play, Mum – they go to the pictures and buy make-up – things that need money.'

She sighed. 'In four months' time, when you're thirteen, we'll talk about pocket money. Not till then.'

Even Aunty Anu, usually sympathetic, was no help. 'One day you'll be glad of your mother's wisdom.'

'One day in this life or the next?'

On Valentine's Day I sent the RE teacher a card from God. It put me in such a good mood I called at Westbourne Terrace. Jan came to the door. 'Fine friend you are: I've been stuck indoors for the last fortnight while Romeo and Juliet slugged it out across the neighbourhood, and you never called once.'

'Sorry.'

'Silly cow.' She put her arm through mine. 'Come on, let's go up to The Regent and get a sundae – like it was summer.'

We crossed under the flyover to the Edgware Road and entered the golden art deco ice-cream bar fortuitously filled with boys from Rutherford talking loudly to each other. 'Hey, Phil, it must be our birthday!'

'Where d'you come from then. India?'

'No, I'm Ceylonese.'

'Silly knees? You haven't got silly knees. Sit on mine, let me have a feel.'

Jan nudged me. 'Go on.'

'His face looks like a pizza.'

We slid into an empty bench as the silliness increased.

'How old are you girls? Gone quiet? Must be virgins, Steve! Or lesbians. Ah, look – they're embarrassed.'

Jan said: 'Ignore it, they'll soon get bored.' She was right. After a few minutes they'd moved on to football and we were forgotten.

'You weren't serious about sitting on his lap?'

'Why not?'

'That's sitting on their thing!'

'I've sat on a boy's lap. And kissed him – in the caff. It was just a bit of fun – not proper snogging.'

'You'd better watch it or you'll end up like Allie.'

But we were both secretly excited by our blossoming charms as we moved on to more mundane subjects. Afterwards we walked down to Hyde Park Square where snowdrops were breaking through the long grass in the church grounds; past the Ceylon Students Centre where my mother had vainly sent me for Sinhalese lessons a few years previously, and into Westbourne Terrace the back way.

As we approached her house, Jan's pace slowed. 'It's been on-off all week. I hate the sight of him lying there with his belly hanging out, putting the world to rights.'

'He's good to take on so many kids.'

'He hasn't taken us on – we've taken him. If she'd fussed around my dad half as much, he'd still be here.' She sighed. 'Anyway, sod Tappett – I've got a treat stashed away.'

In the kitchen she poured me a glass of flat cider.

'It's horrible.'

'It's alcohol.'

We swilled it round our mouths as a rumbling began next door. I said: 'Nothing changes but the cast.'

She got up to shut the kitchen door. 'I can't bear it.' But just as she pushed it to, it was shoved violently open from the other side, hitting her full in the face so the glass smashed against her teeth. As she fell to the floor, blood pouring from her mouth, Jack Tappett came marching in. Pulling a fraying leather jacket off the back of a chair, he wrestled his arms inside as Mrs Connors came running behind. 'No, Jack, don't go. They're just kids – they don't mean it.'

She stumbled on Jan, who was holding her hand over her mouth to stem the flow. 'Get up from there, you stupid girl – it's you that's driving him away! Jack, please: anything.'

But he was heading for the door.

'Bastard! You bloody bastard!'

As it slammed she started to cry loudly. Turning on Janice, she hissed: 'You're ruining my happiness.' When Jan didn't reply she ran into the lounge screaming to Sean and Marie: 'Come here and let me kill you!'

In the morning Allie came round. 'Mala, I'm taking Jan to the dentist. What happened?' I told her. 'Neither of them helped?' I shook my head. 'Right, that's it. I don't need this hassle. I'm going to the Social Services.'

'You can't do that, Allie.'

'Just watch me. Look, sweetheart, I'll have my own baby soon. I'm moving in with Guy – there won't be anybody here to help. And there won't be money for extras because I'll stop work.' She squared up. 'Someone's got to take charge.'

I went indoors fearfully.

'Is that Allie pregnant?'

'Yes, Mum.'

'*Chi!* And no husband, I suppose?'

'She's moving in with her boyfriend.'

'Living in sin? I always thought she was a decent girl.'

'She's very modern.'

'Modern is a new word for cheap.' She shook her head. 'What will it be like for that baby with no father?'

'It's got a father. Anyway, it hasn't done me any harm, has it?'

'*Chi!* I'm a respectable woman – don't compare me with Allie Connors. Only because you haven't had a father can you think his absence hasn't harmed you. Do you think we'd be living like this if he were still here?'

'What you don't know can't hurt.'

'Perhaps you don't know, Mala – but I do.'

Jan was sitting on the wall outside her flat. Her face was all swollen. 'I'm getting caps.' I stroked her cheek but she shrugged me off. 'Caroline's waiting for us in the Wimpy.'

Caroline was sitting by the window. 'Don't panic – I've got money.' She took my *Evening News* and turned to 'The Day in the Courts'. 'What d'you reckon, Mala, is it fair he got six months?'

I ruminated. 'Probably. He'd two previous and a suspended.'

Jan groaned, hating the game as much as Caroline and I enjoyed it. Caroline put the paper away. 'So what are we going to do? Tappett can't just march round slamming doors.'

'That's the way it's always been in our house.'

We ordered egg burgers, thinking they'd be easier on Jan's mouth, but just a sip of Coke made her gasp. 'It burns.'

I said: 'I hope your mum's feeling bad. She didn't exactly help.'

'She never helps, Mala. You can't start having a go at her just because this happened.'

Caroline shook her head, despairing like the soothsayer in *Up Pompeii*: 'Who can we have a go at, then? One day, Janice, the pieces won't stick back together.'

The egg burgers arrived. Jan pushed hers away. I pulled it across. 'If you can't eat your burger, I'll have it.'

'Mala!'

'Waste not, want not, Caroline. We could all be hungry tomorrow.'

At school Margaret and I were being 'brought up to date' by

Flick. She had the latest oxblood loafers and a mohair tonic suit. At lunch-time she pulled down the blind on our classroom door, cleared away the desks and went through the steps of all the skinhead dances. Dave and Ansell Collins's 'Long Shot Kick 'e Bucket'. 'Come on, Mala, two right cross-kicks, two left cross-kicks, jump forward, jump back, jump side, start again. Flamin' 'eck Margaret – you got a poker up your bum or summint?'

During the lunch-time discos we'd line up alongside girls with feather cuts and grey tights like Pan's People.

'Flick, d'you go round with kids who Paki-bash?'

'Don't be stupid.'

'A lot of skinheads do.'

'Blokes, not girls.'

'D'you think it's all right to do it?'

'Of course not. I'd hardly be friends with you if I did – not that you're anything like the real Pakis – you're one of us, aren't you?'

I thought about the skinhead gang that had started swaggering down Praed Street shouting threats and abuse at the Asian commuters, including my mum, in the early evenings.

'They're just stupid, Mala: layabouts,' Margaret had comforted.

'I know that, but they frighten the life out of her and then she stops me going out. They're spoiling both our lives.'

'Some other victim'll soon come along.'

'I'll have died by then – of boredom or old age.'

She laughed. 'If it helps, my dad says Asians are going to revolutionise trading in this country.'

'It doesn't.'

She looked glum. 'Now you'll never let me squeeze that blackhead on your thigh, will you?'

They came for Sean and Marie six weeks before Allie's summer baby was due. We knew something was going to happen; they'd been to the house several times, even when we were there.

'So, Janice, you're the one who gets the children ready, gives them their meals and is generally responsible for their welfare?'

'I don't mind doing it.'

'And when your mum's out at night, you baby-sit.'

'Well, I live here.'

'What about when she's out all night?'

'Most times she's back by one or two.'

'You know this because . . .'

'Because I always wait up – to check.'

Another time, it appeared that Mrs Connors had been given a warning because they were asking if things had changed. 'What has your mother done in the house this week?'

'Well, nothing much, but the divorce has just come through and she's rowed with Jack so she's depressed.'

'What about doing the laundry or the shopping?'

'They're my jobs – why would she do them?'

'And what's Mr Tappett's involvement?'

'Involvement? We're not his kids.'

'Have you seen your father since the notification?'

'Not in the last month.'

Afterwards we went out into the hallway. 'The way they ask questions makes out there's something wrong with the way we live.'

'It's not exactly normal family life, is it, Janice?'

'What's normal Caroline, having a brother who creeps round corners saying the Lord's Prayer? I wish you'd all stop mouthing off and making it worse for us.'

But Mrs Connors was managing that quite well on her own. One of her pub friends had given her a home perm and she looked like Ken Dodd as she recited her list of woes: 'It's a lot of work for one woman. I've got five kids and a troublesome back and I don't get any help.'

'Two of your children are adults, Mrs Connors. It's the three youngest we're concerned about.'

Mrs Connors shrugged. 'Jan's all right but the other two, they're a handful.'

'Are you saying you find it hard to cope?'

'You try coping with them!'

In the corridor we bristled at the unfairness of it. Sean and Marie were certainly tough, rude and dishevelled, but compared to some kids who had no respect for anybody, Janice had done a really good job with them.

It wasn't enough.

'This is not a permanent situation, Mrs Connors, it will be reviewed monthly,' said the woman who'd arranged to take the youngest Connors children into temporary care. 'The sooner you're sorted out, the sooner they'll return.'

The kids, confused and defiant, were loaded into a black cab to be placed with foster parents, their clothes hurriedly jammed into Co-op bags. Marie had found a teddy somewhere, and clutched it to her chest. Sean, small, crew-cut and angry, leered at us all as if it were us being punished by his removal. Their mother was nowhere in sight. Allie stood in the street grim-faced. 'Don't worry, my pets, you'll go to lovely homes until our mum feels better. I'll phone you every week, and bring the baby: I promise.'

Catching my baleful stare, she said gently: 'It *is* for the best, Mala – cruel to be kind.' But as I went indoors to Janice, who was standing at the window with tears streaming down her face, I wasn't sure I agreed. It seemed to me that just because something makes sense in theory, it doesn't necessarily work in practice. While Mrs Connors was just about the worst mother possible, Jan was the best, and she'd been doing the job a long time under the noses of regular social workers. What she needed was enough money – that was all. What good would it do sending Sean and Marie to live with strangers for a month or two? And if it was better than being at Westbourne Terrace, what would happen if they didn't want to come back?

Hours later I left the flat. Allie had gone home to Guy and Mrs Connors was still missing. Jan paced the eerily empty rooms. 'Stay with me, Mala, please.'

'I can't. Come back with me – have some dinner.'

'No. I've got to be here. She'll fall apart when she sees they've gone.'

'She knows they've gone.'

'She doesn't know anything till she sees it.'

'You mean she doesn't know anything till she's lost it.' I squeezed her shoulder. 'I'm sorry, Jan.'

As I left I slammed the front door as hard as I could. To try to comfort her with a familiar sound.

6 ∫

We'd left Jan behind: she made us feel guilty.

'It's like going out with Bambi,' Caroline said, 'except no one's brave enough to shoot the mother.'

I twirled in front of the mirror. 'What about these?'

She folded the legs of the jeans to ankle height, exposing my white socks and black square-toed lace-ups. 'They're better than the ones in Marbles but you still look like a navvy.'

'Get with it, Caroline.'

We headed up Oxford Street to the Souk where I spent my remaining birthday money on bead chokers and a plaited leather wristband. Caroline said: 'Are you a skinhead or a hippie?'

'I'm a Skippy – the friend ever true.'

On the way home we stopped at Jolyons. 'Actually, I don't think I'm a very good friend to Jan,' I said. 'Nothing I do makes it better. They've put the kids into care instead of a foster home. She goes over and over it. I end up feeling worse than her.'

'Misery's contagious: I should know.'

I sighed. 'That must make me the lucky one – all I've got is a mother from the Dark Ages. I bought a Miners mascara and she called me a Lolita.'

'Talking of which, has Allie had the baby yet?'

'Any minute. That'll cheer Jan up. Honestly, I dragged her out after school yesterday and she wouldn't do anything. We ended up riding the Circle Line.'

'And now you're going round in circles too.'

It was a relief to go to Margaret's, to finish our geography project on the Argentinian beef industry. Through the fourth-floor door of a George Street mansion block, we entered a cream-carpeted hall. 'Take your shoes off, Mala, I don't want my mum having a heart attack.'

We passed Margaret's bedroom, its shelves stacked like Hamleys, and settled in the red-flocked dining room. She got me a drink. 'I'm really pleased you've come at last – I wish we didn't have so much work.' Spreading our books on polished mahogany, we charted the journey of a prize bull, carefully sticking Fray Bentos labels in the margins and copying information sheets: steak, hide, corned beef. Margaret's dad had given her a newspaper feature on ranching and she wrote a story around it while I retraced and mapped Argentina: Buenos Aires, Cordoba, Cape Horn, the Andes. It was an impressive piece of work.

Margaret said: 'Stay for tea now – my mum'll be back soon.'

This seemed to me a much better prospect than afternoons at Jan's where even chips couldn't be fried without a house fire, or Caroline's where visitors were only allowed to smell the food. I decided to stay, an option rubber-stamped by the return of her mother with fresh ravioli from Derry and Toms where she worked as a buyer.

My mum wasn't pleased. 'Mala: where have you been?'

'At Margaret's. You said I should see more of her.'

'It's seven thirty.'

'How could I let you know? Semaphore? Tom-toms? Why can't we get a phone?'

She sighed. 'Perhaps the time has come.' She put up a hand to stop me cheering. 'As a safety precaution: not for your friends to be ringing all the hours.' She sighed. 'There's a different climate in this country. Nobody is safe any more. Do you know I was assaulted in the street today?'

A man had jostled my mum as she came out of Paddington Station and then spat as she'd pushed past. 'So many people saw – not one asked if I was all right. He followed me down the road shouting filth – "Paki scum I'll get you" – as if I were an aimless cur. I was so frightened of him learning our address I walked in and out of the shops until he went away.'

'It was just one man, Mum. He's probably sick.'

'In that case the whole country is ailing.' She held my hand as I sat down next to her. 'You must be careful, Mala. You may think you are one of them, but they only see your colour. Their minds are full of filth. They stripped our countries of wealth and now they strip us of our dignity. Bloody skinheads – it's my taxes that pay for them to loiter in the street barracking and attacking respectable people.'

The Saturday after school broke up, Caroline came over and we spent the morning trimming each other's fringes. 'So you're really getting a phone?'

'Yep. Now you'll have to get one.'

'Why don't *you* tell that to my parents?'

We went to the takeaway on Spring Street for Cornish pasties and wandered up to Jan's. She was sitting on the wall outside, talking to a boy.

'Are these your mates, then?' She nodded, embarrassed. 'Nice.' He looked us up and down. Then: 'So what d'you say?'

'All right, Sid.' Sid?

'I'll pick you up later, then, about seven.'

We watched him gangle away: long, thin, pale, bony – male.

'A date, Janice? Aren't you a little young for that sort of thing?'

'He's only taking me up to the Stowe, to watch him and his brother play pool.'

I savoured the last mouthful of my pastie. 'So where did you meet him, Jan?'

'He just walked past while I was sitting here. I think he lives in the flats up Orsett Terrace.'

'So much for love's young dream,' Caroline said, but there was a twinge of jealousy in her voice. 'You *do* fancy him?'

'I don't know.'

'If you don't know, why bother?'

'Because he asked, Caroline.'

'Just as well he didn't ask you to put your head in the oven.'

It was such a lovely afternoon we went to the park. The tourists had descended on the Serpentine and all the boats were out. We stood on the bridge picking out the handsomest faces and nicest clothes as they disappeared into the darkness beneath us. 'Summer holidays – hooray! No Hereford this year, Mala?'

'No: I'm too old. I don't mind. I'll miss the people, but it's more exciting being in London.'

'You've not said that before.'

'I've not been thirteen before.'

We bought ice creams and cut across to Kensington Gardens, idling on the grass around Peter Pan until Jan suddenly jumped up. 'I forgot! I promised the kids I'd write: I must get something in tonight's post.'

She went rushing off and Caroline and I walked lazily on to her place, to watch *Dr Who* before I went home and dolled up for Aunty Mina's engagement party. As I was going, Caroline said: 'Hang on a minute, I'll give you back your *Flambards* trilogy.' I went to follow her into the bedroom when she suddenly stopped in the doorway. I heard the sharp intake of breath before she screamed.

The sound was so unexpected, so eerie, I started shaking. Shoving her roughly out of the way, I pushed past into the net-curtained gloom. Now I saw it.

Daubed across her wall in capital letters two feet high, Josh had painted in black gloss: CAROLINE IS THE ANTI-CHRIST.

'That boy should be locked away. He's completely mad,' my mother said. 'I see him sometimes in Queensway lurking like a hungry wolf in doorways. Always he's incanting: it's not right.' She checked her reflection in the glass. 'Is this sari okay?'

'Lovely.'

'The next time he won't stop at words: these hallucinations make people do terrible things. You don't believe me? My father had a servant who believed he was Julius Caesar: in Hambantota! Everybody laughed until he pounded his own brother to death in a rice mill, thinking he was Brutus. When the police took him away he was shouting in English: "Beware the ides of March". He'd had a better education than we thought. Caroline's mother should send Josh to a sanatarium until he improves.'

'But then everyone will know he's bonkers.'

'You think they don't know already?'

Mina's fiancé was an engineer at Foster Wheeler. 'We kept meeting at Edgware Road station.' He was embarrassingly keen on squeezing her hips and kissing the top of her curling-tonged head as it nestled in his armpit. '*Chi!* He should have better manners.'

There were about twenty of us squeezed into the large bed-sitting-room overlooking Eliot on Westbourne Grove. 'Cheers, Mina, cheers, Ronnie!' He couldn't stop smiling, and she was proud and bashful in equal parts. 'Who would have thought I'd marry an Englishman – my heart was always set on a nice Goygama boy.'

'Mum, what's a Goygama boy?'

'The highest caste: like us.'

'What difference does it make?'

'It makes a difference to us. Caste marries within caste: they have accepted traditions and beliefs. See, even the Queen preferred a Greek prince to an English commoner.'

'But there aren't many Ceylonese in London. Does that make Ronnie all right?'

'It's a shame his father is only a shopkeeper.'

'Mina's only a nurse.'

'But you see, Mala, she comes from a family of lawyers. Her father is head of the Ceylonese Bar.'

Aunty Anu poured herself more punch. 'Ronnie's a good man. And brave to marry a woman with Mina's spending habits – it's a shame she never met Emil Savundra before his downfall.'

We laughed, reminded of Mina's endless purchases. One of my mother's favourite refusal lines was: 'You're just like Mina – you know the cost of everything and the value of nothing.' But, I thought, looking at Ronnie Bromnick's smart suit and hazel eyes, she'd got a good bargain in her man.

'It's a shame you're so picky, Aunty Anu.'

'Why so?'

'Because you could be settled too.'

She looked surprised. 'Settled with a husband? Let me teach you one of life's more important lessons, Mala: men rarely confer happiness on the women they marry.'

Across the room I watched the women taking it in turns to dance awkwardly with the insistently high-spirited bridegroom: John Kongos, 'He's Gonna Step On You Again'.

\*     \*     \*

The next morning I went back to Caroline's. She was alone. 'Mum and Dad have gone to church before work.'

'Work on a Sunday? I thought they'd become partners?'

'It's a co-operative, Mala, the employees bought it to save their jobs. They're working harder to earn the same. Are you going to stand there all day?'

Instead of going to the lounge, I went to her bedroom. The words were still there: still deeply shocking.

'How could you sleep under that?'

'I didn't. I sat and read all night. Will you help clean it?'

We got some Sunlight and started scrubbing at the paint with worn-out Brillo pads, but the best we could do was fade it. The message still stood. Finally we took the only course available and used the remains of Josh's black paint to block the letters out. But it was oily and runny and we couldn't contain it. The words were gone, but they were replaced by an enormous black spider hovering over Caroline's bed, bearing down on her like a curse.

'We can't just leave it like this. You'll have to paint the whole room, Caroline.'

'What with? Soy sauce?'

We forced open the windows to excise the terrible smell and went on to the balcony.

'He's stark staring mad.'

'You know that, I know that, half the world knows that. But it's not a crime to blaspheme in your own home.'

'What about your parents?'

'He's their son, Mala: their darling boy – remember? My mum just splashed Lourdes water around the room and then we said the Lord's Prayer together. What's really bothering her is that he didn't come home. She was clattering through the worry beads all night.' Although Caroline spoke carelessly, her hands were clenched on the balcony rail. I wished I could think of something useful to say or do. Somewhere in the distance, church bells rang. 'Of course she's communing with the Almighty even as we speak.' Her shoulders sagged. 'Nobody ever thinks what it's like for me. All his life he's got attention for failing. He's clever, but he's always let us down. Me, I'm just left to soldier on – "You're the strong one, Caroline".'

I tried to find an excuse for Josh, as much for the sake of my own feelings as hers: disturbed genius, romantic lost soul, exciting eccentric – but I too had been disturbed by the graffiti. The whole thing spooked me: it was like something from a Dennis Wheatley novel – CAROLINE IS THE ANTI-CHRIST; dark, chilling, sordid.

Above us, someone was playing jarringly tuneless electric guitar, and below, two children were fighting in the road. 'I can't stand it here any more,' Caroline said. 'Can we go round to yours? I've got homework; I'll bring it with me.'

She threw various bits into a shoulder bag and we arrived in Craven Terrace just as the Salvation Army band came marching down Lancaster Gate. Uniformed collectors came along the street with tins while at the junction the choir sang: 'Stand up stand up for Jesus, Ye creatures of the Lord!'

An elderly sergeant approached as we turned down the steps to the flat. 'Can you spare a few pennies, ladies?'

'I'm sorry,' Caroline said rudely, 'but I'm feeling rather anti-Christ at the moment.'

That Wednesday Jan took us to see Allie's new baby. We walked from Victoria Tube to the flat in Pimlico that Allie shared with Guy. 'Hello, girls – you all seem like old grannies now there's a real baby in my life.'

She'd bought angel cake and a Swiss roll. China plates were laid out on a wooden table at the far end of the knocked-through sitting room. As we chomped she described the birth in colourful detail and we oohed, aaghed and made vomit noises as it became steadily more gruesome. Still Jon remained asleep in a basket under the window, one arm thrown carelessly across his pillow, the fist of the other resting against his mouth. 'Isn't he a doll?'

There were lots of phone calls: Allie was chatty and assured. I realised suddenly how little we knew about her other life – her grown-up, genteel life. Her figure was almost restored and the fashionable clothes were familiar, but somehow, in this strange place, that made her more of a stranger, not less. 'Day dreaming again, Mala?'

In the corner the baby stirred. 'Come and look.' It seemed to me that Jon was an impressive specimen. Not yet three weeks, his face was full and comfortingly unwrinkled as his eyes flickered open momentarily. We gazed upon him, like the fairies in 'Sleeping Beauty', wishing all sorts of good things, yet fearing the unknown. He had his father's surname, which seemed to me a guard against the jinx of the Connors, but who knew what secrets Guy Johnson might have hidden?

Allie put the kettle back on. 'Guy and me are taking Jon to meet the kids this weekend. D'you want to come with us, Jan?'

Over fresh tea we talked about fostering and children's names and Pimlico and Guy's yard. We all sighed over Mrs Connors, who'd had the banns posted despite Jack Tappett's continued refusal to commit himself until Social Services stopped sniffing around. Caroline told her about Josh: 'It's my home and I feel that he's ruined it.'

Allie said: 'I feel like that about Westbourne Terrace. Too many bad things have happened there. But if you let it get to you, Caroline, he'll have won.' She laughed. 'Looking back at life with those two maniacs, it's a wonder I didn't end up as mad as Josh.'

I left them to it and went to the loo where a paper dragonfly was hanging directly over the bath and sanitary towels, discarded knickers and all kinds were on show – the nuts and bolts of making love, not war. I hovered, rather than sat, on the toilet seat and, turning to flush, was strangely elated to see a Polaroid of Allie, naked and pregnant, stuck to the cistern; bizarrely, her belly button had popped out, and I stood and gazed in amazement at her strangeness until Jon's cries roused me.

In the sitting room his aunt was holding him proudly.

Allie was saying: 'He's got your gorgeous blue eyes, Jan, and the dark Connors hair, but the rest of him's like his dad.'

Caroline wrinkled her nose. 'His nappy's leaking.'

Jon's wet Harrington was duly deposited into a lidded bucket and I found myself staring at his strangely male genitals. His giant testicle was nothing like the diagrams I'd pored over in my biology textbook; he looked more like the Staffordshire bull terrier in Brook Mews.

'Is he normal, Allie?'

'Normal? Oh, that – it doesn't fall into place until they're older.' She started laughing. 'I do miss you all.'

As we left we could hear her singing to the baby: the New Seekers, 'Never Ending Song of Love'.

We walked from Allie's to St George's Hospital, and then jumped on a bus, continuing our detailed inspection of the afternoon's events.

'Jon Johnson – he sounds like a film star.'

I told them about the picture in the toilet: 'Her belly button had popped out like a Rolo!'

We were just passing Park West when, looking out, I saw Bethany. I was quite sure it was her. The curls were now more mouse than blond, but were pushed behind her ears in that familiar, irritated way. The set of her shoulders was defiant and she had a definite bosom. She still loped as if her legs worked independently of her body. She seemed very tall and I thought fleetingly that I might be mistaken, but it was Beth all right. I jumped up and started shouting her name at the top of my voice through the open half-window. She looked around confused, hearing me in echo: 'Bethany! Bethany!'

Instantly Caroline pulled the bell and we jumped off near the Victoria Sporting Club. 'Are you sure it's her?'

'Of course I'm sure. She was outside Strikes.'

We walked back towards Marble Arch, but she wasn't there. Caroline even checked inside the shops and cafés but came out shaking her head. 'Maybe she's hiding down a side street.'

'Why would she do that?'

'Because she hasn't contacted us in nearly two years?'

We split up, Jan and Caroline continuing towards Marble Arch and me doing an about-turn as far as Sussex Gardens. Nothing. Meeting up again outside Milletts Jan suddenly said: 'Look, it's her. It is her!'

I followed the line of her arm and found myself looking directly into familiar grey-green eyes. Bethany was sitting in a stationary number 6 bus at the traffic lights on the other side. All three of us started jumping up and down, beckoning: 'Come over here! Come here, Beth.' She just stared. I ran across the road and pounded on the bus window as it moved off. 'Get down at the next stop. Walk back!' I was grinning like an idiot – like Mickey Dolenz. The others ran across to join me, but Beth just sat staring with what I would later hope was, at the very least, a deep sadness, like the waxwork woman in Madame Tussauds, hovering in the shadow of the guillotine.

Caroline said: 'If she was happy to see us she would have smiled. The plain fact is she was doing a runner.'

Jan said: 'You're better than Ironside, Caroline.'

I wailed: 'What did we ever do to her?'

We stood like pantomime dames, suspecting all kinds of goings-on but doomed to complete ignorance: 'It's behind you!'

Caroline concluded the meeting: 'It's not what we've done to her, it's what she's done to us.'

In the Coronet cinema on Praed Street, an elderly man was doing business with a woman in a crushed cream raincoat and a blue plastic rain hood. Initially there had been an empty seat between them, but now he leaned across, money changed hands and he filled the gap. Caroline, Jan and I retreated so the transaction didn't spoil our view of George Harrison on the massive stage at Madison Square Garden: save the people of Bangladesh.

Jan sighed loudly. I'd forced them to part with a few bob on the promise that the popcorn was good, but on a wet summer afternoon it tasted like earwax and she wouldn't stop whispering: 'Is that man paying her to sit with him or to go with him afterwards?'

'I don't know.'

'But it is weird, isn't it? Why not go down Sussex Gardens?'

'Will you shut up a minute and let me listen?'

'To that Maharishi bloke? He looks a right state and the music's horrible.'

'It's not the Maharishi, it's Ravi Shankar.'

'How am I supposed to know? They all look the same.'

'Oh, bloody great.'

Afterwards we went back to her place. 'All that hippie stuff, I can't stand it!'

'So what does Sidney the kidney like?' Caroline said. '"Leap Up And Down (Wave Your Knickers In The Air)"?'

'You're just jealous, Caroline Chong. He's all right.'

'Do you kiss him?' I asked. No answer. 'You must kiss him.'

I found it impossible to conceive of a relationship where some form of kissing or fondling didn't go on because, if it existed, it wasn't getting reported in the magazines I was reading – and they told you everything about everything.

Jan reddened. 'Well, he does now, yeah.'

'On the lips or with tongues?'

'I don't know; both really.'

'Really? What does it feel like?'

'It doesn't feel like anything – it's just something you do.'

'It must feel like something: does it make your tummy seize up like when a boy's looking at you, or what? You can't just say it's something you do, or we'd all be doing it all the time.'

She thought about it for a few seconds. 'Okay, if you must know, it's a bit like chewing a sponge.'

Josh was brought back a week later by his college welfare officer. Dishevelled and distressed, he'd been found by the caretaker, dossing down in a disused stockroom. 'This boy is in need of medical help. I suggest you call your GP.'

When Caroline and I pitched up, we found her mother in mute attendance and the doctor recommending Josh for psychiatric treatment. 'They've got a place at Shenley. It's out of the way, but they get results. I'll order an ambulance for tomorrow. In the meantime he's very fragile.'

'Fragile?' Caroline said. 'What about the rest of us? Do you know what he did to my room? If anyone's fragile, it's me!' She turned coldly, angrily to her brother, huddled in a corner of the worn sofa. 'I hate you.' Mrs Chong moved forward, hissing something at her daughter. Caroline turned away contemptuously. 'He can't do a bloody thing wrong, can he?'

'Now, Caroline, I know you're all under stress, but that sort of attitude doesn't help. You all need a break from these dramas.'

'What dramas, Doctor? He's the reason for everything that goes wrong – he's bloody mad, that's why.' She turned away.

'He's not mad, he's suffering from a mild psychosis. He's been overtaken by events: he feels threatened. He'll get better at Shenley.'

'How? The drugs don't make any difference.'

'He hasn't been taking them.'

'So he's brought this on himself?'

On the sofa, Josh started rocking gently, his thick black hair falling over his eyes like a weeping willow, the fronds highlighting the smooth beauty of his pale cheeks. He started to hum; a long despairing note. We all stopped and stared for a moment and then Caroline said loudly: 'Oh yes, look at him now – full of self-pity – not a thought for how he's destroyed us. Pathetic, that's what you are; pathetic. A great big useless . . . pusillanimous pipsqueak!'

'Leave him *alone*.' I squatted on the floor by Josh and put my hand on his. 'It's all right. She's just angry. Don't be upset.' He took no notice, and suddenly I was pushed aside by Mrs Chong who climbed on to the sofa as I sprawled on the floor and clutched his thin body to her small, hard frame, trying, vainly, to still his movement.

# 7

Flick and I were on the top of a number 16 bus to Park Lane, eight-hour candles and a box of matches clutched to our chests. 'If these are the best days of our lives, there's no hope for the future,' I said glumly.

'Biology's not that bad.'

'It's hell. I told them I wouldn't do a science – they said I had to. I said I couldn't do maths – they said it's a core subject. Why call it O-level choice when actually there's no choice at all?'

'Well, at least you'll get them – not like me.'

We tensed as the sound of distant screaming was carried to us on the late afternoon breeze. How can I be sure, in a world that's constantly changing: how can I be sure?

From the moment the new school year had started, all we'd done was study, study, study. We were each down for ten O-levels – the whole class. I sighed. 'We're only fourteen – don't we deserve to live a little?' It was like having a sack dropped over my head and secured with chains so there was no escape, like the escapologist outside the Tower of London. Except, of course, he did escape.

The screaming was louder now: unmistakable. He must be there, he must have arrived! I said: 'I've never felt this about anyone before.'

'What about Marc Bolan?'

'Well, maybe Marc Bolan.'

We got off by the Grosvenor House and turned south; halving our Curly Wurly as a group of teenagers wandered up towards us. Flick asked eagerly: 'What's all the noise? Have you seen him?'

The biggest one shrugged: 'It was just a curtain twitch,' and indeed there was only the sound of traffic now to be heard. As we neared the Dorchester we saw them, dozens of girls clutching LP covers and satchels, crying over new photos in the *Evening Standard*. 'Aren't they pathetic?' I said. 'No self-control.'

Flick nodded. 'We've far too much sense for all that.'

We sat on the pavement and moaned about the house music competition, the source of much bad feeling. I was cheesed that, despite being the only entrant in the middle-school guitar section, I'd been placed second; and there was general anger about Tudor taking the cup when the York house performance was infinitely better. 'It's only because Caz Lazarus is head of house and sucks up to the teachers.'

'I wish I knew how to suck up to teachers.'

'You could stop chatting all the time for a start, Mala.'

'At least I don't argue about everything, like you.'

'Well, they get up my nose – they're only interested in the *nice* girls. That's why they save all the good stuff for them – like the school skiing trip.'

'We wouldn't have the money anyway, Flick.'

'My parents *have* got money. They just don't want us – that's why they didn't announce it till all the places had already gone. All this stuff about equality – it's like *Animal Farm*: some are more equal than others. Roll on comprehensives.'

How can I be sure, in a world that's constantly changing, how can I be sure, that you're the one for me?

Above us, there was a sudden movement on the balcony, and we were seized with acute excitement. The French window opened, and even though nobody was immediately visible, they all started screaming again: 'It's him! Oh my God – it's him!'

I jumped to my feet, and rather than run forward like the others who clutched the outside walls as if to touch him through the brick, I stepped back on to the kerb and looked upwards so that, as he came out and looked around, his glance spanning Hyde Park directly ahead and then moving back to the gaggle of girls below, it seemed to me for a split second that we were looking at each other – not just at, but into each other, like Elizabeth Bennet and Mr Darcy at Pemberley, sharing secret excitements – and that, with all the women in the world falling at his feet, David Cassidy, the divine David Cassidy, only had eyes for me.

Caroline read *Harpers* while I relayed my adventures in the labyrinthine confusion of the Dorchester Hotel: 'We were on the sixth floor when this kitchen hand saw us and blew the whistle – I thought I'd die!'

'Brilliant. You get into a back staircase while everyone's screaming round the front, and before you reach your destination you're found and sent packing – how intrepid, Mala.' She feigned a yawn. 'You'll be taking over from Tony Curtis and Roger Moore soon.'

I stood up crossly. 'At least I do things – not like you and your boring magazines full of stupid women in stupid clothes.'

'You just don't appreciate quality, Mala.'

'I can't afford quality, Caroline – not on two pounds a week.'

My Saturday job at Andre's earned me a pound plus tips for shampooing old ladies: it was hardly the good life, scrubbing hairlines for lice and going home with tingling fingers discoloured by bleach. Worse: a punter had complained because the cold rinse I'd recommended for extra shine had given her a head chill. Even in my sleep I could smell Life-tex.

Caroline was still talking. 'All you need to create style is imagination. Some of these outfits work because of the little details – the buttons, the cuffs. I could do it with a bit of practice and you wouldn't know the difference.'

I sighed. 'Give it a rest and let's go walkies.'

We got a bus to Kensal Green cemetery and wandered along the canal side swapping jokes and building stories around grave stones. 'Look at this – seven children from the same family – isn't that awful? This one's a bit grand: "Here lies Grace Tappett, dearest wife of Arthur, adored mother of Nan" – d'you think she's related to Jack?'

That summer, Mrs Connors had finally become Mrs Tappett and Jan had got herself a job at Clive's paper shop, arriving at 6.30 a.m. to mark papers for delivery and then working behind the counter until 8.45 when she literally ran up to North Wharf Road in time for register. 'His wife's taken a turn for the worse. He needs help and I need money.'

Sean and Marie had been moved to a home in Sunbury-on-Thames, which wasn't even London, and their mother showed no inclination to have them back. 'You can't say now that I was wrong to have them moved,' Allie said. 'At least they're reading and writing properly: I even get letters.'

Allie was pregnant again and Jon was a scrumptious, bald, wobbly-legged bundle. 'He does have some hair, it just doesn't show.' It was the only thing in her family that Jan felt positive about. 'I hate what that man did to the kids and even more than that, I hate what he's made my mother into.'

'What: Mrs Tappett?'

'No: a selfish, hard-hearted bitch.' A pause. 'Don't laugh at my family, Caroline.'

'If I didn't laugh, I'd cry.'

The angel watching over Grace Tappett gave nothing away: no district, no descendants, no detail; but, I thought, tracing the outline of her chiselled wings, she was too bold a representation of love, loss and cash to have come from the same branch.

We sat on a moss-covered mausoleum as the sky darkened, watching the trains in the sidings on the other side of the canal and the late afternoon narrow-boats heading for the Paddington Basin to tie up for the night.

'You used to get spooked by this place, Mala.'

'Because my aunties told such dreadful ghost stories.'

'You still remember them?'

'Not really. You forget the details unless they're being repeated to you.' In the half-light, a giant cross was illuminated by the dying rays of the sun. 'All these people long forgotten. When did Grace Tappett last have a visit, overgrown with grass like that?'

'You drop out of the race and in the wink of an eye you're a distant memory,' Caroline said, getting up. 'Come on, before it gets dark, or we'll both be spooked.'

There was curry for dinner and Anu and Prisky were there. 'No homework, Mala?'

'Plenty.'

'But you still go loafing? What is it tonight?'

'History: the First World War.'

'You must keep ahead. It'll be very disruptive when your school turns comprehensive. The timing is terrible.'

'Not just the timing, the whole idea.' My mother shuddered as she mixed together coconut and chilli for the pol sambal. 'We were always told English schools were the best, but all we hear is gangs, fights, drugs. They commit nothing to memory: at Mala's age we could recite poetry, conversions, capital cities – everything. Now . . .' She fine-chopped an onion. 'The whole system is verging on collapse.'

'It's not till next September, Mum.'

'Importing the worst to destabilise the best.'

'That's not fair,' Anu said. 'The philosophy is admirable. Even Tony Benn sends his children to Holland Park Comprehensive. The real problem is that some of the mergers are ill thought out.'

'I don't like the thought of boys being in her school, Anu.'

But I did, and Anu smiled at my subversive expression. 'Come on, Miss Lazybones, let's have a look at that homework.'

As we worked, Mum and Prisky gossiped. 'Ronnie's had a bit of a shock. You know these English boys – they expect Asian girls to be submissive.'

'A submissive girl wouldn't date a Western boy! He should have been warned that if Mina's alone in a lavatory, she would argue with the toilet roll – that's her way.' They both laughed.

I dropped my voice. 'Aunty Anu, you know what you said about men at the engagement party? Are you asexual?'

'*Anaa*!' She got up, shaking her head: 'Mala is trying to make sense of the world through cracked spectacles. She wonders why I'm still a spinster.'

'Mala is right, Anu. The bloom of youth will soon fade. Why don't you marry that lovesick Shanta, all the time gazing goo-goo eyes like a bush-baby.'

'I spend all day with children, Prisky, enough is enough.' She sat down again and sighed. 'Now, Mala, how did Princip's action play into the hands of the Kaiser?'

At the mirrors, Mr Andre's hands were busily fashioning a rigid black beehive on an old lady's head and Katya was whittering away about Benidorm to a cut-and-blow-dry with chlorine-damaged split ends.

I gazed idly out of the front window as I rinsed perm solution from an anonymous scalp and cursed my luck – if only I knew the Lambeth Walk and could talk bingo as easily as my Saturday counterpart Lisa, I knew I'd get better tips. But she was one of them and I was acutely aware that I wasn't. I didn't do the same things in the same way: I shared similar experiences, but differently. The punters liked me – that much was clear. But while I gave better shampoos, I didn't have the same value to them: I got 5p tips, she got 10p. Was it my chat or was it something else I didn't want to express? Something that made me deeply uneasy.

Sighing, I switched off the taps, got a fresh towel and patted the excess water from the rubber-clipped curlers. 'I'll just get Katya to put the neutraliser on. Would you like a coffee?'

I was exhausted after six hours on my feet. 'Can I take my lunch now, Mrs Andre?'

'Haven't you been? I'll see you back at half past two.'

I took off my overall and went to the ABC bakery in Church Street for a cheese roll and a cup of tea. Two elderly men visibly shrank away from me. I sniffed the perm solution on my skin and hoped that was why: then told myself off for thinking otherwise; it wasn't Lisa's fault, after all – I just wished she didn't gloat over her spoils at the end of the day as if they were a measure of her good work when all they represented was her Englishness. Her whiteness. Even the cheeky chat-up line of a knicker-stall boy couldn't lift my gloom, my sense of injustice. All right, so my mum was obviously a bit different: but wasn't I just the same?

Returning in a lull, I got lumbered with the worst job of all – cleaning the glass shelves with meths. This was worse even than carrying bags of wet towels to the launderette for drying – at least that got you out. Lisa was filling the shampoo bottles. 'Pulled the short straw, Mala?'

Working my way round the room, my own glum face stared balefully back at me in the mirrors: right now is where you are, in a broken dream. Ow! Katya gave my hair a playful tug. 'It's getting really straggly – let's do that restyle I keep promising. You look like you need cheering.'

Magically the spring returned to my step. My best customer, Mrs Webster, who regularly gave me 10p, opted to wait until I had finished sweeping the floor rather than have Lisa do her hair, and both she and Mr Andre agreed that I was turning into 'a real looker'. In a bleachy blur, the afternoon, which had been passing in a slow ache, started to speed up. As Katya's last customer was paying at the front desk and Lisa boasted that she'd reached her £2 tips target, I didn't even think about the paltry £1.20 in my pocket. Instead, I got her to wash my hair so that, when Katya returned to her cutting chair, I was already in place and ready for my new look.

My mum had bought a second chest of drawers for the alcove. 'I can't ask the landlord. Since the tenants took him to the rent tribunal, the goodwill has gone.'

Next to the ugly old walnut, the new rosewood piece from Frederick Lawrence was glossy, burnished and beautiful. 'The first good thing I've bought since we came here – an heirloom. I'll rearrange everything and use this for linens and towels.'

She pulled out the bottom two drawers from the old chest and laid them on the floor. In one were scores of little pocket hankies neatly ironed and rolled so that each was immediately identifiable; dozens of them like flowers fighting for dominance in a cottage garden: scarlet, violet, pink, purple, cream, navy, lemon; white, vermilion, sandstone, puce, ochre, grape, sienna; an artist's palette with each shade ranged alongside complementary hues so the brush instinctively dips into the right corner. And on each an individual mark – some embroidery, an initial, a scalloped edge, an inset of lace, a pattern like Biba wallpaper.

'Why keep all these, Mum?'

She shrugs. 'We clutch the past to make sense of the present. To shape the future.'

'But they're hankies.'

'Even hankies tell a story, Mala.' She picks up a small white lace square – too many holes to be anything but decorative – and holds it against her cheek. 'This was my mother's, part of her trousseau – French lace. She gave it to me on my wedding day.'

'What for?'

'A symbol, perhaps: purity, hope, beauty.'

'Bogies?' We both laugh and she puts it affectionately on the little pile I am making, ready for transfer to their new home, and shakes out a large grey man's handkerchief with a blue 'L' needleworked at each corner. 'This is a rare thing, a hanky your father didn't lose.'

'Let me see.' But there's nothing there: no fragrance, no texture, no markings. L for Lucky, Lucky Fonseka; full name pronounced Luckshman, spelt Laxman. Unlucky Lucky, machine-gunned in the arteries: Biff! just like that. Hello, wife and daughter, goodbye, wife and daughter – oh, and by the way, there's no dosh in the kitty, okay? Poor sad sod, long gone, long forgotten; pushing up the daisies in . . . where? Kensal Green? Willesden? Where?

'Mum, where's he buried?' A flicker; a hesitation. 'He's cremated. I sent the ashes home to his family.' Aren't we his family?

I wonder how these events passed me by: you forget the details unless they're repeated to you. She studies her fingers awkwardly. 'There was no point keeping him here.' Of course not. There are enough ashes in Paddington from bonfires in the park, from the workings of the railway, from the pyres of family life. Poor old Lucky. No chiselled angels, no beloved father of, just thanks for nothing and hit the road, Jack. And why do I suddenly care because of a big grey hanky?

'You seem disappointed, Mala.'

'I thought there'd be something more – something to hold on to.'

'I can't remember when you last mentioned him.'

We both look away. How have I lived ten years without even noticing his absence, except as a source of great relief – when Jan's relived a bruising encounter with Mr Connors or Caroline's complained about her father's meanness: thank God I haven't got a dad who's always standing in my way.

How strange; how sad. And yet there must, even now, be so much to say about who he was and what he meant: more, surely, than the contents of that old Grundig tape with 'Volare' and 'The Banana Boat Song'; but my mother has already folded up the hanky and put it on one of the piles. 'Look, this one with the embroidered pig – I bought it for you in the old linen shop

– always you were at the window asking "Can I have that one, or this one". When I bought them you had no interest.'

'Did I really want hankies? What for?'

'Because they're necessary.'

'And they look good in drawers.'

She starts to transfer the first pile, rerolling them lovingly. 'This was my sister's. She gave it to me on the boat – to dry my tears. This I bought in Oxford, see – the picture is Magdalen College – we went with the Ceylon Women's Association: do you remember?'

'And Rani's daughter broke the flask of iced coffee.'

We laugh, remembering how the child cried and the women sang *baila*, louder and louder to try and drown her wails.

'Whatever happened to her?'

'She'll be going to university next year – and she isn't as clever as you.' She sees my feigned yawn and smiles. 'Anu gave me this silk hanky when I joined the GPO – what a difference that made to our lives. This one with the flowers I found in our old room – I don't know whose it is.'

I take it from her hand. 'It's Bethany's. We both had sixpences and wanted something special. One of the old sister's who ran the linen shop said it was ladylike.'

She is silent, fingering the hankies still fresh and unused, unlike the plain yellow-and-blue checked scraps that are always ironed and tucked in her sleeves, her handbags, her coat pockets; available for general use at the hint of a sniff; but she, who sniffs often, resists the need to sully her pocket-sized perfections, resorting instead to Kleenex tissues.

'So many memories,' she says, putting away the last one.

'And all tightly folded.'

'One day,' she says, 'you will take charge of them, and shake them out, and dust away the cobwebs.'

'You're a 32B?' I marvelled at Jan's pointy cones and felt excited that my own must look similar.

'I'm still an A: it's so depressing.'

'Well, Chinese girls aren't really big on top, are they?' Allie said, playfully wobbling her own bosoms. 'It'll change when you get pregnant, Caroline. Mine come up like melons.'

'So does the rest of you.'

Allie cleared a space amongst the coloured glass and crystal earrings on the table and brought out a sherry trifle. 'Because I don't see you enough.' She gave Jon a bottle of Delrosa. 'I hope he's not jealous of the new one. He's got used to my attention – except when I'm selling.' She laughed. 'Isn't it Sod's law that I fall pregnant just as it all takes off?'

Allie had started making and buying jewellery as a hobby, but recently it had become a profitable sideline. She sold from a folding card-table outside Sloane Square station. 'I've been doing really well but the cops get heavy and I'm too fat to run. Guy's trying to get me a proper pitch.'

I picked up an exotic pair of dangling garnets and sapphires, holding them against my face. 'Those suit your skin, Mala, try them on.' I clipped them on to ears exposed by my new wedge cut and smiled. 'You look beautiful. Like an Indian princess. Keep them; really. They're only paste – part of a job lot.'

I went over to the mirror. I looked about twenty. I looked about twenty and gorgeous. The new haircut slimmed and framed my face and the earrings reflected light into features that I'd always thought too symmetrical for true beauty – amber eyes, small nose, full mouth: balanced and bland. No, not quite. I saw it now: balanced and bland and, sometimes, beautiful. How strange because, while I could see the allure of Jan's palely freckled creaminess and the passion that lurked in Caroline's black eyes and ruby mouth, I'd never thought of myself in the same league.

'Who'd have thought this motley crew would grow into jailbait?' Allie said, and laughed.

Later we put Jon in the pushchair and went to the King's Road to be part of the parade of beautiful people, a pleasure heightened by the awareness of our own allure against the backdrop of Allie's pregnant state. The air shimmered with possibilities. As we passed Mr Freedom I imagined the appreciative looks of delicious boys with curly hair and flared denims. On the way back we sat outside the Campion. Allie got us Cokes and a group of lads from a local building site came over: 'Blimey O'Reilly, our own harem,' but she sent them packing with a smile and despatched us homewards up Sloane Street and across the park.

As we crossed the Bayswater Road, Jan stared up at the pinky-orange cloud formation over the Royal Lancaster Hotel. 'Sometimes I feel we live in the most beautiful place on earth.'

'That's because we do,' I said, wrapping warm fingers around the red-and-blue stones of the earrings in my pocket.

I knew before Caroline told me. I'd seen them in Leinster Terrace that morning: Josh Chong in his old alpaca jumper, a bag under one arm and a large redhead in the other. They looked lopsided: she was nearly as tall as him in her leather maxi-coat, and twice his slender width. His head was leaning lightly on hers as she talked: absorbed, listening, focused. So why did the sight of the woman who'd pulled it off fill me with resentment?

'It's the pits,' Caroline wailed. 'It's bad enough having one loon in the house – now *she's* here every day.'

I wanted all and any details, but just then Josh returned with her in tow. 'Hello, Mala, still coming to coven meetings?' I didn't answer. 'Sorry: I know you save spell-making for full moon.'

'Shut up, Josh,' Caroline said.

'Honestly, Caroline, you complain when I'm flaky, you complain when I'm stable. Perhaps the problem is yours, not mine?'

She snorted. The girl said: 'That's enough from *both* of you.'

Josh said: 'This is Ellie.'

She smiled and put out a hand. Close up, she was prettier than she'd seemed in the street: a round face with a reddish blond down – like a peach. Her eyes were prettily made up, but her neck was blotchy and she'd dabbed concealer on a crop of drying spots under her mouth. She was old, maybe in her late twenties. Inexplicably I felt relieved – this could never last.

I turned to Josh; he was looking at me, brooding, as if he'd read my mind. 'We're getting married. Has Caroline told you?'

I shook my head slowly. For what seemed an age but probably wasn't, he held my gaze. Then Ellie laughed and took his hand. 'Come on, before I go off you.'

They went to his room. In the corner Caroline had picked up a magazine. I went to the window feeling hot and cheated. Why? It wasn't as if I had something going with that loony tune or, indeed, as if Josh had ever treated me as anything other than one of his sister's troublesome friends; but we had an unspoken bond, a bond which allowed me to see his face when I was daydreaming about love and David Cassidy or Marc Bolan or the sandwich boy at Caprini just didn't fit the picture. An understanding which meant he shouldn't have punished me with his news, but told me gently. She was old and acned. He must be madder than he ever was when they took him away.

I whispered as much to Caroline. She said: 'They're both barking. She had a complete breakdown after someone spiked her drink with a couple of LSD tabs: reduced to a gibbering wreck within twelve hours. It's taken her three years to recover.'

We listened to them laughing behind closed doors. What a strange thing – to hear Josh laughing normally instead of baying like a wild thing. And how like the old Josh he'd been. 'Hello, Mala. Still coming to coven meetings?'

'You never said he was getting married.' My voice, falsely light, as Caroline put down her tattered *Vogue*.

'I was saving the worst for last.'

'She's ancient.'

'Thirty.' Ten years older!

She uncurled herself. 'He spent months in Shenley being sorted out, then does the craziest thing ever. Let's get out of here.'

In their dreary idyll, Josh and Ellie put on a record. Johnny Nash: 'There Are More Questions Than Answers'.

We arrived at Jan's just as she got back from work. All quiet on the West Two front: she put on the kettle and sat down to massage her soles. 'Clive's wife's gone into hospital. I've been doing it all on my own.' She slumped in her chair. 'Make the tea, Mala.'

I threw some bags into the old brown pot, stirred and poured – thick, brown and horrible in chipped cups. 'Honestly, coming from Ceylon you should know how to make it.'

We sat silently warming our hands on the steam: daydreaming.

'Has Caroline told you Josh is getting married to a red-haired girl?' I swallowed my sigh. 'I wonder what it is about her that makes him happy.'

'Probably her tits,' Caroline said coarsely. 'Big – to match the rest of her; ten-ton Tessie. No accounting for taste.'

'Well, he wasn't going to end up with a duchess, was he?' Jan said. 'It can't be easy taking on a bloke like that.'

The door flew open: Mrs Tappett, still in her dressing gown, her hair in bushy strands on her shoulders like Mr Rochester's wife. 'Are you talking about Jack?'

'No, Ma, Caroline's brother.'

'I don't want you saying things about Jack: he's my husband and you'll show him respect!'

'We were talking about my brother, Mrs Tappett; he's just announced he's getting married.'

'Is he now?' She came into the room and collapsed on to the remaining chair. 'I'm worn out; pour me a cup.'

Jan got up and we all squirmed uncomfortably. I said: 'Are you well, Mrs Tappett?'

'I haven't been well for years. The bastards have tried to wear me down but I'm still here, though God only knows what for. My life's ruined.'

'You've got your kids, Ma.'

'What good have they ever done me? And now another on the way: what did I do wrong?'

Jan passed her her drink. 'Jon's as good as gold. The new one won't be any trouble.'

'I don't mean Allie's baby: I mean my baby. Bloody thing!'

Mrs Connors stumbled up and lit a cigarette off the cooker. She took a deep drag and her shoulders sagged. Jan was next to her. 'What baby is it we're talking about?'

'Haven't I just told you? The baby in here.' She slapped her stomach as if it had cheeked her. 'This baby: Jack's baby.' She saw Jan's face and her voice suddenly softened. 'Yes, love, you're going to be a big sister all over again: now isn't that grand?'

# 8

I had never once, I thought, spent more than ten minutes in the presence of Mr or Mrs Chong before they removed themselves to the kitchen. Yet here I was in a hideous green outfit my mother had conjured up, sitting around a restaurant table with them, as if I had some place in their lives or they in mine. I was isolated at the far end, consigned to sit opposite Caroline and minimise potential misdeeds. I willed her to return from the loo, gazing wistfully across the road to the Kam Tong where glorious Chinese boys in black bomber jackets and flares stood making merry on the pavement before steaming in for dinner. Around me, plain bamboo wall hangings discouraged the eye. Even the heat from Josh's thigh, sending tremors through my body, could not overshadow the ghastliness of being caught in the crossfire of his friends' vacuous chitchat: 'What would you like to do when you grow up, Mala?'

Grow up! As if anyone who wasn't an ancient crone over twenty was a kid. 'I'd like to be a reporter.'

'Oh, that'll be really interesting.' As if you give a stuff.

'Mala has a knack of being in the right place at the right time,' Josh said. 'She melts into the background like a wallflower at a dance. She'll do very well.' He turned to me. 'Of course, you'd have to learn shorthand, but then you do have quite short hands, don't you?' A dagger through my heart!

I drank the bitter dregs from my end-of-pot pouring of jasmine tea. Where on earth was Caroline?

'Are you at school with Josh's sister?'

'Mala's the clever one, Alex – she's at a grammar.'

I looked down the table at the Chong parents, sitting on chairs at the end of the small, cramped booth – uncomfortable, out of place – and yet this was their place: the Lotus House, number-one co-operative, soon to start breaking even. Next to me Josh shifted uncomfortably but did not move his leg. 'These banquettes are too restrictive.'

'They're made for small Chinese people.' Ellie, on Josh's other side, neck blotched from two glasses of vinegary wine, framed by Chinese faces, father and son. Had Caroline been kidnapped by toilet robbers?

Alex and Pia had sagged into the gap she'd left. 'It's a shame your parents couldn't make it, Ellie.'

'They think we're making too much fuss.'

'Because Josh is Chinese?'

'Of course not, Pia. It's just . . . you know what parents are like.' She looked up the table. 'His are the same. They don't think we're settled enough – no steady income – but they're paying for tonight and mine are paying for the wedding. Quid pro quo.'

They laughed and I saw Mrs Chong wince. But Josh was laughing too: of course he was laughing – it's not every day you get married at Caxton Hall! And here we were, just one week after his coming of age, already halfway through the twenty-four-hour countdown to D-day. 'She'll probably wear a furry dress like Lulu marrying Maurice Gibb,' Caroline said unkindly. 'Except then the groom was the ugly one.'

And here she was at last – behind a tray of chicken and sweetcorn soups. She sat down and contemplated the glutinous glory in front of her. 'Crap – sweetened and thickened for Western tastes.'

'I thought your mum organised the cooking?'

'That's how I know.'

I didn't care. I wolfed it down as the table began to sag under a sizzle of dishes – *char sui*, beef in black bean sauce, sweet and sour pork, ribs with chilli and plum, egg fried rice, Singapore noodles: I marvelled that these concoctions must have started life in that miserable Hallfield kitchen while I waited hungrily outside. And still they sat, the Chongs, the meaningless conversations of their son and his friends washing over them: going through the motions to maintain face.

Josh had organised an extra college year to finish his degree and Ellie was training to be a social worker. A pair of loons in love – at least he thought he was; what chance did they have? Under the table Caroline kicked me as Pia started talking about the new sex shop, Ann Summers, that had opened at Marble Arch: 'I don't understand the fuss; most of it's perfectly respectable.'

'You went inside?'

'We both went inside. It's not just vibrators and dirty mags – they have underwear and manuals. Like in Amsterdam.'

'I couldn't.'

'Of course you could, Ellie – it's a sex maniac's paradise.'

Ellie clapped a hand across her mouth and nudged Josh. 'Only since you.' What a tart!

Caroline and I exchanged sneers and, as always, he noticed. 'This is all a little bit over your heads, isn't it, girls, when, in actuality, it affects the parts below.'

The tablecloth rustled as Ellie said crossly: 'Leave them, Josh, they're only kids.' But while Caroline frowned at this put-down, I didn't care – because, as he delivered his barb, Josh, probably jokingly, tickled me behind my knee and ran his finger halfway up my thigh; and the ensuing rush of blood had not gone over my head, but most decidedly into it.

'You know, Mala,' my Aunty Mina said, 'Englishmen are so much more . . . well rounded as husbands.'

'You mean they're fatter?'

'No. I mean they're more . . . adventurous. Their imaginations encompass the needs of women – of their wives.' I waited. 'They spend time finding out what . . . makes you happy.'

'Like spending money on clothes?'

'Not quite.'

'You mean Ronnie's kinder to you than a Ceylonese man?'

'No. I'm talking about husbands and wives and being in love. Englishmen have more . . . knowledge about the rudiments of the human body. Carnal knowledge.' Oh. 'You're almost fifteen. Soon these things will start to matter to you. There are cultural differences, attitudes. It's important to have self-respect, but it's also important to realise that an element of . . . carnal knowledge . . . is useful.'

I tried to form an equally oblique response. 'You don't think there's anything bad about it, Aunty Mina?'

'No. This is a different society, a different culture – you are part of both. There is nothing to be ashamed of where emotions are legitimately engaged.'

'Thank you.' Awestruck but horrified, I turned my attention to Aunty Anu, who was listening politely to the small talk of our guests of honour – a visiting great-aunt and uncle: 'You know the only way to buy sterling in Colombo is on the black market? The rate is terrible. I spoke even to the minister about it – Ranjit Dimbulawala, he's my sister's husband's third cousin on the mother's side – but there's nothing to be done. Anyway, we had to come because Anil has a supplier here and Kumari wants all sorts of electrical mod cons for the new house – she married that Arugala boy, did I tell you? His aunt was the Prime Minister's father's piano teacher.'

We nodded appreciatively and Anu said: 'Mala must have been only five or six when last you saw her.'

'And now such a big girl – towering over her mother – I must tell her grandparents. What a shame, no? They haven't seen her since she was four. Are you well behaved, Mala?'

'Oh, I'm just brilliant.'

'They grow so quickly these days: my three sons – all went to St Thomas's – have long since flown the nest. One is a lawyer in Sydney, the other an eye surgeon in Seattle, and the younger boy has just returned from a year at the Sorbonne. I call them my international citizens. I'm sure you will do as well, Mala.'

'Some hope.'

'What's this about hope?' Ronnie, creeping up from behind.

'We're talking about universities.'

'And I thought it was something interesting.'

As Anu palmed off the old aunty, he turned to me. 'Where's my little girl gone? You're a young woman, Mala! How's life?'

I stared at his long, slim fingers, casually wrapped around a glass of Bull's Blood, and wondered about carnal knowledge. I tried to imagine them unhooking bra straps and – what was it she'd said? – exciting the rudiments of the human body.

'Cat got your tongue?'

I shook my head.

He was amused. 'What were you and Mina gossiping about over there?'

'Nothing.'

'Oh, come on, Mala – let me in on the secret. Is she complaining about her diminishing wardrobe or singing my praises?'

'Yes.'

'Which?'

'Praises.'

'Well, that's good news. I have to say, marriage is good for the soul as well as the body. I recommend it.' He grinned. 'But don't you go rushing into it like some of these silly teenagers we read about – first have some fun.'

What was wrong with the pair of them: oversexed? Had she told him about our conversation? I tried vainly to find something to focus on – not his face; not his smiley mouth.

'You've gone all coy, Mala – don't tell me you've already got a boyfriend?' Now teasing. 'Oh – is it a secret? Don't worry, I won't say a word – I know what the Ceylonese ladies' mafia is like.' I was dumbstruck. He put his free hand on my shoulder. His grip made my neck tingle; his voice was gentle, worried. 'Is there something wrong?' I shook my head. 'You're all on edge. Have I upset you?'

'I'm fine.' I pushed his hand away.

He looked suddenly awkward and, turning to the wall, appeared to fiddle with himself. Disgusting! This was taking 'physical needs' too far. But in seconds he'd turned back – visibly relieved. He gazed at me in bewilderment. 'Sorry, sweetie, but you've been staring so hard at my crotch, I wanted to check my flies weren't undone.'

At Shelleys the new look was raffia platformed T bars. We elbowed our way through the crowds of girls trying them on and climbed the dark stairway at the back to the incensed gloom of Virgin Records: *Ziggy Stardust*, £1.99.

Lounging on floor cushions, we listened to *Dark Side Of The Moon* and *Talking Book* on headphones before going up to the counter. Beside us, against us, leaned snake-hipped young men who smelled of patchouli oil and bore traces of last night's mascara. Heaven. 'Hi, babe,' one of them said as he passed, and I sniggered gratefully.

'Load of old hippies,' Jan whispered. 'He's got nail varnish on.'

'Like Brian Eno. Don't be such a square.'

But she was uncomfortable so we paid for my haul and returned to the mid-morning glare of Tottenham Court Road, sitting for a while by the fountains under Centrepoint before heading north up to Warren Street where the new London radio station, Capital, was sited. It was a cold but sunny April day. Jan tucked her arm through mine. 'Let's save bus fares and walk.'

We wandered homewards, stopping to giggle at French boys in the queue for Madame Tussauds and the Planetarium. Outside Marylebone register office a young couple posed in a graffittied Morris Minor: Better Luck This Time.

Jan made a face. 'No chance.'

'How do you know?'

'Well, look at my mum.' She shook her head. 'I don't know how Jack can fancy her with that big belly, she's like a set of bagpipes.'

We both got the giggles. I told her about Mina's pep talk. 'I think she was saying it's all right to sleep around before you settle down.'

'Well, it is, isn't it? Look at Allie, she's had the best of both worlds.' She smiled. 'You should see Rebecca – she's so tiny, like a little doll. And Jon loves her.'

'I'll come next week.'

At the Harrow Road ABC we started running. 'Last one into the station buys the teas.' We cut down the taxi route on to the mainline concourse of Paddington Station. Jan found a bench on Platform 1 and I got the teas. 'D'you remember the first time you went to Hereford and we all came to wave goodbye?'

'My heart broke.'

'But you kept going back.'

'Because it was brilliant.' I sighed, fleetingly transported to the Herefordshire countryside and a lifestyle so different from ours. 'That's what I'd like one day, a big house, lots of green, and rooms with lined curtains.'

Jan jumped up. 'Clean curtains'd do. Come on – I've got to do the laundry before tea.'

'But it's the first day of the Easter holiday!'

We found Mrs Tappett lying on the doorstep like a giant udder. 'Where've you been? I've been locked out for hours.'

'What happened to your key?'

'I can't remember.'

'Well, it's your own stupid fault, isn't it? You're forty-four years old, Ma: you're disgusting.' Stepping over her mother at the thinnest point, Jan opened the door. 'The doctor's told you to stop drinking. You better go up and rest.' Obediently, Mrs Tappett rolled to her feet. Janice leaned against the door frame so they didn't touch. 'Dirty cow – I could smell her coming up the path. My dad would never have stood for it. Tappett's a turd.'

I walked home trying to imagine Jack Tappett mounting his wife. Given that both their stomachs were in the way, his penis must surely be at least fifteen inches long to make contact. How could he possibly jam this ketchup-bottle monstrosity into a pair of Y-fronts? It defied belief.

Back in the flat, I sorted through my back-catalogue Bowie and danced: Oh you pretty things, don't you know you're driving your mamas and papas insane?

'You are like a woman crazed, Mala, asking all the time about boyfriends. Have you nothing better to think of? Is this what they teach you at your grammar school? You'll end up like that Janice, always at a lamppost with delinquents.'

'Oh, don't start that again.'

'When I was your age we appreciated the important things in life – education, exams – respect for your parents.'

'Bloody hell! All I asked was how old I'll be before I can have a boyfriend.'

'Don't say bloody. I've told you: eighteen.'

'I could be dead by then.'

'*Chi*! At home we *never* had boyfriends: only husbands. Always girls were chaperoned.'

'Mum: I'm talking about someone asking me to dance or a youth club – things I already do with my girlfriends. Could I go?'

'And end up at the lamppost?'

'What is all this about Janice and lampposts? You should be pleased she isn't sneaking up alleyways and shagging.'

'Shagging? What is shagging?'

'Sleeping with them.'

'*Chi*! That you have such thoughts.'

'It's not me that's having the thoughts, it's *you*.'

She sighed. 'You want to play with fire, Mala.'

'In thirteen months I'll be old enough to leave home; old enough to marry. It's ludicrous to say you won't let me have a boyfriend until I'm eighteen.'

'Why don't we wait till someone asks, Mala – you may be eighty before a boy takes an interest.'

'What d'you mean, lampposts?' Janice said.

'My mum said you hang around lampposts with blokes.'

'Like a dog,' Caroline added helpfully.

'Is that what she thinks – that I'm a dog?'

'I didn't say that, Caroline did.'

'So you think it, Caroline?'

'It was a joke, Janice; keep your knickers on.'

'Oh, ha ha.' She looked away crossly.

I giggled. '*Do* you keep your knickers on, Jan?'

'What? Don't you join in as well, Mala. I haven't gone half as far as some of the girls round here.'

'How far is that?' Caroline asked. 'Scunthorpe, or beyond continental Europe?'

'You're just jealous, Caroline.'

'What: of that pimpled pipsqueak Wayne?' Wayne!

'I'm not with him any more – I'm seeing Craig.'

'Craig?' A look of utter disbelief. 'Craig Olleranshaw?'

'That's right.'

The air tensed and quivered like a cat's-cradle between them. I'd never seen Craig Olleranshaw, but the girls at Sara Siddons swooned at the mention of his name. Now Jan was dating him! Caroline looked sick. 'He's the cleverest of all the boys at Rutherford. What the hell do you talk about?'

'Lots of things: sport, school, films. And he tells me things too.'

'Like what?'

Jan shrugged. 'The names of all the inert gases; the difference between a sea and an ocean and . . .' She was saving the best till last. 'He's told me I'm the best kisser he's ever been out with.'

Silence.

Caroline said: 'Well, they say practice makes perfect,' which wasn't meant as a compliment, but somehow sounded like one.

On the way home she was disbelieving. 'Why would a boy like that date Janice?'

'Because she's pretty?'

'You mean she's got tits.'

'No, I mean she's very pretty: thick dark hair, big blue eyes – blokes go for all that.'

'She's thick as two short planks.'

'She's not thick – she's just not interested in learning.'

'Same difference.'

I sighed as we meandered along the green perimeter railings of the Hallfield estate. 'I can't imagine kissing a boy. My mum's still so touchy about us going comprehensive, she thinks I'll get pregnant if I pass one in the corridor.'

'You're not missing much.'

'How would you know?'

'Because I've tried it with a couple of the boys who hang round our school gates.'

'Caroline!'

'It was horrible – wet and slobbery. I hate the way they press their *things* against you.'

As I tongued the back of my hand that night in another failed attempt to get a handle on French kissing, I was overcome with despair that the fruits of love seemed forever destined to fall into someone else's basket. I took out my English homework: write an essay from a captive viewpoint.

'I am the serpent in the garden of Eden,' I wrote, 'and I'm fed up with people finger-pointing when all I've done is expose the common desires of man. I didn't ask to be born – specially not here where everyone's paired but me. Adam and Eve don't know how lucky they are pitching up here simultaneously – they've been saved years of yearning.'

\*　　\*　　\*

Jan's mum had her baby a week later. A girl, Tammy, born by Caesarian section after Mrs Tappett turned up drunk in the labour ward to report that her waters had been leaking for two days. 'Probably thought she'd pissed herself,' Allie said angrily.

While she recuperated, her husband wetted the baby's head in the Mitre, the Railway, the Swan and the Craven Arms. Tammy was the toast of the neighbourhood.

On the Sunday, Allie and Jan brought Sean and Marie up to London to meet the new addition. I met them afterwards, outside St Mary's and we got a Tube to Piccadilly, to the newly opened McDonald's on Haymarket.

'So, was she born with blond hair and cowboy boots?'

Jan grinned. 'They all look the same.'

'She's not as pretty as my Beccy,' Allie said.

'I wish I could live with you, Allie.' Marie held on to her arm and looked up with wary, grown-up eyes.

'I do too, pet: but there isn't room or money. You're better off where you are – your house mother's a darling.'

'When you're there. There's rules for everything – even going to the toilet. She's always bossing us about.'

'That's what mothers are supposed to do, Marie – keep you on the straight and narrow.'

In the restaurant, Allie and I got the food while Jan took the infants and juniors upstairs to the seating area.

'So, Mala, what d'you think of Sean and Marie?'

'I wouldn't have known them – they've grown so much.'

'Oh, they've grown all right. Marie's a hard-faced little bitch, and I caught Sean trying to nick sweets at the hospital kiosk.'

'They're only eight and ten, Allie.'

'The rot's already in, Mala. Jan and me, we fought it, but those two didn't have the chance. My mum's always been a dozy cow, but my dad going was the final nail.' She paid for the order and handed me a tray piled high with paper-wrapped burgers. 'You'll be all right: your mum's a fighter – she's got on with her life. But those two . . . Sean's got Eamonn's ways and Marie's always looking for someone else to blame – just like our ma. There's nothing I can do to change that.' She laughed. 'Now aren't you glad there's only one of you? That's what they call damage limitation.'

That night Caroline and I went to see *Tales from the Crypt*. 'Is this what it's like at your youth club: grisly deeds in the bowels of the church?'

I ignored her jibe as we queued for Frankies, knowing she was still spitting because I hadn't asked her to join, but it was Margaret's church. I'd been invited to join by her mother. Like school, it was something separate to my friendship with Caroline. And it was fun: there were books and periodicals, a TV, table tennis, a stereo system, guitars, volleyball, a performance area with various props: and, most importantly, boys. Truly heaven-sent.

'Maybe I should join?'

'But you're a Catholic.'

'And you're a Buddhist. It's not as if you go there to pray: what does it matter?'

It mattered to me. I didn't want her there, laughing as Margaret and I mimed to Slade on the stage, or played volleyball badly because it was the only means of physical contact with the club heart-throbs, Terry and Marek.

'They'll never look at us,' Margaret had sighed. 'We're too boring.' But the previous night, as we'd got our jackets and left, they'd caught up with us and we'd walked together as far as Praed Street. 'See you next week, girls.' Just the thought of this small exchange made me palpitate!

'Youth clubs are boring, Caroline.'

We smothered our hot dogs in ketchup and I ran through the highlights of my outing with the Connors children: 'And then, just as we were going, Sean got so angry that Allie wouldn't buy sweets, he threw his drink at her. The top fell off and it went over Beccy. She started crying – it was a madhouse. Then Jan shouted and hit Sean across the head, Marie kicked Jan, Jon started screaming and Allie was just standing there, soaked, while I mopped the floor with serviettes.'

Caroline shook her head. 'God, what a show. Why do they bother?'

'They're family. You wouldn't write off Josh.'

'Only because it's impossible. They were round today cadging lunch. Ellie calls my mother "Mum" – my parents hate it.' She wiped her mouth clean. 'Still, you can't have it all; he's been a different man since she came on the scene.'

'You've started to like her?'

'They've been out of the way for four months: long may it continue.'

'And they're happy?'

'I think so. She's a bit moody, but he's not exactly God's gift, is he?' She stood up. 'What does it matter in the great scheme of things?'

After my birthday I handed in my notice at Andre's. I'd got a new Saturday job at a boutique on Queensway where my mum had bought my presents – a sleeveless cheesecloth smock and matching flares. I teamed them with my yellow Ravel platform clogs to meet Margaret. 'Mala, you look great. The cream is brilliant against your skin. I wish I was all smooth and brown.'

'You'd probably get Paki-bashed.'

'Your mum hasn't been getting it in the neck again?'

'Isn't she always? A stall-holder in Church Street refused to serve her today.'

'Outrageous.'

We linked arms and walked up the road together, slowing outside the Regent where a group of rowdy lads from the Lisson Green estate were blocking the pavement. As we stepped sniffily round them they wolf-whistled. One pointed at me and shouted: 'Cor! Cop an eyeful of that.'

Immediately we straightened our backs, raised our heads and strutted on as elegantly as we could. Round the corner Margaret said: 'We'll have to sell you to the Race Relations Board – you're obviously doing something right,' and we both giggled.

At the club it was show night: some of the older members had been working on a mini-production of *Godspell*. Margaret was a fast-growing weed; I was front-row prompt. 'I'm glad a career on the stage is not for you, Mala,' my mother had said drily, and I was grateful that she'd relaxed since confirmation that my class would remain single-sex in the autumn.

The Quintin Kynaston gang, with the help of an art teacher,

had made the backdrops, and now they perched alongside me as troubleshooters.

A blond head next to mine. 'Break a leg,' Terry whispers.

'What?'

'Break a leg – that's what they say on theatrical first nights.'

'Is that what this is: theatre?'

He grins. 'Loosely speaking.'

'Well, don't speak too loosely,' I say, holding up the script. 'I haven't got any lines for you.' And he grins even more.

Oh, joy! In the dark my heart was beating double time, drowned by excited chatter and then everyone saying at the tops of their voices: 'Shhhh.'

Suddenly Marek pranced on stage in a green woolly jumper, purple flares and red baseball boots and we all burst out laughing. 'He's not exactly David Essex,' I said under my breath to Terry.

'No,' he shot back, 'more like Ilford, Essex.'

But it was good; and by the end virtually everyone had run on for five minutes of fame, and when we all jumped up and clapped madly the cheers were genuine. Afterwards there were jugs of fruit punch and plates of garibaldi biscuits laid out on a table at the back of the hall, and the stage was cleared and turned into a dance-floor by the Rev. Marchmont, who had us in hysterics with his Fluff Freeman impersonation.

As the 'disco' got going a group of us helped clear up. I was wandering about with a damp tea towel when Terry asked me to dance. 'Come on, you had the easiest job of all tonight, sitting there holding bits of paper – it's time to get off your bum.'

'But then you'd see it.'

'You can't miss it.' He took my hand and pulled me into a circle of people. 'I warn you now, I'm a useless dancer.'

'So am I.'

'We're well matched, then.'

I wobbled around on my platforms while he deliberately made an ass of himself. 'I told you I couldn't dance.'

'That's all right; the men in white coats are waiting outside.'

'Will you come along and nurse me?'

'Only if you'll take your tablets when I say.'

'I'll take anything you tell me to.'

Beam me up, Scotty, before I die of happiness!

He pulled me closer and we did a pretend slow dance: Medicine Head, 'One And One Is One'. Across the floor, Margaret held up crossed fingers.

And then it was ten o'clock and the extended party was over. I had fifteen minutes to get home. As we left, Terry and Marek joined us as if it were now an established routine. But at Praed Street, instead of going his own way, Terry said he'd walk me home. We hardly talked. For God's sake, Mala – think of something to say! At the corner of Craven Road I stopped: he must think I'm such a wally.

'You'd better leave me here,' I said. 'My mum's a bit . . . old-fashioned, you know. She'd have a fit if she saw you. Without warning, I mean.'

He smiled. 'I know. How old are you?'

'Fifteen. How old are you?'

'Nearly eighteen. Do you like older men?'

'I've not had any experience of them.'

'Oh dear. Then I'd better help you get some.'

My head was exploding!

He took my hand and held it a breath away from his mouth before dropping it and saying: 'What the hell!' and bending down to place the gentlest of kisses on my lips.

'Can I take you out, Mala Fonseka?'

'That would be . . . massively great.'

# 9

This time I caught Bethany napping. Literally. Well, sort of. She was slumped in a doorway on the Portobello Road. Her head was jerked back against the peeling black front door. Inches away, a young boy in a Stetson was playing electric guitar, his small foot jammed on a wah-wah pedal, a discordant drone resonating from the amplifier on the pavement: The Who, 'I'm Free'. Beth, can you hear me?

Caroline had gone ahead to the grotty end in search of a fox stole to jazz up her winter coat. I searched the mêlée for a glint of her slick black bob: nothing. No helpful instructions to be had from her glossed lips.

Sitting down next to Beth, I felt the peculiar boniness of her hip through the floor-length cheesecloth dress. 'Beth, it's Mala. Are you all right?' Nothing. I crossed my arms and waited until, in her stupor, she shivered and straightened, eyes open, staring ahead. 'Beth, are you all right?' I put my hand on hers. 'Say something, for God's sake.'

'Mala?' She turned to me. 'What are you doing here?'

'Shopping. What are you doing here?'

'What does it look like?'

'Getting out of your brain.'

She laughed without energy. 'Is that what you tracked me down for – to give me a telling-off?'

'You don't need me to tell you you're on another planet.'

She turned away, angular, angry. Her mousey hair was tangled and badly cut. This wasn't how I'd imagined a reunion. I waited for her to say something. It wasn't what I'd expected. 'I'd better go, I'm meeting a man.'

'Your boyfriend?'

'Something like that.'

'Where've you been, Beth?' No answer. ' Why didn't you leave a note or write to us?'

'I couldn't.'

'Because your mum wouldn't let you?' A shrug. 'So where are you now?'

She started to get up. I put a hand on her arm to keep her there. 'You're not going till you tell me how I can contact you. I mean it. What's your phone number?'

'We've grown up, Mala; we've got our own lives.'

'There's room for you in mine.'

'Bring out the violins. I don't want it: I don't *want* to see you.'

'We can write.'

'I won't write back. We've nothing in common. Look at you, all ponced up just to walk down Portobello Road—'

That was choice coming from old Panda-eyes! There was smudged kohl on the rise of her cheek and her toenails were painted black. 'Have you seen *yourself* recently?'

'You sound like Caroline.'

'She'll be here in a minute.'

She went to get up but I grabbed her hand. 'Give me your address first.'

'Don't be stupid.' I tightened my grip. 'I haven't any paper.'

'I'll remember.'

'Like your times tables?' She tried to wrestle free.

'I never had a problem with them.'

She was angry, but I was stronger. 'Forty-six Grays Lane, Harlesden.'

'I'll write.' I let go and she wandered off past the lonesome cowboy who'd provided the soundtrack for our exchange: the strangled echo of tunes at once recognisable, but impossible to name. My former friend, my dearest friend, in tie-dye blue and white, a silver bell chain round her left ankle, probably off to meet a pusher. I wondered why, having waited so long for this moment, I felt neither happy nor excited; just dull, almost insensibly dull; and inexplicably cheated.

*     *     *

Forty-six Grays Lane, Harlesden; it was easy enough to remember, but I didn't tell Caroline. Maybe later I'd mention it to Jan when we went out on our first foursome – Jan, me, Terry and her latest boyfriend, Phil, to see 10CC at the London School of Economics. Maybe.

Dear Beth,
    It was great to see you last week. I hope you're all right. Guess what? I live in your old flat!! It's a bit different now, though. It was awful when you just disappeared. We've all really missed you. There's so much to tell. I've got a boyfriend now – we've been seeing each other for ten weeks!! He's just got great A-level results so even my mum can't moan! That said, she'll moan about anything. She hates the fact that we're a comp now – but at least my year's still kept separate. Will you ring? Or write and arrange a meet? I can't do Saturdays before five because I work.
    Love, Mala. x

I opened my desk and put away my writing things: twenty minutes to bell and a deadly double maths session grappling with fractions of fractions and compound calculations. Instant death. Grabbing my purse, I went down the central staircase where the horny black boys spent their breaks loitering against banisters: 'Hey, Mala – looking hot today.' I grinned and sailed past, relaxing only in the cold calm of the street.

In the phone box first-year girls were giggling into the receiver: the dirty caller strikes again. I laughed at the thought of our regular sicko, stationed somewhere in the flats opposite, sharing his fantasies with the new intake. At the sub-post-office, I ran into Jean Malin, former Head of House. 'It's a bit different now isn't it?' She smiled. 'I always wanted to be in a mixed school – now I keep wishing the boys away. Thank God this is my last year. Will you stay on?'

'I haven't got a choice.'

I posted the letter. With any luck, Beth would receive it tomorrow. Maybe she'd even turn up at Craven Terrace out of curiosity. She'd be surprised at how much better it looked: bigger. My mother was not in an alcove like Mrs Stephens, doing business behind the yellowing muslin curtain. The sofa bed was opened only at night. If not for the saris draped over the back of chairs or the shoes hidden in corners, it was a normal sitting room. In the yard, which she had never seen, were pots of busy Lizzies and geraniums; on sunny days the door was open and sometimes a passing cat would visit. Beth would be amazed.

I debated whether to buy some Treets or a Marathon. No, sod it, diet week. I bought some sugar-free gum to share with Margaret.

'I'm too heavy, Mala – five foot six and nearly seven stone. Why don't we diet together – you're always moaning about your bum.'

She didn't need to lose an ounce really, but did any of us? 'I don't think you should lose any more, Margaret.'

'You sound like my mum and dad.'

'You're just perfect. Like Twiggy.'

In truth, her brown eyes were over-large in her emaciated face. Her chestnut hair was dull and limp around her shoulders. The previous day, when it had suddenly turned cold, she'd shivered uncontrollably despite wearing several pullovers. It didn't help that we all had to run the gauntlet of admiration. 'Those boys make me feel so self-conscious – as if I'm just a body. I hate it.'

'It's because they all fancy you.'

'It's not because they fancy me, it's because I *don't* fancy them.'

The more she turned her nose up, the more they craved her attention. I nearly cried with her when a smart-alec third-year leered at her boobs: 'You'll never need a life jacket with those!'

But we were faring better than the girls whose classes had been integrated. Now, as I passed a fourth-year classroom, I noticed two kids snogging in a corner. Miss Maylin, our ancient physics teacher, slowed to see what had caught my eye. 'All control has gone, Mala. Welcome the new dawn.' She opened the door and barked: 'You two children get out into the playground immediately before you're put on report.'

I giggled at their shocked faces, then froze as the boy said clearly: 'Why don't you fuck off, you old cow?'

In our form room, I got ready for afternoon lessons. Outside, a master wrestled down a large lad who'd tried to hit him. The bell went. Other teachers hauled them apart. It was over in the flick of a switch: the flick of a knife. Welcome the new dawn.

Unexpectedly, it was Josh who opened the Chong door. 'Caroline's gone to the shop, she'll be back in a minute.' He drew back to let me pass. 'Come in and wait.' A pause. 'Not scared of me, are you, Mala? I don't bite.'

I went through to the sitting room. 'Where's Ellie?'

'She's at work. I was hoping the old lady would feed me.'

I sat in the armchair, shiny now with age. He perched on the settee. 'I hear you've got a boyfriend.'

'Yes.' Why didn't that come out as proudly as it should have?

'Is it serious?'

'Yes. Well . . . not really. I don't know. I think . . . '

'Therefore you am. You're too young to get serious.' He cocked his head. 'But you're so pretty and naïve, it's almost inevitable.'

I didn't say anything. Instead I tried to concentrate on what Terry had said the previous night: 'Mala, you are a scrumptious plumptious princess with a bounce in your step and two in your jacket.' Bliss. Now Josh was throwing little darts of doubt into the equation.

He laughed. 'Who am I to talk: a married man. Very happily married in case you were wondering.' I shrugged. 'You get that look sometimes.'

'What look?'

He moved across the room and leaned over me, bringing his face close – so close I was forced to meet his confusingly dark eyes. I could smell garlic and toothpaste and Eau Savage: a bouquet garni of manliness. The heat from his breath warmed my mouth. 'That look: that muddled-up little-Mala look.' He pushed closer so our noses were almost touching. I tensed, terrified he would kiss me. Terrified and thrilled. 'You were like it the day you first turned up on our balcony: too frightened to come in, too curious to run. Is that how you feel about me?'

'I don't know.'

'Don't you?'

The front door opened and Josh lazily straightened himself.

Caroline said: 'What's going on?'

'I've just been giving your friend some therapy.'

'Why, has she gone nuts too?'

'Call it shock treatment.' He blew me a kiss and I remained immobile until he left, saying he was going to eat with his parents.

Caroline turned on me. 'What's up? Has love coddled your brain?'

'Who said anything about love?'

'You did.'

'I'm only fifteen.'

'Wasn't that my line?'

She threw a copy of *Tatler* and two chocolate tools on to my lap. 'A gift from Clive. Something old, something new.' As she settled with *Vogue* I thought about my encounter with Josh, and my follow-up letter to Bethany.

Dear Beth,

Did you get the note? If not, my address is at the top: does it look familiar?!! I really want to talk with you. Please get in touch – even if it's only to say you're okay.

Love, Mala.

Sighing, I turned the page and found myself looking at an article on Eastern mystics. If I didn't fancy Josh any more, why was I so unsettled? I snapped the pages shut. 'Let's get out, it's stifling in here.'

We walked up to Queens and drank hot chocolate while watching the skaters bump and slide. Then it was time to head home and knuckle down to serious work: mocks were two weeks away and I needed decent results to keep my mother quiet. 'I feel like I never stop,' I moaned to Caroline.

Tammy Tappett was like a perfect Tiny Tears – pink, bald, fat and always crying. Whether you picked her up or just left her, she cried. On Jan's front steps you could hear her even before the door opened and the red puckered face appeared, usually under her big sister's arm like the pig-baby from *Alice in Wonderland*.

'Can't you shut her up?' Caroline begged, and we'd all root

around for something small to shove in her mouth. Today was no different. Jan appeared looking cross and tearful. 'I can't believe it. The old cow swore she'd only be gone twenty minutes – that was two hours ago.'

In the kitchen Tammy was slumped in an old high chair. 'I had to put her down somewhere – I'm getting muscles like Henry Cooper.' Jan gave her a teething rusk and put the kettle on. 'She's driving me mad. She cries all night, but they just sleep through it. Why have babies if you can't look after them? The old cow's already got two in care! They should have taken this one the minute the doctor slapped her wrinkled arse.'

While Jan ranted, I straightened Tammy and put the fraying leather straps around her twice so she was secured in a rigid but upright position. I dusted off her rusk and put it in her hand. She sucked quietly. Jan said: 'She'll start again in a minute – that's too hard for gums at five months, but who cares?' She sighed and poured two cups of tea. 'She's not my responsibility. I did all this for Sean and Marie, I'm not getting caught again.'

'You sound just like Allie when she was your age.'

'Yeah – and what's the first thing she does? Settles down and has babies. I tell you, Mala, I'd rather glue my privates.'

At this, Tammy suddenly started a high-pitched cry. Jan jumped up. 'That's her serious noise. Bloody hell, Mala, what have you done with these straps? It's all right, doll, Jannie will have you out. There you are, darling, all safe.' She rocked the baby against her shoulder and, miraculously, there was silence. 'She's fallen asleep,' Jan said. 'Peace at last.' She took her upstairs and returned crossly. 'I've done everything now. Bloody old cow must be drinking away the dole money.'

'Isn't it always the way in this house: the grown-ups piss off and the kids do the work.' She saw my expression and started to laugh. 'Sod her – tell me about Terry. I thought he was gorgeous.'

I sighed. 'So did I.' But before I could expand on my new uncertainty, Mrs Tappett came gaily through the door, still fat from having a baby. 'Here I am, girls.'

Aunty Anu dropped by the next evening. 'How are the mocks going, Mala?'

'Not too bad. Well, maybe French oral – I get embarrassed talking to strangers in a foreign language.'

'*We've* done it all our lives.'

'That's not the same.'

'Your mother and I were taught by Irish nuns. We spoke English to each other, Sinhalese to the servants.' I tried to show interest. 'Now of course we speak and think in English, but at home they've reverted to Sinhalese.'

'That doesn't matter to me because I'm British.'

My mother laughed. 'Mala thinks she's white.'

'Being British doesn't mean being white.'

'It does to the British.'

'But I'm British.'

'Then one day it will matter to you.'

Anu put up her hand. 'We're talking about French. Try and speak it as well as your mother speaks English, Mala.'

'No chance.'

'I have warned you,' my mother said, 'that if you don't get good results you can forget that boy of yours.'

'It's not his fault I muddle up *la* and *le*.'

'The two evenings you're out with him could be spent learning the difference.'

'Too much ooh-la-la, and not enough *la* and *le*.' Anu smiled.

'I hope not,' my mother said darkly.

'Oh, Mum – I'm the most virginal fifteen-year-old in the country.'

'*Chi!* That you say things like that! This is the British for you – sex, sex, sex from the cradle to the grave – dictionaries by the dozen but interested only in three-letter words.'

'I wish I'd never opened my mouth,' I said.

Dear Mala, I am okay. Okay? Stop bothering me. Bethany.

'Wow, this is very swish.'

'Special treat. We're celebrating.'

A waiter took my coat and seated us at a table overlooking the canal. Celebrating what? Was he going to pull out an engagement ring or something? Surely it was too soon for all this. Yes, he's gorgeous, but I'm still so *young*. I studied the menu – the main-course prices started at three pounds: a front-row ticket for Roxy Music.

'Terry, are you sure you can afford this?'

He grinned. 'What d'you think I've been earning all this time – chocolate buttons?' He was filled with secret excitement. I began to feel anxious.

'Would Madam care for an aperitif?'

'I beg your pardon?' So much for French.

'Two Cokes,' Terry said, and the man went away.

I ordered chicken because I didn't recognise the other things on the menu. I practised various responses to his proposal in my head: I really love you but this is premature/Let's get university behind us/You're a lovely man but I must say no. He put my hand to his lips. I needed the toilet. Jumping up, I forgot the damask napkin on my lap. The manager made a fuss of picking it up. When I returned, he made a fuss of putting it back. I was so embarrassed I wanted to cry.

'Shall I tell you why I'm buzzing?' I nodded. Again he took my hand. 'You know I met Marek and Gabe yesterday? Well, we're going to do the European adventure: leaving after Christmas and back in June. What d'you think?' Suddenly his brain engaged. 'I know I should have told you before but it was only an idea until now.' A gentle squeeze. 'I'll send you cards. I'll phone. We'll still have three months before I take up my place at Exeter. By then, Miss Fonseka, you'll be sweet sixteen: lots and lots of fun.'

The waiter brought the food. I seethed: so Goodbye Yellow Brick Road, where the dogs of society howl.

I said: 'There's no point us seeing each other, Terry. You'll be away for as long as we've been together.'

'And in that time you'll sit your O-levels without distraction and be ready for some growing up on my return.'

'To sleep with you, you mean.' So much for the ring.

'That would be nice.' He shrugged. 'Look, it's not important – I just said it to be funny. You didn't think I was going to spend my whole year off in the print room of an engineering company, did you?' I didn't answer. 'It's just a blip.' He cut into his steak. 'This looks great – try yours.'

'I'll choke.'

'Mala, I love you.'

'And that makes it all right?'

The chicken was almost begging me to eat it, so I did; but I left my sautéed potatoes as a protest.

Our waiter returned. 'Madam has left her vegetables?'

'Are they compulsory?'

Terry hissed: 'Don't be so rude.' I felt tears welling up. 'Don't get all soppy on me, Mala, I'm not going for two months.'

'I'm not crying to be soppy, Terry. I'm crying because I'm angry.'

Dear Beth,

I'm glad you're okay. I think I am. I've just split up with my boyfriend and I'd only just got used to him. My mum's pleased, of course! Oh well, plenty more fish in the sea. Janice has had so many blokes we've lost count, and Caroline's so sniffy she'll never get *one*. I bought a brilliant tie-dye shirt last week. Do you have a Saturday job? We're coming up to Harlesden to see SNAFU at the Mean Fiddler next Friday. It must be near you – why not join us? That would be great.

Love, Mala xx.

'Even the good ones let you down,' Jan sighed.

'I didn't know you had experience of good ones,' Caroline said. 'Would their names fill the back of a postage stamp?'

'Give it a rest, will you?' I'd had enough of their bickering. 'Isn't this where we get off?'

Jan squinted out of the window, looking for a road name. 'There's supposed to be a clock tower.'

'We passed a clock tower ten minutes ago.'

'Shit.'

On the pavement we learned we'd overshot by three stops.

'I can't walk in these heels,' Caroline said. 'Let's just cross and get a bus going back.' But after five minutes at the stop we were forced to get moving to ward off frostbite.

'Does SNAFU mean anything?' Jan asked.

'Situation Normal All Fucked Up.'

'That just about says it,' Caroline snarled.

I got the Babychams while Caroline and Janice bagged a table near the stage. 'I don't know why you bothered. We'll have to stand when they come on anyway.' I looked at Caroline in her ridiculous Sacha wedges. 'No wonder your feet are hurting in those, they're six inches high at the back and half an inch at the front.' She looked at me coldly and I rolled my eyes. 'You should buy proper platforms like the rest of us.'

'Stop it,' Jan muttered, 'you're getting as bad as her.'

Crossly I knocked back my drink and waited for someone to get in the next round, but they just ignored me. A beautiful dark man at the bar smiled. I turned away: what could I do about it?

A duo based loosely around T Rex came on and did a warm-up. 'I wouldn't mind his hands on my bongos.'

'Mala!'

We all laughed and I relaxed: cross with myself for being cross; not even knowing why. Was it the thought that Beth might turn up? Or the fear, perhaps. I still hadn't mentioned our meeting to anyone; or the exchange of letters. There had to be something concrete to say first. I looked around, but I knew in my heart she wasn't there. What the hell!

The main band came on. Everyone moved to the front. Jan got lemonades the second time round, and we pushed our way to a better spot. 'Caroline's staying put,' she shouted above the opening chords. There was a whistle in one of the amplifiers. When it was fixed the effect wasn't much better. A couple of tall guys muscled in front of us and blocked the view. I felt fluey and achy and wished I hadn't come. The music wasn't my sort of thing. I checked the time: ten o'clock. Much too early to go home! Jan caught my eye and mouthed 'awful'. I nodded and jerked a thumb in the direction of our table and we tunnelled our way back. Caroline had a copy of the *War Cry* and was doing the crossword. 'A Salvation Army woman came round with them. She thought I needed saving from myself.'

'In case you fell off your shoes.'

'How do you spell Deuteronomy?'

Jan said: 'There's still a quid left in the kitty. Shall I get more lemonades?'

I went with her. The dark man was still at the bar; he winked as we approached and I smiled despite myself. 'Looks like you're on a promise, Mala.'

'I'd never get him past my mum: he must be thirty.'

'You'd better take him home for her, then.'

We giggled as she ordered the drinks. The crowd was thin at this end. In a corner an elderly gent was locked in an embrace with a woman whose skirt was riding up her thigh. 'She shouldn't show legs like those,' Jan said, 'they'd frighten horses.'

He came up for air. 'Isn't it Clive?'

Her eyes widened. 'And his wife only dead three months! No wonder he was so bloody happy this morning.' She turned her face away. 'I don't want him to see me here, it's too embarrassing.' She paid for the drinks while I savoured this glimpse into a secret world. 'Stop gawping, Mala.'

Caroline had put away her paper. 'I'm better versed in the catechism. Can we go after this – I've got buzzing in my ears.'

We passed on our juicy titbit. She pulled a face. 'What did you think he'd do, stay home dusting the ornaments?'

Finishing our drinks, we pulled on our coats and prayed for an early bus. As we headed for the doors, Clive was alone and directly in our trajectory. I tried to hide my delight as his face dropped at the sight of us. 'Hi, Clive – fancy meeting you here.'

Jan dug me in the ribs. 'We're just on our way out.'

I said: 'I didn't know you were into live music, Clive.'

He struggled to find the words.

A figure placed herself between me and Caroline: the smell of 4711. I turned around, knowing instinctively: and it was her. She studied me and suddenly the penny dropped, but instead of being embarrassed she gave the most enormous smile. 'Mala? My goodness, you've grown lovely.' She turned to Jan and Caroline. 'It's a full house.'

We all stared. Mrs Stephens said: 'Of course, you all know Clive, though I don't suppose you knew we were friends.' She looked coy. 'Well, more than friends now.'

Clive said: 'We've just got engaged.'

I didn't mean to, but I started laughing. I didn't know what else to do and I had a bit of a headache. I put my hand over my mouth, embarrassed but unable to stop. Jan looked mortified. Caroline ignored me. 'When's the wedding?' she asked coldly; politely.

And for some reason, this made me laugh even more.

# 10

I sat on the bed coughing and feeling sorry for myself. In the main room my mother was boiling up coriander seeds in an effort to finish me off. 'I've got antibiotics, Mum, I don't need this.'

'Natural remedies are best. You ignore what I say – going out in scanty clothes – that's how you get bronchitis.'

I sighed and chewed the end of my pen. How to begin?

Dear Beth,

I suppose your mum's told you that we ran into her and Clive. What a laugh! I couldn't believe my eyes!!

No, that wouldn't do. My mother came in with a soup cup of foul-smelling brew. 'It will loosen the phlegm.'

'Disgusting.'

I crushed the piece of paper and started again.

Dear Beth,

I'm sorry if you're cross about us meeting your mum.

It was a real surprise, but Clive's a nice bloke, isn't he? The band was deadly. I don't know why they stayed. Your mum says your boyfriend imports Thai silver. I bought a Siamese silver ring at Marbles – two dolphins – is that one of his? So Clive's going to be your stepdad: no wonder he always slipped you packets of Twizzlers!! Jan said he didn't seem too put out when his wife died!!

I stopped; this didn't quite capture the mood either. My mother put her head round the door. 'I am not moving until every last drop is drunk.' Painfully I forced the *cothamali* down. 'What are you writing, Mala?'

'A note to Beth; about Mrs Stephens.'

'That cunning Mrs Stephens – not happy mixing with the cheap and the low, she took the heart of a man with a dying wife. She'll return in her next life as an ant. You'll see.'

'Why, am I coming back as one too?'

I gave her the cup and she sighed. 'Over here, you marry only till the first distraction arrives.' She sat next to me. 'You know, Mala, in our village there was a fisherman, married to the *dobi* woman; they had seven boys, all boisterous. Both of them had wrinkled hands – he from the sea, she from the river. Look, even here my hands are ruined from washing clothes. Believe me, Mala, you could hear their arguments halfway along the Hikaduwa road. Every day he drank toddy and beat her with the yard broom. Today they are still together and have seven fine fishermen to show for their pains. *That* is marriage.' The bell rang. 'At last Mina and Ronnie. I better make the roti – she's only expecting one baby but she eats enough for three.'

Mina came through the door with a green velvet poncho stretched over her bump. 'Don't come too near me, Mala, I don't want to catch your germs.'

Ronnie grinned. 'A mere three months to go – we must take precautions.'

My aunt pulled up the black leather pouffe and, plonking herself in the only decent chair, put it to use as a footstool. 'Ronnie, ease my boots off, darling, my feet are swelling like sausages.'

Good-naturedly, her husband pulled off the fur-lined slip-ons and put them aside. 'Just think, I'll soon have two babies to slave for. I need a stiff drink every time I think of it.'

My mother gave him arak and orange. 'This is the easy part.'

'Don't say that, I'm already looking for escape routes.'

'It's the fashion.'

Ronnie looked confused. 'What is?'

'Escape routes. Give a man a ladder and he's gone.'

'Are you saying Ronnie will run off when the baby comes?'

'I am saying, Mina, that men are easily led away in a free-love culture.'

'That's very pessimistic.' Ronnie knelt down next to Mina and patted her stomach. 'I'll always be here for both my darlings.' He grinned. 'What are you laughing at, Mala; I'm not just a pretty face, you know.'

'Not even, you mean.' I told them about Clive's secret love affair and how Mrs Stephens had moved away to prevent gossip. My mother pursed her lips. 'All this time behind the counter holier than thou.'

'The majority of men are not like him,' Ronnie said.

'I don't know why we're even discussing this,' Mina whined. 'Can we eat now, Mum?'

We passed round the plates. Ronnie served his wife first. 'Here you are, honeybun, it'll build you up.'

'Honeybun?'

'Don't take the mickey, Mala, one day you'll be grateful if someone calls you honeybun.'

'I hope not,' my mother said sourly.

'Something is wrong with you today, Vino. Stop picking on Ronnie – he's a good man.'

'The only thing wrong with me is that nobody is eating. Of all of us, Mina, you must start; you have a baby now to nourish – your health is most important.'

Mina burst into tears.

'Now what's the trouble? Who have I offended this time?' Getting up, my mum pulled out a pink lace hanky from one of the hanky drawers and handed it to her. 'Here, your face paint is streaking, I hope it washes off.'

Mina sniffed: 'You haven't offended anyone, it's just that I get so tearful when I think of this little thing inside me.' She put her plate on the floor and hugged her stomach.

'My mother said she was very emotional during *her* pregnancies,' Ronnie said. 'It must run in the family.'

'But Mina isn't your family,' my mother replied, 'she has her own parents. It is the baby who'll inherit your mother's characteristics.'

Mina started crying even more.

'What's the matter now, Aunty Mina?' I asked gently, fearing that the turn of conversation had gone too far.

She let out a big howl: 'I don't want the baby to have his

mother's characteristics – she has large nose hairs and inoperable bunions. She's a good woman, Ronnie, but she's never worn a pretty dress in her life. If I have a baby like that I shall be forced to cut off my own head!'

Dear Beth,
   I'm not really sure what to say. You must know that we met your mum with Clive last week. I didn't tell her anything about writing to you. We were so surprised, we didn't say very much at all, actually. Why can't we meet? There's so much more to tell each other now the secrets are out. Please write.
   Lotsa love, Mala xx

'Well, there's a turn-up for the books,' Allie said the next afternoon. She emptied a can of Heinz spaghetti hoops into a Tupperware bowl and gave it to Jon in the high chair. 'She's a sly one, that Bethany. Must have known all the time and never said a thing.' She watched impassively as Jon's face began to resemble a Caribbean sunset. 'Mind you, Clive's wife was a real misery. I can't say I blame him.' Now Jon sank his fingers into the bowl and smeared hoops over his tray and bib. She wiped him clean with the same J cloth that had just been used on the sink. 'Was the old tart looking grim?'
   'She had a skirt halfway up her bum,' Jan said.
   'Ah well, you can't blame them for grabbing at happiness.'
   She wrestled the spoon from her son and tried to distract him. 'I'm so tired, but there's no rest for the wicked.'
   'Can't Guy help?'
   'He's depressed. They've closed the yard – no orders. Who wants repro card-tables in a recession? He was out half the night schmoozing some bloke who's opening a theme bar on the King's Road, but he won't get the contract – he hasn't got a clue about building work.' She plucked Jon from his seat and put him on the floor in front of a pile of bricks. 'That said, my stall's going a bomb. I cleared a hundred quid last week – after Nancy's wages.' She opened the wooden workbox on the coffee table. 'See these? Austrian crystal – really good stuff.' She picked out a stone and held it to the light. 'They can fool you into thinking they're real. I'm selling for half the price of Butler and

Wilson. All the clasps are gold-plated too.' Jon started grizzling. Allie got up and turned to Jan. 'It's your turn, Aunty, I want to gossip with Mala.'

She came and sat next to me. 'How's your boyfriend, then?'

'I haven't got a boyfriend.'

She listened to my tale of treachery. 'You don't sound too upset.'

'I feel better now.'

'It's always like that. First you panic, then you realise life's just as good on the other side – better, even.'

'You don't feel like that about Guy.'

She smiled. 'Who knows how I feel?'


'It's a fucking world-size disaster,' Bethany said.

'His wife's dead. It doesn't matter any more.'

'She might as well have shouted it from the rooftops.'

'They're engaged – you can't keep something like that secret.'

How weird to come out of the Tube station cramming chemical compounds and find Beth at the Bakerloo exit as if the previous four years had never happened. Even in the December chill she was wearing a long floaty dress under her mohair cardigan, last night's mascara shedding shafts of smudged darkness that fashionably accentuated the circles under her eyes. But where I exclaimed in joy, she glowered angrily. 'What right did you have to go there?' As if she owned the Mean Fiddler! I said crossly: 'Don't have a pop at me – it's not me who did a bunk because my mum was shagging the local paper-man.'

'Fucking bollocks.'

'Do you have to swear every other word?'

'Do you have to be such a stuck-up goody two shoes?'

We carried on in silence. I was annoyed by her alternate anger and distraction. She kept scratching her arms and it irritated me.

'So did you come here just to have a go, or have your squatter friends in Westbourne Park thrown you out?'

'Who told you about them?'

'Your mother.'

'She's got no fucking right to discuss me.'

'It's true, then?'

'I have a life you can't even imagine, Mala. Not like you – poor little mummy's girl.' I didn't respond. 'What else did she say about me?'

'Nothing. I didn't ask: none of us did. We've moved on too, Beth.'

She kept walking along beside me. Outside Clive's I slowed, but her step didn't falter and I had to catch up. At Savory Moore I said: 'I'm going home now. You can come if you want.'

'Home to *my* old flat?' She started laughing. 'I get Clive, you get my old bedroom. Who d'you think got the best deal?'

Linking arms, we walked in step down Craven Terrace, to the stairs by the railings: just like the old days.

'Your life's like a number six bus,' Margaret said in the dinner hall.

'What does that mean?'

'People just jump on and off. Things are always changing.'

'They're not changing, they're becoming clearer.'

'They've changed for Beth: she'll have a father figure now.'

'Clive? He's about ninety. She was better off before.'

'How do you know?'

'I've got eyes.'

She shook her head despairingly. 'Will you see her again?'

'We don't have anything in common.'

I looked up as Royston and Lior, the celebrated sixth-form superstuds, stopped at our table with trays of cottage pie. 'Is this a private conversation or can anyone join?'

'It's private,' Margaret snapped. I thrilled to their disbelief.

'You could regret this. Every girl in this room is wetting herself to sit with us.'

'My seat's quite dry.'

'Very sassy, Mala Fonseka.'

'Gentlemen, we're not interested,' Margaret said.

Royston gave a little roll. 'Neither are we.' He gave me a wink. 'I want someone who's got a little meat to grab hold of.' I felt the colour rise in my cheeks. They swaggered off, laughing.

'He's so bloody rude.'

'I know. But you are looking very thin.'

'Don't you start as well.'

'I wish you'd eat more.'

Margaret looked forlornly at the untouched cheese roll on her plate. 'My dad says if I don't start gaining weight, he's going to admit me to hospital.' She forced herself to take a mouthful. 'So why don't you and Beth have anything in common?'

'Because she's so . . . she's on the Pill. She's sleeping with her boyfriend! I think he's a druggie. She's probably one too. And you'll never believe this, Margaret: she lives with him half the week and her mum doesn't mind. She's only three months older than me.' I threw up my hands. 'When she came round to our place she asked if I had any Crosby Stills Nash and Young. As if!' I ate my last chip. 'Margaret, please swallow – you've been chewing that mouthful for five whole minutes.'

Across the room Royston caught my eye and winked again. 'That bloke thinks he's Casanova, doesn't he?' I said to nobody in particular, but I felt a vague and dangerous flutter within. I picked up her paper plate. 'Let's take this up: if we identify what went wrong in the mocks, we'll sweep the board this summer.'

As we left, someone wolf-whistled and Margaret stiffened. 'It's probably for you.' But while I yearned to look back, I still bore the memory of the awful day a classmate had done just that and the boy had shouted: 'I didn't mean you, Four-eyes.'

So I merely straightened and sauntered to safety.

Upstairs, Flick watched us come in. 'The two of you are looking like Cannon and Ball.'

'Am I too fat, Margaret?'

'You look great – everything's just right.'

'But you're so thin it makes me look fat.'

'Please don't nag, Mala.'

'What size would make you happy?'

'It's not about being happy,' she said sadly.

'Are you happy, Jan?'

'With what?'

'I don't know. Life.'

'Am I happy with life? What sort of question is that?' I didn't respond. 'How am I supposed to know?'

'You must know.'

She shrugged and served a customer, tidying up the stack of evening papers before coming back to me at the comic stand. 'Is that what you came in for – to ask if I was happy with life?'

'No, I came in for some cartridges.'

She took a packet down from the display. 'We've only got black. Is that all right?'

'A bit funereal.'

'Are you happy, Mala?'

'With what?'

'Life. Only you seem a bit cranky today.'

I gave her the money. 'Who can say? What is happiness? What is life? And why are my trousers too tight?'

'Everyone seems so low at the moment,' I said to Caroline as she drew on Canaletto arcs of blue eyeshadow. 'It must be something in the stars.'

'Hot gases.'

'The aspects are wrong. It drags you down.'

'The trouble with Chinese eyes is you can't see the lids.' She studied herself in the mirror. 'This looks awful, doesn't it?'

'Nauseous.'

She looked up. 'So what's wrong with you?'

'I don't know. I just feel heavy.'

'You are heavy – you should give Margaret your chips and do her diet.' She got up from the tester table. 'A few sequins and I'd pass for Danny La Rue.'

We left Miss Selfridge through the main shop, stopping for sample sprays of Rive Gauche and Chanel 19. 'Just what I want for Christmas,' Caroline said. 'Something sophisticated, cool and understated to send baronets crazy with desire.'

In South Molton Street we stopped for a milk-shake at Widow Applebaums, spotlit by the limy glow of a neon apple. Elegant women in full-length furs flitted past. 'This is class,' Caroline said. 'There's so much money around these days, but no style. Look at the Edgware Road – fat kids in Rolexes and ten Arabs on every street corner propositioning you.'

It was a favourite theme. We'd all suffered harassment since the Middle Eastern swarming of Marble Arch. Even my Aunty Anu, who applauded the Third World backlash from the rise of

OPEC, found it a culture shock. 'They see us as courtesans or servants; be careful, Mala, don't be tempted into conversation.'

All the posh flats in Park West and the Water Gardens were being snapped up for cash. The ricochet of rocketing property prices had even filtered the half-mile to Paddington where, my Uncle Shanta complained, a flat over an Indian restaurant in Star Street was now too expensive to rent. 'Twenty-five pounds a week to smell like a curry puff.' The area was an all-night activity centre dominated by burly men with fine features.

'London is changing,' Aunty Anu said. 'There are more black and brown faces on the streets – it is not just a swinging city, it is a cosmopolitan city. Don't listen to stupid talk about repatriation. What we are seeing is the future – and it's a future in which people like us will at last have some influence.'

Now Caroline was saying: 'It shows money can't buy class.'

'Who says they've got it in South Molton Street?'

'You can see for yourself. There's an essentially English way of showing wealth without boasting.'

'That's about culture, not money.'

'It's about style. Look at Marie Helvin and Vivienne Ventura. There's an essence, an understatement. It's not where you come from, it's what you represent.'

'So what do *you* represent?'

She shrugged and I snorted, causing her to frown. 'Your problem, Mala, is you don't understand style.'

'And yours, Caroline, is you don't understand substance.'

'Hello, Mala.'

'Hello, Terry.'

'You're looking great.' I turned away. 'Don't be like that. I've missed you.'

'That's your problem.'

We stood awkwardly, not moving.

'So why did you come tonight – to kiss the vicar goodbye?'

'Maybe to kiss you goodbye.'

Around us were the sounds of hilarity and excitement – the club's Christmas panto was about to get under way. I'd finished my work as wardrobe mistress. Margaret was an ugly sister.

Terry and Marek had stopped coming after leaving school, but both were here now, full of news and enjoying the adoration of the girls. Someone was shouting: 'Three minutes to curtain-up – take your places, please.' A few of the parents had turned up too: not mine, because I hadn't told her.

Now Terry and I sat centre front. 'Déjà vu.'

Margaret came on in what looked like a fish tail. I was struck by how terrible she looked. Terry put his hand on mine. I didn't respond.

At the end of the evening there was long and loud applause. Then the music came on, the parents left and it was disco time. He didn't ask me to dance. 'I won't push it, Mala.' I said nothing. 'Unless you want me to?'

I shook my head. 'There's no point: you'll be gone in three weeks.'

'But I'll be coming back. People always come back.'

'Yes, like bad pennies.' Whatever they may be.

Ding dong merrily on high: a week from Christmas and there is no room at the inn for my mother. On an overcast December day, just twenty-four hours after drinking too much sherry at the office party, she is stranded like Rapunzel at the top of a tower. Except this tower isn't in a forest but on the Euston Road. Her captor isn't a wizard but an HEO with the catch-phrase 'Why don't you go back where you came from?' The prince is in fact a princess – Prisky in her old gold Humber, coming to the rescue two hours after my mother's colleagues have decamped to unofficially continue the previous evening's celebrations elsewhere.

My mother is crying with anger, the plain blue hanky covered in wetness, bare feet tucked beneath her. Her shoes have been locked away in a drawer. The key is hidden amongst someone else's personal effects. No wonder they left in such high spirits! An impractical joke.

'I hate that man,' my mother cries. 'He deliberately gives me bad reports – I can't even apply for a transfer.'

'You should tell him to drop dead.'

'How would we pay the rent, Mala?'

'Report him under the Race Relations Act.'

'And get myself into even more trouble?'

So much for good old Buzby. The only lines of communication open to my mother were between her and the heavens: so we went off to make a vow in the hope that her fortunes might change. 'It's your duty to come with me, Mala – you haven't been for two years.' The temple at Christmas!

We bought flowers for the prayer room and provisions for the temple kitchen – cornflakes, All-Bran, Weetabix – and got the train to the Vihara in Chiswick.

'I thought Buddhism wasn't a religion.'

'It isn't. It's a philosophy.'

'So why do we kneel in front of statues and make offerings?'

'At home we prostrate ourselves even before our parents.' She sensed my opposition. 'It's our way of showing respect. If you're not happy with it, just put your hands together and bow your head.'

In the Vihara hallway we took off our shoes, adding them to the neatly lined row left by other worshippers, and climbed to the small prayer room. The blackout curtains were drawn to keep out the intrusive winter light. A shimmering golden Buddha of almost ceiling height dominated the dais against the facing wall. All around him were flowers – red, blue, white, yellow, purple; huge pink lotuses floated in jars of water and hundreds of incense sticks burned in special holders. The whole space was alight: alive. An orange-robed monk sat contemplating in a corner as we distributed unseasonably bright blooms into vases and joined him on the brown carpet. So warm, so womb-like: the joys of central heating. My mother was preoccupied with her own problems; I concentrated on mine. The previous day Caroline had fired a warning salvo: she wanted to leave school despite her parents' protestations. 'What good has it done Josh? By the time I'm his age I'll be established, Mala. In charge. I'll be sixteen in a few weeks. I want to get out there and sniff the air.'

I had a sense of impending doom: but why? Unthinkingly I sighed out loud, an action that seemed to set off a chain of events in which two novice monks entered the room, reeled out the prayer thread so everyone had a handhold, and started chanting: *Buddhung saranang gachaami, Dhammang saranang gachaami, Sangham saranang gachaami . . . pranatipata veramuni sikhapadang samadiyami.* At the end we all put our hands together and bowed: '*Sadhu Sadhu*' – Teacher Teacher – and now we queued to have part of the prayer thread tied around our wrists: auspicious; before the long walk back to the station.

'If there really was a God, we wouldn't have wars.'

'Buddha was not a god, he was a philosopher.'

'But if there really was a God—'

'If there is a God, Mala, I wonder what he thinks of all this nonsense with trees and present-giving. Modern society is so materialistic: the Buddha taught that we should control desire – not let it control us. The man who relinquishes desire has truly found nirvana.' But not the woman? I didn't ask in case my sense of relief was quashed by an unfavourable response.

## 11

'It says here that full oral sex increases your bust,' Janice said. 'I wonder how that works?'

I bit the top off my Cadbury's Ripple. 'Maybe the more you talk about it, the more air you get in your lungs. Like a bellows.'

She looked at me blankly. 'That must be it.'

Throwing *Cosmo* to the floor, she lay back on the settee and announced: 'My New Year resolution for 1974 is to get a job, get some money and get away from home.'

'That's what Caroline says.'

'If she sees it through.' She folded her arms. 'Come July I'll have served my time. I've got my typing speeds up, and I can manage shorthand.'

I savoured my last mouthful of chocolate and sighed. 'I'll be the only one staying on. You'll both have money and freedom while I'm still stacking shelves to pay for concert tickets.'

'Yeah, but I'll always be a typist and you'll have a career. Anyway, there's nothing to stop *you* leaving.'

'My mum'd have a fit. And I need five Os and two As to be a reporter: that's what the careers woman said.' She'd also said I didn't stand a chance and would be better off going to university and becoming a doctor or a dentist: 'Asian people do very well in the medical profession' – as if I wanted to spend my life prodding pustules or hoovering halitosis holes!

'How much can you earn, typing?'

'About twenty-five quid, I suppose.'

'What I could do with twenty-five quid.'

She looked at her watch. 'What time are we meeting?'

'The support film starts at seven.'

'But that isn't Bruce Lee, is it?' She closed her eyes. 'Richard Chin showed me his you-know-what. Wanted me to touch it. His dad's Chinese: I thought it would be different – like black ones are supposed to be bigger.'

'Are they?' No wonder Royston was always promising me a good time. 'What did it look like?'

'Just the same. I wouldn't touch it in case he got ideas. I don't really fancy him, he's too full of himself.'

'Would you have touched it if you did fancy him?'

'Why not – if it makes them happy. Didn't you do it for Terry?'

'Only through his trousers!'

She rolled on to her side and looked at me. 'Would you go all the way if it was someone nice?'

'If I was in love. The first time's got to be special. Would you?'

'I think so, but I always get put off when it gets too close.'

'Cathy & Claire say you have to be absolutely certain.'

'You don't learn about sex from *Jackie*.'

Chastened, I got our coats and we headed for our martial arts appointment at the ABC Queensway. Caroline was not alone. 'You don't mind us tagging along?' Ellie said. 'I'm a Bruce Lee fan.'

'Oriental overkill,' Josh said.

'He's the first Chinese screen hero since David Carradine.'

'Ellie, David Carradine isn't Chinese.'

'But he's meant to be: grasshopper.' We all stared at her. 'I'm just being silly – but I do love karate.'

'Kung fu and karate are hardly the same thing,' Josh said dryly, 'though it's true they both begin with a K.' Turning away from his wife, he organised the collective kitty. 'Come on, Mala, we'll get the tickets, the others can queue for sweeties.'

Unwittingly I found myself back in the cold, at the end of a ticket queue stretching up the side alley, Josh next to me. Remembering our previous encounter, I remained silent. A mistake.

'You're a sweater girl, Mala; you should leave the short skirts to Janice.' Excuse me? I scanned the nearby paving stones for a suitable hole in which to bury myself. 'Have I embarrassed you?'

Embarrassed me by suggesting I've awful legs? My eyes found a new fixity ahead.

'Still working hard?'

'Yes.'

'Me too. I'm taking finals a year late. Ellie's a saint: she keeps me focused when I have the odd lapse.'

'I didn't know you still . . . lapsed.'

'When things get heavy. There's an instinctive need to withdraw under stress. You don't see me then. But I'm strong and I'm beating it. The prognosis is good.' I assumed this was positive because he'd put on weight and was looking better than he ever had. His uncontrollable hair was thick and glossy. Self-consciously I moved on to the steps ahead of him: please don't let my legs be more horrible than Wendy Garner's bowed peculiarities. 'The only trouble is, the better I get, the more depressed Ellie becomes.'

'She seemed fine just now.'

'She's trying hard.'

Unexpectedly he put his hands on my shoulders and a tremor of excitement shot down my back. 'You're so tense, Mala. Relax. I'm not going to pounce – I'm a respectable married man, remember?' Yes: because you always remind me. Yet here you are, gently manipulating the pressure points under my jacket and turning my jelly-like legs into . . . jelly. Josh said: 'Ellie's been getting anxiety attacks – needs to wash her hands all the time.' He held my gaze as the woman at the ticket window counted out our change. 'What about you, Mala, what makes you anxious?' And when I didn't answer – because I wasn't sure – he said half to himself: 'I think I do.'

We joined up with Janice and Caroline. Josh said: 'Sis, check the toilet and tell Ellie we're going in.'

I went with her. We found Ellie washing her hands, just as he'd said. Her arms were almost raw to the elbows from overuse of soap and water: dry, white, cracked. 'Are you all right, Ellie?' Caroline asked as I went to the loo. 'We're about to go in.'

'I'm fine. I'll join you in a minute.'

'I'll wait with you.'

'You don't have to.'

'No, I'd like to. I have to guard Mala's popcorn against germs.'

'The whole place is full of them.'

'But yours are washed off now.' God bless Caroline for caring.

Josh was waiting outside the door. Plainly relieved when we came out, he put an arm round Ellie's waist. 'Come on, sweetness,' he said gently, 'the first film's already started.'

Sweetness? Oh, such pain.

Dear Beth,

You could have sent a Christmas card – it doesn't take much. My mum's very low at the moment. She's been getting a lot of flak from one of her bosses but now she's complained to the union so maybe it'll stop. Maybe. Jan and Caroline are both threatening to leave school in the summer. I'm so jealous!! Talk about putting the heat on – six weeks into the new term and the teachers are virtually whipping us up to working harder! I hope everything's all right at your end.

Mala xx.

Whipped into action with a masculine mixture of Brut, brutes and Brutus: 'Did you realise today's the Ides of March, Margaret?'

'Does it matter?'

'Well, it ties in with our reading.'

At the end of the corridor a small battle was being waged between two oversized white boys. Egged on by his mates, one kicked the other in the stomach and he toppled to the ground. Our new headmaster came racing down the central stairway, pulling the injured lad to his feet and grabbing the assailant's ear in a single smooth action. 'Okay, you two, into my office.'

'I'm leaving this place,' Margaret said. 'My parents have found a private crammer in Holborn. I'll do my A-levels there.'

'What? You can't just walk out.'

'Why not? I can't cope with all this aggression, Mala – if these guys aren't coming on at us, they're beating each other up. I joined a girls' high school, not a mixed comp: I'm a bag of nerves. This summer is as far as it goes.'

Now it was me who was winded, and I must have looked that way because Royston Bailey swaggered round the corner in a cloud of cheap aftershave with the school slag and said: 'Never mind, missy, your turn next.' Aaaggghhh!

I said: 'Margaret, you know it's only teething troubles. My Aunty Anu's a teacher, she says there's always a settling-down period when pupils react against the new regime.'

'Well, I'm a pupil and I'm reacting. I know it'll get better, but not soon enough to help me.' She saw my downcast face and ran a finger across my cheek, chasing an invisible tear. 'Come too, Mala. Maybe your mum could do a bit of overtime and pay for it?' I shook my head and she looked away. 'It's a terrible thing, but there you are.'

'No, not there I am. *Here* I am.'

Daffodils were pushing their heads through the Hallfield railings. 'New beginnings,' Caroline said as we walked up to Jan's. 'I'll use the Easter holidays to see what the temp agencies have on offer. I want to try a bit of everything.'

'I hope you've made the right decision.'

'Of course I have.' We turned into Westbourne Terrace. 'All exams provide is proof of individual ability, but employers can judge for themselves. I'll be getting a two-year head start.'

We found Janice in an agitated state, scrubbing the front-room floor with bleach while the increasingly pretty Tammy Tappett crawled around her smiling. 'She's just icked everywhere.' She washed out the bucket and went upstairs. Now, finally, she was ready in a jeans skirt and simple white blouse. 'Lend us your mascara, Caroline.'

We sang as we waited for the bus. Ringo Starr: You're sixteen, you're beautiful and you're mine. Two down, one to go. As the number 7 nosed its way into Piccadilly Circus I savoured the choices that would soon be on offer to me too: leaving home, marriage, work, sex – a smorgasbord of options from which I could fill my plate. And if I chose to postpone that meal, it was my choice and mine alone because, for the first time in my life, I could say 'No' and have my own way. Like Jan, though no one would stop her; and Caroline, whose parents had tried.

At the Shaftesbury Avenue bowling arcade I bought the drinks, got the first game out of the way and then leant back to survey the players in the surrounding lanes: young guys in smart casuals, a couple of families, an office party, and us. Specifically my two friends, one polished and assured; the other gentle and unassuming; both beautiful and each merging into the other as if somehow their qualities were interchangeable. Now Caroline was teasing Jan. They beckoned to me but I shook my head. 'I'm happy watching.' Caroline raised an eyebrow: reading my mind as I contemplated whether the long blond-haired man in the dog-print shirt was more attractive than the dark boy with eyeshadow in Lane 3. She shouted: 'You're a bloody hormone homing device.'

Afterwards we headed up to Goodge Street, to the Spaghetti House, which went up and up and up and didn't cost too much. Jan was determined the evening would be low key: 'I'm off thrills and surprises.'

And of course we'd had one surprise already tonight when Mr Tappett came crashing down the stairs in a methane aura to announce his wife was missing: 'She's disappeared from the bed.' He opened the fridge and took out a beer. 'Like Mary Poppins.'

Upstairs we could hear Jan moving around. Suddenly she shouted: 'She's on the floor. The silly cow's fallen out on her side. For God's sake, Jack, come up and help.'

I straightened the quilt as Janice and her stepfather lifted the unconscious woman on to the sagging mattress.

Mrs Tappett, her frizz contained in kirby-gripped sprigs, lay on the bed like Hilda Ogden. Her breathing was heavy and her cheek had a carpet burn. 'Will she be all right?'

'It's only a tumble.'

Downstairs, Tammy began to cry. Jan said: 'I'm going out, Jack. She needs changing – you'll have to look after her.'

'I don't know what to do.'

'You'll soon get the hang of it.' But it wasn't until we'd slammed the door behind us that he realised she was serious. 'I've got to train myself to walk away from it,' Jan said. 'The rest of my life started today.'

So here we were, the three of us, eyes bigger than our bellies as we grappled with overloaded plates of antipasto: happy. I laughed to myself, overwhelmed with affection for them both: my friends. How stupid to worry that we'd grow apart after the summer. We were as closely knit as a packet of Shreddies. You'd need one hell of a strong spoon to prise us apart: it would take more than leaving school to do it.

It was Easter Sunday and I was having a lie-in when the phone went. My mother had already left on a Ceylon Women's Association day trip to the races, but I couldn't face the curiosity of the punters when four dozen saried ladies alighted from a coach and sat on the grass with patties, cutlets, iced coffee and the *Sun*.

'A job must be done properly,' my mother had said, reading the form. 'Really, this paper is disgusting – full of loose women jiggling their breasts.' But she had put aside five pounds for a gamble and decided to risk 50p a time, each way.

Now, as I staggered out of bed at 9 a.m. on a weekend, I cursed the thoughtless idiot on the other end. 'Yes.'

'Mala? It's Bethany. Can I come over?'

'When?'

'Now. I've a favour to ask. I'm at Paddington. I'll be with you in five minutes.'

A favour? Of course: why else would she ring. After all, she hadn't written for months. I felt out of sorts. Pouring myself a glass of milk, I turned on the telly and awaited her arrival – *Morning Service*: Oh Lord our help in ages past, our hope in years to come, our shelter from the stormy blast and our eternal home.

The bell rang and Beth entered her own eternal home with a red holdall in her hand. 'How come you're still in pyjamas? Get dressed – I'll put the kettle on.'

When I came out of the bathroom, the holdall was open. Beth's head was in the cupboard under the sink. 'What are you doing?'

'Looking.' She emerged, flushed and a little bit frightened. 'Promise you won't tell.'

'Won't tell what?' All we had in there was a box of Brillo pads and a plunger.

'They're putting the squeeze on Sam – he's under surveillance. They think he's importing drugs in his silver shipments.'

'Is he?'

'Only for himself!'

I brushed my hair. 'So what's the favour?'

'I just want to leave the stuff here for a while. It's our personal stash. I've put two packets in the U-bend of your sink.' She handed me a cup and sat down. 'I like your hair like that.'

I sipped the tea. It was lukewarm and weak. 'Beth, what exactly is it that you've put in the cupboard?'

'A couple of packages.'

'What's inside them?' Sudden enlightenment. 'It's not drugs, is it?'

'Personal use only.'

'You what? You've hidden dope in my mother's U-bend?'

'Fuck's sake, Mala, no need to shout like that!' She looked around anxiously, as if someone might pop out of a corner. 'Don't draw attention to us.' I gawped, disbelieving. 'Anyway, it's not dope, it's smack.'

'Smack?'

'Heroin, you know: it's all pure, no rubbish.'

I collapsed in the chair. She looked at me as if I were mad. *I* were mad! Christ almighty: I had two bags of heroin in my flat and my mother was at the races dispensing cheese footballs and applauding my reverential application to my studies.

Thoughts presented themselves in slow motion: Dinah Cargill sniffing Zoph during the fourth-year trip to the Isle of Wight. The ceremonial destruction of the bottle after she hallucinated her father's death. Yasmin Brown's crowd had been to a party where people smoked marijuana. This was the full range of my encounters with the drugs underworld: not forgetting a weary proposition from a pusher on All Saints Road. But that was Lucozade, and this was whisky.

Bethany, meanwhile, was watching a gardening programme. 'I haven't seen a black-and-white TV in ages.' She turned to look at me. 'You're still tired, aren't you? I'll go.'

'No you bloody won't!'

'Fuck's sake, why d'you keep shouting? All right, I'll stay. Is there anything to eat?' She got up uninvited and opened the fridge. 'Can I have that salami?' She popped the slices straight into her mouth, wiped her fingers on her dress and sat down.

'I can't keep it for you.'

'Why not? It's perfectly safe. It won't burst or anything.'

'I'm not worried about it bursting, Beth: I'm worried about being arrested.'

'Nobody knows I'm here – not even Sam.'

'Bethany, listen to me: I will not look after these drugs for you. Let Sam sort it out.'

'He can't – the police have fucking got him.'

So even as we sat there, Mr Plod might be chaining his bike to our railings. I said: 'Beth, take the stuff away or I'll throw it.'

'You're supposed to be my friend. You're always writing to tell me you're my friend.'

'I *am* your friend – but I don't do left luggage.'

She started to cry. 'I don't know what to do. That's our future in there.' Her future in my U-bend!

I searched desperately for inspiration. Finally I found it in a large bottle of Horlicks that was due for despatch to my ageing grandfather. Emptying it down the loo, I retrieved the packages, shaking their contents into the bottle while Beth sponged down the thin layer of powder that settled on the worktop. 'Take it away, nobody will guess.'

'Thanks, Mala.'

When she was gone I could barely function. I went to the toilet and found the Horlicks floating in unflushable lumps. A small reservoir of boiling water and it cleared: the fish would sleep well tonight; but I was a nervous wreck. Beth had brought her own peculiar brand of disorder into my life and now my Mott the Hoople money would be spent replacing the bottle. How could I revise when I was eaten up with fury?

That evening, it would be my first visit to the Bird's Nest, Paddington. I was so excited I could barely string together a sentence; but my future depended on it. Thankfully the multiple-choice comprehension section was easy and the essay subjects lent themselves to a serious exercise of the imagination. It was pure luck that today was English and not maths.

At the end of the room Mr Berrill caught my eye and frowned, as if looking up somehow implicated me: another hour to go. I pulled myself together and got on with it: *Walking the Fine Line*. 'There is,' I wrote, 'an invisible thread that is the boundary between Childhood, when only the here and now has meaning, and Adulthood, where dreams and expectations are grander, more long-term and achievable. Choosing to be part of one or the other is the easy option. Far harder is to walk the fine line between the two – trapped within the limitations of the child while constructing the game plan of the adult. This fine line is called "being sixteen and staying on at school".'

Yes, I thought, as we filed out silently, that's me – teetering while Caroline and Jan prepare to cross. And yet I was looking forward to the lower sixth because, that morning, we'd been shown the newly painted common room complete with easy chairs and a kettle: very grown up in its own way.

On the main landing, Margaret came alongside. 'That wasn't too bad, was it?'

We left the building and walked up Elgin Avenue to the Harrow Road. She treated me to a cappuccino and a toasted sausage sandwich and, under pressure, bought herself an iced bun. 'Happy birthday, Mala, I'm really going to miss this next year.'

'Oh, I don't know: there are loads of coffee bars on Kingsway.'

We talked about our essays and the exams completed so far. I had only art and history left, she biology and geography. 'We're not going to see each other, are we?'

I grinned. 'There's no point coming back once the exams are done. Ten weeks off – brilliant.'

'Then I won't see you at all this summer. We're off to Corsica in two weeks and after that I'm being sent to my granny in Sussex for fattening up – like a turkey.'

'Oh, Margaret, why can't you just make an effort? Please eat that iced bun instead of shoving it round your plate.'

'It isn't that easy.' Her face crumpled – as it always did under pressure. 'The sight of it makes me sick.'

'Then I'll have it,' I said, doing her a last favour.

Tonight's the night I've waited for – because you're not a baby anymore, you've turned into the prettiest girl I've ever seen, Happy Birthday Sweet Sixteen: and we believed Neil Sedaka as we sat round the circular dance-floor at the Bird's Nest, glowing in a tumescent, adolescent sort of way. Martini and lemonades all round, barman, please! Already I felt giggly as Jan escorted me to the loo. 'Have you seen our bras under the ultra violet?'

She giggled and put on some cranberry lip-gloss: 'It's Caroline's – try some.' I shook my head. 'Allie's earrings look fantastic on you – I'd forgotten all about them.'

We went back to find Caroline resisting the charms of an acned youth with fresh sweat rings under the arms of his nylon shirt. 'I said no thank you. Please go: I'm engaged to be married.'

'Living For The City', Stevie Wonder; we put our mimsy little bags in a pyre on the dance-floor and bobbed up and down like buoys on a stormy sea. Behind Caroline a man and a woman were dancing the Hitchhiker and we grinned at each other because it was funny; but when 'Sugar Baby Love' started, the laugh was on us because a group of squaddies with short hair and legs moved in for the kill and we had to hot-foot it to safety. 'No finesse,' Caroline said.

We got more drinks and she made a toast: 'Here's to the future. Yours in academe, ours in the world out yonder.' Academe? We sat chatting and joking as, somewhere behind us, we were coming under scrutiny:

'I like the look of the one in cream.'

'You've got to be joking – she's a Paki.' Bastard!

'Come on,' I said, 'the squaddies are at the bar – let's shake a leg.' We'd show them.

And then destiny smiled on us all. Across the dance-floor came three young men with Roxy Music haircuts and a hint of mascara: heaven in green platform shoes. First they danced near us: Mud, 'The Cat Crept In'. Then they were dancing with us: Bad Company, 'Can't Get Enough'. My stomach felt tight; I caught Jan's excited eye. Behind her hard-to-get face I sensed that Caroline too was warming up. The mood changed; the boys moved in closer. Momentary confusion. The Hollies: Sometimes, All I Need Is The Air That I Breathe.

One of the group, lanky, hairy, effeminate – gorgeous – leaned across and pulled me against him. As we started swaying, first awkwardly and then with a semblance of rhythm, my head leaned uncertainly towards his chest. Suddenly, gently, his mouth grazed my ear: 'Has anybody told you you've got come-to-bed eyes?' I couldn't suppress my grin of pure happiness.

Happy Birthday Sweet Sixteen!

# 12

The week after she left school, Caroline got a temp job at the West End estate agents Park & Wright and never left. Unlike Jan, who sat the London Transport exam and got a job in the Telstar House typing pool, she was on a permanent high. 'This is it! This is what I want to do. You should see the way these guys live – money money money. Property is the future, Mala.'

When I went to meet her after work, she whispered: 'Look at the carpet, it's Axminster, specially made.' Lovingly she tidied the information sheets on her desk: mansion flats near Baker Street and 'town houses' off the Edgware Road. Town houses! Talk about stating the obvious. I sat in a leather swivel chair and watched as she set the switchboard and locked the safe. 'We're getting push-button telephones – have you seen them?'

She brought out her handbag – faux black snakeskin. 'Fiorucci: beautiful, isn't it? Two weeks' wages.'

Even Jan, emerging into the early evening gloom on Eastbourne Terrace, was cloaked in the confidence of the unfettered consumer. 'D'you like this shirt? I wasn't sure if crushed velvet was my thing, but I deserved a treat.' And though she complained her job was boring as hell: 'I type everything in triplicate – top copy for the addressee, blue copy for our files, yellow for the department of issue,' she also boasted that the building was full of young men. 'They're down the pub every night. I'd go too if I wasn't frightened of running into my mum or Jack.' She grinned. 'Come on, let's get a pizza – my treat, before the old cow tries to cadge my pay packet for the housekeeping.'

Stacking shelves in Boots each night, I cogitated and agitated.

I moaned to Margaret: 'I've become the poor relation, dependent on handouts like the needy people in my mother's village going to my grandfather's house for feeding. Caroline and Janice treat me like a duty. They've grown up and I'm still a schoolgirl.'

'You don't grow up in three months.'

'No, you just grow apart.'

'What are you, frigid or something?' Royston demanded. 'A lesbo – is that it?'

We'd gone for a walk in Paddington rec and, as usual, as soon as we got into a clinch, his fingers were infringing my modesty.

'Take your hands *out* of my loons, please.'

'You're so repressed, woman – and such a squeezable arse.' He pulled away, laughing. 'You tease me, Mala, it's not good for a man. You might force me on to someone more willing.'

'I thought you'd had half the girls in the school.'

'That still leaves half.' The arrogance!

I spotted a lone conker at the base of a tree and popped it in my pocket. What d'you call a bloke who's walking on autumn leaves?

Russell.

'I won't wait much longer.' Royston lunged, large hands grabbing conical bosoms.

I pushed him away angrily. 'Why are you always threatening me? If it means so much to you – go find someone else. I don't care.' We started walking back. I took his hand, trying to make peace. 'I read *Soledad Brothers* over the weekend – you're right, it's life-changing.'

He shrugged. 'Glad to help.'

'Don't be mad with me. If I did sleep with you, you'd think I was a dog.'

'I wouldn't be with you if you were a dog.'

'Why not? You've been with plenty of dogs.'

He pulled away and marched ahead. I let him. I didn't want to look overkeen – there was enormous pleasure to be had from someone wanting you so badly. I'd sort it out in the morning.

But the next morning he was supporting a wall with Denise Gyngell! She too was apparently unforthcoming because, within a week, he was parading round with Seema Khan who everyone knew was panting for it before being shipped to her arranged marriage in Pakistan. Finally, as the end of term neared, he hitched up with Regina Bright, who claimed to French-kiss her spaniel and had slept with every boy within a three-mile radius. What a set of slags. So why did I feel so miffed?

Mina's baby Rohan was, she claimed to my mother, bilingual.
   'But the child can't talk yet, Mina, he's only ten months.'
   'Nonsense – he says mummy, daddy, cat, dog.'
   'In two languages? He must be a genius.'
   'You can laugh, Mala,' Ronnie said, 'but it's extraordinary what he understands.' He leaned across to Rohan, who was chewing a rusk on the floor, and said slowly: *'Bo-ho-ma hon-dye nay-der?'*
   'What is he saying, Mina?'
   'What do you mean, what is he saying? It's perfectly clear! *Bohomer honthai nayther*: it's very good, isn't it?'
   My mother suppressed a smile. 'Does the child speak like his father or like you?'
   'Why do you have to make fun? He's very gifted.'
   Ronnie said: 'Look at him smile – he understands every word.'
   'What's the point of talking to him in Sinhalese?' I asked.
   'So he appreciates the breadth of his heritage.'
   'But he's got no use for it here. Mina always speaks English.'
   'But often I think in Sinhalese.'
   'He won't.'
   'It'll help him communicate with his grandparents,' Ronnie said. 'They're due to come over in March.'
   'Ronnie – my parents speak beautiful English – far better than yours. For goodness' sake, we have the highest literacy rate in the Third World.'
   'But if he doesn't need it in Sri Lanka and he doesn't need it here, what's the point? Wouldn't French be better?'
   'But I don't know any French, Mala.'

'Perhaps we should buy him a course at Berlitz as his Christmas present?' I started to giggle.

'Perhaps we should have bought you one,' my mother said. 'Then you might have got an A in French as well.'

Ronnie sighed. 'I'll introduce some French once he's a little more fluent. He may be a genius, but if we crowd his mind with too many cultural cues he'll just be confused.'

'That is always the case,' my mother said, and looked sadly at me, but when I met her stare she was the first to look away.

A week after finding three Valentine cards on her desk, Jan announced she was leaving home to share a flat with Merle from work: 'Merle's in a horrid bedsit and I need to get away from home. It's the obvious thing to do.'

'But this is major, Jan.'

'I said I'd do it. Will you and Caroline help me move? It's only round the corner, in Chilworth Street.'

That weekend, while the Tappetts were out, we carried her belongings up three flights to the top-floor flat: two bedrooms with a shared kitchen on the landing and a bathroom.

'Nice, isn't it?'

I smiled and nodded, even though I saw the poky attic as yet another fence post in the division between us. 'I'm really happy for you, Jan.' But not for myself!

I cleaned out a small chest of drawers while she put things away and Caroline went for Cokes. The old wardrobe and the sad single bed weren't how I'd imagined a place of one's own would look. In my own displacement fantasy, my new address was always far superior to our pathetic surroundings in Craven Terrace. But if this was what Jan wanted . . .

'This isn't what I want, Mala – it's what I can afford. I'll do it up over time. Anyhow, it's better than what I left behind.'

'One street away isn't very far behind,' Caroline said, and she was right. The next day Mrs Tappett came round and dumped Tammy.

Later that week we shared a sandwich at the Caprini. Jan said: 'Ring the bell three times when you come – I don't want to answer if it's my mum. She asked Merle to take Tam yesterday – she got short shrift for that.' She finished her sandwich. 'Honestly, Mala, you don't know how lucky you are: you don't have to work, you don't have to run, you're doing exactly what you want.'

'Mala Fonseka.'

I turned around. 'Yes, sir.'

'I wanted to have a word with you about your last few homeworks.' Mr Hardy motioned me into the library and sat me down. 'They're good, but lacking your usual spark. Is all well?'

'I think so.'

'I know conditions aren't ideal. Few of the grammar-school girls have stayed; but you used to be one of my brightest students. Don't lose it now.' He smiled at my expression. 'I'm saying this for your own good. In fifteen months you'll leave this building for ever. Recharge your batteries over Easter – for me.'

In the common room, an argument was under way – something to do with quarks and atoms; way over my head. I curled into the chair and struggled on with 'The Wife of Bath'. Lost my spark? I'd show him.

Somebody was humming – loudly and close: Hey, Fattie Bum Bum, sweet sugar dumpling. Bloody Royston Bailey. 'How's the virginal Miss Fonseka?'

'All the better for being reminded of my wisdom.'

He laughed and walked away shouting: 'Too bad you missed your chance,' as if I'd ever thought about it!

'He's a real Lothario, isn't he?' Lothario?

A deep friendly voice with long black hair and treacle eyes: Tony Carlettidou. Tall, dark, funny, clever, final year – and engaged to a Miss Junior Tupperware finalist from Marylebone Grammar. I smiled. 'It wouldn't be so bad if girls didn't throw themselves at him.'

'He's very good-looking.'

'No more than you; it's just that he's available.'

'So am I.'

'Everyone knows you're engaged.'

'Was. Not any more. My dad was right – I'm too young.' Then, casually: 'D'you fancy a cappuccino?'

We went across the road to the greasy spoon. 'You didn't mind me breaking your concentration?'

'It was already broken.'

'I take it you're over Royston?'

'Over him? I only ever got a chance to get under.'

A smile. 'How d'you fancy going out with me one night? Nothing serious – just to see a film or something?'

'I'd like that.' Nothing serious. I stirred my drink feeling strangely elated.

Caroline said: 'You'll be glad to know I've surmounted the problems of a lowly birth and scant qualifications. I'm going to help show the new development in Crawford Street and Martin says if I pull off two sales he'll make me junior negotiator on my eighteenth birthday.'

'But it's not yet May and your birthday's in January.'

'Time flies when you're enjoying yourself.' She grinned, showing small even teeth against healthy pink gums. 'I reckon I've got one sale in the bag already – the man was falling over himself to sign up.' Jan feigned a yawn and slumped. 'I wouldn't do that if I were you, Janice, you're already getting round-shouldered from hunching over the Remington Noiseless.'

'Piss off, Caroline.' She'd been miserable all night.

We paid our bill and went outside. Jan said: 'I'm going home.'

'That's just great,' Caroline said. 'I turn down a chance to view the new Regalion development because *you* want to go out – and now you're off to bed.'

We saw her on to a bus and walked back to Chilworth Street. 'What's wrong, Jan?'

'Nothing, really.'

'Something's up – I'm not stupid.'

'I've just made a complete idiot of myself, Mala – that's all.'

We went upstairs. She said: 'That bloke Eddie – the one I said kept hanging round my desk. Last Friday I gave in. We had a drink after work and then he came back for coffee.' She stared down at her hands. 'He started kissing me and it felt quite nice, you know. But then he suddenly got heavy. Pawing. Horrible. Hands everywhere.' She shuddered. 'Everywhere.'

'Didn't you tell him to stop?'

'I didn't know how.'

'For God's sake, Jan!'

'I didn't want to upset him. I see him in the office every day. I thought he'd stop because I kept pushing him away. But then he pulled my pants down, Mala, and started doing it.' Tears rolled silently down her face. 'I couldn't move. I just let him. And then he rolled off and fell asleep on top of the covers and in the morning he said he hadn't known I was so experienced.'

'You're not: are you?'

'Of course not. And when I said I wasn't, he said I was lying.' She pulled up her sleeves and showed me bruises at the top of her arms. 'He just laughed.'

I wondered how something new and exciting could be so dirty and incidental. I was astounded that Jan could be so stupid. I didn't know what to say. I put my hand on hers. 'You're not going to see him again?'

'Not like *that*. But he works in the same office.'

And all the lads were looking at Jan and laughing: 'Vergin' on the ridiculous, I'd say, eh, Janice?'

'I just feel so cheap. I could've said no and I didn't.'

'He should have stopped. It could have happened to anyone.'

'But it didn't happen to anyone, Mala, it happened to me.'

Dear Beth,

I swore I wouldn't write after your last visit, but . . . a lot of water has passed under the bridge etc. I've spent the entire summer holidays working in Boots – and I've learned my lesson. I can't wait till school starts on Monday!! Caroline is selling properties. She's been doing it nearly a year now and is already in line for promotion! Jan's had a bit of a bad time, but she's getting over it. She's moved into a flat with a girl from work who cooks amazing Trinidadian food – better than chips in Westbourne Terrace! My mum's got her transfer at last, so she's happy. I've got a smashing new boyfriend called Tony. Well, not that new any more! He's gorgeous. Have you left school – not that you went there much as I recall!! Do write.

Lotsa luv, Mala xx

Caroline was powdering her nose and talking to Martin as I arrived. At the lettings desk, Jonathan looked up and wolf-whistled. Martin grinned. 'Naughty boy. What are you two lovelies doing tonight?'

'Late-night shopping – Christmas is but weeks away.'

'Don't I know it. The old lady wants Gucci loafers, my daughter's passed her test and needs a car, and the boy's pushing for tennis coaching in Florida. I'll be bankrupt at this rate.'

'That's not true,' Caroline said, putting away her compact. 'It won't even dent one of your accounts.'

'Have you been reading my bank statements?'

'I don't have enough time.' She picked up her bag.

'And what does my favourite girl want for Christmas?'

'You know what I want: a card saying Junior Negotiator.'

'You drive a hard bargain, Caroline.'

'That's why I deserve it.'

Martin winked at me. 'As if I needed telling. Shall we take her out and celebrate, Mala? We could make it into an office outing.'

I liked Martin; he was old but fun. 'That sounds great.'

'It's a date, then. Now, don't go mad, will you, ladies, or I'll start to think I'm paying Miss Chong too much already.'

We trailed around Take Six. 'What're we looking for, Caroline?'

'Something for Josh. A sweater maybe.'

'What about Ellie?'

'I don't know. She's so busy scrubbing. It's got to the stage where she washes the sink and bath before sitting down to a pee.' She picked up a striped tank top and held it to the light. 'She's had to give up work. Just as well Josh is getting shifts computer operating. It's good money. They've asked him to go on a programming course.'

'But he *still* has to work nights.'

Caroline shrugged. 'Maybe it's a relief to get away.'

*     *     *

Janice was full of smiles. 'I've got a new job at a law centre near King's Cross, starting Monday. I'll be away from that bastard Eddie at last. When I think of the *decent* blokes I could have lost it to!' She put her arm through mine. 'Come on, let's go up to Flanagans – my treat. I fancy a little bit of piano, some posh fish and chips and a giggle with my best mate.'

A man in a butcher's apron took our order. 'Won't they be deadly serious in a law centre, Jan?'

'It'll stretch me: that's what they said at the interview. They weren't in suits and all that. It was really friendly.'

'Will you have to go to court?'

'No – I'll just be typing statements and letters.' She grinned. 'There's a lot of big words but they're giving me a dictionary to check my spellings. I can't wait.'

'It'll be brilliant.'

'It won't change the bad bits.' She screwed up her face. 'I've looked after Tammy three nights this week. If the old cow's not after my time, she's hanging out on Eastbourne Terrace cadging my money.' I started to laugh. She said: 'It gets worse. This weekend I've got to see Sean and Marie *and* I'm baby-sitting for Allie all day Sunday.' She cocked her head sadly. 'I don't have a bloke and I'm paying rent – it's not the life of Riley.'

'Caroline went to the Talk of the Town the other night to see Tony Bennett – she said he was amazing.'

'Because the people she works for are loaded.'

'She's got us tickets for a river disco on Sunday night. We can collect you from Allie's.'

On the way back we passed the midden in Westbourne Terrace. 'Looks like Tammy's up, her lights are on,' Jan said. 'I hope she's all right.' We turned the corner. 'Why am I worrying anyway? Tam's hers, not mine. Why have children? She hates the sight of them. It's a miracle really.'

'No, Jan, a miracle is the loaves and two fishes. Your mum's one of life's insoluble mysteries.'

'Like Stonehenge.'

'More like *The Twilight Zone*.'

'You're both in time to give me a big send-off,' Allie said. She was standing at the front door with two red leather suitcases, a blue trunk and a number of small vanity boxes. Beccy was asleep on Jan's shoulder and Jon was sitting on a cardboard container marked 'Fragile'. Allie buttoned up her camel coat with the fox-fur collar. 'It's bloody freezing.' She looked for her purse. 'The cab'll be here any minute – I didn't want a dramatic exit.'

'What's going on?' Caroline said.

'We're leaving.' So chirpy.

'On holiday?'

'No, a bit longer-term than that.' She put on a *Watch with Mother* voice: 'Jon and Beccy and I are going to live in a lovely big house in Hammersmith, aren't we, cherubs? With Uncle Peter, who owns the building where Mummy sells her jewels. There's a smashing garden for my darlings and we'll see the river from our windows.'

'You're leaving Guy?'

She put a finger to her lips and moved us away from the children. 'I don't want them to get upset – you know how kids are.' She saw our confusion. 'Don't look like that – it's been coming for a long while. It's only me that's been holding the place together. Guy's chasing dreams all the time: he's talking about making jumps for Hickstead when he doesn't know one end of a horse from the other.' She pinched my cheek. 'That's not the way I am – you know me – I like my finger on the button.' She straightened. 'It's all very civilised. We've not had words or anything, it's not like my parents. We could have carried on, but why bother? It's not as if he's ever around.' She put her arms around us conspiratorially. 'Anyway, I've met someone new, someone dynamic. We'll marry as soon as his divorce is through. He's more like me – started out selling door to door and now he's a millionaire – all kosher money too. His name's Peter, Peter McGibben: you'll love him.'

A cab pulled up. 'We'll have to go. I wish you'd come earlier, you could have heard all the gossip.' She directed the driver to her piles of luggage. 'Sorry it's such a squeeze.' Then she scooped up her children affectionately and climbed into the back, smiling through tears. 'Janice, thanks, darling – I'll give you a ring as soon as we're settled. And you two, come and visit – it's a great house.'

As the cab drew away and the children's uncertain faces were swallowed up in the crocodile of traffic, I felt inexplicably sad; it was as if Allie's departure highlighted a hiatus in hope. She was so warm and kind and full of love. If it could go wrong for her, what hope for the rest of us? Caroline looked across and snorted. 'Not still hoping for the fairytale ending, Mala? Haven't you learned that life isn't all about happy-ever-afters?'

'You're wrong,' Jan said from behind. 'This is her fairytale ending; this is her happy-ever-after: can't you see?'

Janice's new office was the complete opposite of the controlled grandeur of Park & Wright. A neon light constantly buzzed in the reception area where Jan and Ritu worked. Behind them were two haphazard rows of desks, like at school, and at the very back a small kitchen where they made teas and heated food. The smell of steak-and-onion pie merged with that of the kerosene heaters and cigarette smoke to produce a prison canteen effect during the months when the front door was closed against the elements.

Behind the girls were two women in their late twenties; a counsellor, Carin, and the rights adviser, Miriam, who dealt with calls and organised meetings for themselves and the two solicitors who, hidden behind a sandbank of brown files, made up the third and highest tier of the workforce: Al and Evie. The phones never stopped ringing. A sign behind Ritu's desk said 'Welcome to the Madhouse'. As I walked in she waved for me to sit down. 'Jan's nipped out to get Al's fags.'

I sat near a sad woman in dirty clothes who was slumped in the waiting area gazing blankly at the wall posters. Her make-up had faded on the left side, as if she'd fallen asleep in it. I studied a leaflet on civil rights for several seconds before realising it was printed in Urdu.

Jan came in, threw the Benson & Hedges across the room to the other side of the filing system, and grabbed her coat. 'Let's get out of here before someone else cadges another favour.'

We walked up Gray's Inn Road to Chancery Lane. 'Are you sure you want to go carol singing, Mala? I've got to go because Al promised to send a rep from the office. You could be having fun.'

'This is fun. Anyway, the tree's always lovely in Trafalgar Square.' We cut through to the Aldwych and down the Strand, singing 'Oh Little Town Of Bethlehem'.

'The hopes and fears of all the years are met in thee tonight.'

The lights were shining as we drew up outside the Knightsbridge Sporting Club. The doorman, in maroon serge, took the keys to Martin's Porsche and ushered us inside. Jonathan and his girlfriend were waiting in the wood-panelled lobby from which a mirrored corridor led to the gaming room.

There was a girl in the loo whose only job was topping up complimentary bottles of scent and giving out fresh towels.

'We'll tip her at the end of the evening,' Caroline said. 'That's what they do.' Seeing my look, she raised an eyebrow. 'Mala – in the world of the rich everyone gets a cut. Just watch *me*.' She laughed as she said it, and as we re-emerged Martin was pleased that we were pleased. 'The old lady said you'd like it here.'

We walked to the gaming room. 'This is where it all happens. What would my rising star like from the bar?'

Wandering curiously around the dozens of tables, we passed Jonathan settling to a game of blackjack. A girl in a frilled apron came past with a huge tray of short-eats. 'Would you like sandwiches?'

'How much are they?'

'They're on the house, madam.' She handed across a mixed plate of smoked salmon and chicken mayonnaise. Bliss!

'It's to encourage you to stay and spend,' Martin said, slipping alongside. 'Your drinks are at the table directly behind. Now if you'll excuse me, ladies, I've just spotted a business contact coming through the door and I want to grab him before someone else does.' He pulled out a wad of notes and unrolled two fivers. 'Go and cash these into chips and have a go yourselves. After that you're on your own.'

At the cashier's office we each got 50p chips and did the rounds of the roulette tables, vainly hoping we could spot a discernible pattern in the numbers that came up. 'If it's there I can't see it,' Caroline grumbled.

'Then bet on colour,' said the woman over whose back we were leaning. 'That's fifty-fifty. This square's for red, this one's for black. And learn the first rule of gambling – silence.'

Caroline put all her chips on red. I put mine on black. The ball landed on zero, which is green. We lost ten quid!

'Now you know why there is no such thing as a certainty in gambling,' the woman said.

'Like life,' I muttered darkly. We returned to our drinks.

'What a waste,' Caroline said. She finished her Tio Pepe. 'Mala, d'you mind if I just go and see what Martin's up to? I think he's talking to one of the guys involved in the Welbeck House deal – it's big bucks.'

I flagged down another plate of sandwiches, but they were soon gone so I went in search of Jonathan and his girlfriend Natalie.

'Where's the boss?'

'He's schmoozing some bloke in the lobby with Caroline.'

'Oh yes? I wonder what that's about.'

Natalie said lightly: 'Now don't get all anxious.'

'I can't help it – it's a slippery business.'

'That's why you're so successful.'

'Thanks, babes.'

I hung around vacantly until I saw Caroline come back in with Martin and a good-looking Asian man. She was smiling and his hand was resting on her thinly strapped shoulder. Jonathan looked up: 'Oh, it's only Luxy. Martin thinks he's got investors in Bahrain who're gagging for property, but Luxy's all mouth.' He sniggered. 'Your friend seems well in. If I were you I'd slip across and tell her not to waste her time: the most he'll give her is a shag.'

'*Jonathan*!'

'Sorry, Nat, but she's a very ambitious girl and he's not worth it.'

Smarting on my friend's behalf, I walked over to the trio who were still deep in conversation. Luxy's fingers had moved inside the straps of Caroline's dress and she wasn't doing anything about it.

I stopped by a backgammon table and watched them. She was laughing now at something the man had said and Martin was looking at her admiringly. I tried to see her through their adult eyes: classy, exotic, confident, smart. And she was loving it.

Once, just once, as they stood there joking, those long tapering fingers slipped, almost accidentally, beneath her bodice. Martin didn't seem to notice, but my stomach was in knots. I didn't know this Caroline, but it was exciting. It was exciting *me*. I wondered what magic Luxy had in his touch. Practice makes perfect – and God knew he was old enough to be her father.

Now Martin moved across to the bar, and I saw that hand again go where it shouldn't, and casually trace the swell inside. Was she so bloody frigid she didn't realise: or did she want him to? I crept up and said loudly: 'I was just about to send out a search party.'

She wasn't at all embarrassed. 'Where've you been?'

'Talking to Jonathan.'

'What's he doing?'

Out of the corner of my eye I saw the hand return to neutral. 'Playing blackjack. And losing.'

'Won't you introduce your charming friend, Caroline?'

I ignored his interest as Martin returned. 'Mala – thanks for being so patient.'

Caroline said: 'Luxy, this is Mala.' Luxy. Like a soap or a radio station.

'Mala? Do I know you?'

'I don't think so.'

'Let me see you.'

I looked him defiantly in the eye, embarrassed by the attention, knowing where his hand had been, aware that Caroline was uncomfortable with his interest. 'Mala Fonseka?' He must know me: where from?

I trawled through the catalogue of half-forgotten faces: Uncle Oliver's brother; Aunty Anu's old flames; worshippers at the temple. Surely I'd remember sculpted features like these? Nothing. I became anxious that I might get into trouble for being there.

'Do you know who I am?' he asked.

I coloured. 'I'm sure I know you, but I just can't . . .'

'You certainly should know me.'

'It's on the tip of my tongue.' I struggled and gave up.

He was staring at me with wonder. 'Surely you know me?'

'I'm sorry, I don't. I really don't.'

And now the same fingers that had brushed Caroline's breast just moments ago broke free and gently pushed my fringe away from my face. 'Darling child – I'm your father.'

# 13 ∫

Because I do not understand, I argue with him. But he is spilling out details that no stranger would know. It becomes incredibly important that he cannot remember my birth date, but he knows where I was born. My father is dead and his sad ashes are with his family: perhaps preserved in the glass-fronted bureau of an estate bungalow or scattered on a southern Sri Lankan paddy-field. I do not know. But he has been dead for as long as I can remember. Yet this man has his name. Luxy Fernando: Lucky as was, short for Laxman – lax man – pronounced Luckshman; and he is smiling.

Caroline is suddenly very closed and Chinese and Martin – Martin is trying to civilise the disturbance by suggesting we sit somewhere quiet because I think I am saying: 'You are not my father, my father is dead!' rather too loudly in a room where silence is the key to success.

Trapped in the vice of quiet insistence, I go with them to a secluded part of the lobby, and Luxy tries to take my arm but I shake him off. Instead he puts a hand on Caroline's waist to guide her into a chair. I sense something there and I am sick: sick that he might be telling the truth; sick that, if it is true, it had to be him; and sick that his hand has been inside her dress.

I am primed for sex, pregnancy, marriage, work – even orgies on canal boats – simple little things that Molly Parkin in *Petticoat* says happen to girls my age all the time. But there is no advice on recovering fathers from the grave: grim reapings.

If this is a moment of great joy, why do I wish him dead? Again. This man in an Austin Reed suit and pigskin loafers. If

I have nothing against which to measure my feelings, are they feelings at all? I sit and I listen and sometimes I respond, but all the time I am screaming inside.

Like a teacher running through the great dates of history, he says: 'It was a lifetime ago. I intended to send for your mother but within weeks of arriving I met a woman in Paddington.' He stops and calls a waitress. 'Two dry martinis for the men, sweetheart. Caroline, what about you?' She shakes her head. 'Mala?' I look down. 'And a box of matches.' As the girl goes I am struck by his voice: not singsong like my mother and aunts but exotic – like Ilie Nastase. He takes out a small silver cigarette case and offers it round, taking one for himself and tapping the ends on the arm of his chair. 'She was a woman with a certain reputation, Mala, but we got on well. Too well: she had my baby.'

Martin says: 'You are a dark horse, Luxy. A stallion.'

Luxy laughs. He leans across the table towards me. 'It was all so new. I was lonely. The child was beautiful – Ayesha, she looked a little like you. Then your mother telegrammed that she was taking the boat.' He stops, draws on the unlit cigarette and, finding no pleasure, places it precisely on the table so it is in line with the edge. 'Two days after I got her letter the worst thing happened. The baby died. That stupid woman. She left her alone with the older girl – out doing business, no doubt.' His face hardens. 'We don't know how . . . She came back and the baby was dead in its cot. When you arrived, I couldn't cope. I gave your mother what I could, and went.'

The waitress comes back with the drinks and he gives her a fiver. 'Keep the change, sweetheart.' He raises his glass to Martin and Caroline. 'Here's to Welbeck House.' I go for my coat.

At the counter Caroline joins me. 'This is unbelievable.'

In my mind's eye I am reliving the fantasies I had about my father after his 'death'. In all of them he was not this man. He was somebody good and kind who put my needs first; whose last thought was not of his own sad demise, but my sad future, deprived of love, money, security. Alone with a mother who never stopped working or bossing.

I say to Caroline: 'Have you slept with him?' Her mouth

forms a perfect O. Too perfect. 'I saw him with his hand in your dress.'

'After the party to celebrate the Park Lane deal.'

'Why?'

'Why d'you think? Because he's gorgeous, he's rich, he's experienced, he's well connected and he's . . . he's good fun.'

'You didn't tell me.'

'It was only once. He'd got a complimentary room at the Inn on the Park. We went back and it happened. No hearts and flowers like you picture it, Mala; no pathetic regrets like Janice: it happened the way we both wanted it. That's all.'

'You slept with my *dad*.'

'He wasn't your dad then.'

I have lost the ability to exclaim. I am flat, flat, flat – like the front of Caroline's dress where my father had a feel.

'If you must know,' Caroline hisses, 'the thought of it makes me pretty nauseous right now.'

Coaxed back upstairs, I sit square and silent. 'I've remarried twice. It's never worked out. You can see I'm not your mother's type.' How can I see? My mother has given up on types. He says: 'Of course, she wanted to maintain the façade to keep the folks at home happy, but what's the point? The great thing here is that nobody cares! Divorce is taboo in Sri Lanka but here it's a badge of pride. She couldn't accept that.'

Martin says: 'Don't tell that to Carmel or she'll try and take me for everything I've got.' He stands up. 'I'm going to find Jonathan. There's a flat in Lisson Street I want him to see tomorrow.'

Caroline says: 'Weren't you curious about Mala?'

Luxy shrugs charmingly. 'We agreed it was better to sever all ties. Vino concocted some story about being widowed. It meant I could establish myself without endless family duties. It was in Mala's best interests.'

I say angrily: 'If it was in my best interests, why tell me now?' He is charming, like a brown Lionel Blair. 'Because I was so surprised – and thrilled; you've grown into the most beautiful girl.'

'I was happy when you were dead. Now nothing will ever be the same.'

He smiles fondly. 'You're just like your mother, Mala: emotional, judgmental, hasty. You should calm down.'

I stand up. 'I never want to see you again.' I look across at Caroline, who gets to her feet and says almost apologetically: 'I'd better go with her,' and the stranger nods – and gives her a wink – and for a moment she is excited. And then she picks up the jackets that I'd collected from the cloakroom, and guides me outside. 'Let's take a taxi – my treat.'

'Did you really want the truth, Mala: that he is a philanderer, a liar, a cheat? That two weeks after we arrived in this country he informed me he had fathered a prostitute's child? That even as he was telling me this, he was having an intimate friendship with the West Indian woman in Room seven? Is that what you wanted to know? *Chi*! What a dirty fellow he was.'

My mother walked across to the front window. Wet feet in galoshes trudged by the railings. 'When we took the boat to England, do you imagine I expected to live in a hole in the ground?' She turned and threw up her arms. 'Look at me – a woman of forty and I haven't even my own bedroom. Such dreams I had – and he was seed-spreading like a labourer in the field. You remember his first words at Tilbury? "Why have you come?" This he said as you clung to his coat crying "Papa! Papa!" Better he was dead.' She spat the words angrily. 'Not one letter, not even a birthday card – that is your father's contribution to your life. He *is* dead!'

'You should have told me.'

'So you would know his tainted blood ran through your body? Always you would have looked for signs of him in yourself. Instead you believed he was good – and you've grown up good.'

'We live in the same city, for God's sake.'

'He said he was going to Paris with a French girl.' She sighed. 'When a marriage is built on lies, how does one recognise the truth? Even he believed himself. Remember, it was *he* who said he wanted nothing to do with us. I honestly thought, Mala, that we would never see him again.'

She returned to the drawer full of hankies, pulled out for new handles to be fitted. So many colours tightly packed like marker flags, the pattern or embroidery on each little square representing a pivotal point in my mother's life; in our lives. So many memories tightly folded away. What was it she'd said, one afternoon so long ago: 'One day, you will take charge of them, and shake them out, and dust away the cobwebs.' I laughed bitterly. The webs I'd uncovered were spun by a black widow: my mother herself!

'You are thinking bad thoughts, Mala.' Kneeling, she pulled out a rough-cut square of silk. 'I cut this from my wedding dress. It was borrowed from my sister. No bride should wear another's cast-offs. It was an inauspicious start – our horoscopes were ill matched. Foolish, foolish pride.' She rolled it and put it back. 'I asked him to stay until we could return home without scandal – he refused. I would have taken you back to my father's house, but not as an abandoned wife. What would they have said about our family? Such a small sacrifice. Three, four months, I could have found a way, but he packed his bag and left. Don't be angry with me – be angry with him.'

'You lied.'

'To protect you.' She got to her feet tiredly. 'My only comfort has been seeing you grow; making something of your life.'

'And what's my comfort?'

'That your father returned too late to do any harm.'

Aunty Anu said: 'So he's a rich playboy now? In that case, only his bank balance has altered.'

'So everyone knew but me?' Silence.

Aunty Mina chided gently: 'Don't blame your mother. We all agreed it was better to present him as dead. In time the truth would be forgotten. It eased the load for you.'

'Poor Vino. Probably he wants the credit for her success.'

'What success?'

'In raising you, Mala.'

'Raising me? I've raised myself!'

'All these years she's pushed you – never forget that. Was your father at your school concerts? Did he hold your hand when you were sick? Where was he when you took exams or won the handwriting competition—'

'Oh, the immortal Brooke Bond handwriting competition!'

'Never once did he come looking for you.'

They continued their harangue until I rose crossly and left: victim turned perpetrator. Back on Inverness Terrace I headed for Caroline's. I met her coming into Hallfield from the Cleveland Square end. 'What are you doing here?'

'I just wanted to talk . . . about Luxy.'

'He's nothing to do with me.'

'He's my father, Caroline.'

'End of story.' She stopped by the stairs. 'I'm going out tonight. I need to be bathed and back at the office by seven thirty. I'll try and find out what I can.'

'You're going out with him?'

A hesitation. 'Not *with* him. He'll be there.'

'I'm not angry, Caroline – you didn't know. I just need to talk. My mum's half demented. I don't know who I am any more – it's like I've become a stranger to myself.'

'You're exactly the person you were before, Mala – except your dad isn't dead, he's absent.'

'Is that what he says?'

A vague toss of the head. 'You've always said it's great not having a father to hold you back. You can't have it all ways.'

'I haven't had it any way. Don't go out tonight, Caroline – I need to clear my head with you.'

'No can do, Mala: this is about the Welbeck House deal. I'm about to become junior negotiator, remember?'

'You're going to sleep with him.'

'Don't be stupid. And don't ever mention it again. Martin hasn't a clue.' She turned to go. 'Come round tomorrow and we'll go out. Who knows, I might even have picked up some useful information, like whether it's worth squeezing some money out of your old man. Martin says he's loaded; but it's mainly back-handers.'

'It's too bloody late for his money.'

'It's never too late for money.' She sighed wearily. 'Listen, Mala – in this world, you play for everything you can get. Meeting Luxy was serendipity – a happy accident. You'll see.'

\* \* \*

'It's a happy accident for her: a fucking disaster for me.'

Margaret put the kettle on. 'This is the most extraordinary thing I've ever heard. It'd push me over the edge. You're very calm.'

I sighed. 'Perhaps it would have been different if he'd wrapped his arms around me or been interested in me as a person, but he only took notice of how I looked. He couldn't even remember my birthday.'

'That's shocking.'

'I'm glad someone understands.'

She made coffees. 'What will you do?'

'Nothing, probably. ' I shrugged and leaned miserably across the table.

'Poor you. What a dreadful thing to happen.'

'Yes, it is, isn't it? It's bloody dreadful.'

I reached across to pick up my drink but was suddenly overcome by a dreadful weariness. I started crying: huge sobs; unbearable wailing; as if the weight of the world had fallen not on to my shoulders but off them, leaving me stranded in an unrecognisable limbo. Margaret sat quietly, occasionally putting a hand on my shoulder: 'That's right, let it out – that's what my psychiatrist says,' as if it was *I* who was mad and not the people around me. I cried even harder. What a pathetic way to carry on.

Later, when I'd stopped, Margaret said: 'Sometimes I feel like that – like an outside force is trying to push me off course.'

'Is that why you don't eat?'

'Yes. Though I'm trying. With you, there really is an outside force. Do you honestly not want to know him?'

I leaned back in the chair. 'What for? He doesn't want to know me – he just wants me to forgive him.' I stopped. 'I'm not even sure of that, actually.' I picked up my cup – the coffee had gone cold. 'If he'd just taken a little bit of interest, imagine – I could have gone to a good college like you. Our lives would have been so different. I could have had twenty Ben Shermans.'

'But you haven't. Don't start all that "what if" nonsense. It's so negative. He doesn't exist for you, even now.'

'You know why this makes me so bloody miserable? I realise I'm no better than Janice Connors.'

'Mala!'

'All this time I thought I was special, but I'm just the same as everyone else. Everything has lost its shine.'

'Mala, nothing's changed but history. This is just a pre-Christmas blip.'

'I keep imagining—'

'Then stop: you're starting to sound like John Lennon.'

Imagine there's no heaven, it's easy if you try.

That night I rang Tony. 'You're right. I mustn't let it get to me.'

'Good girl. Do you want to come round?'

'Your mum doesn't like me.'

'It's not you she doesn't like. It's me finding another woman.'

But the formidable Mrs Carlettidou, sitting at the kitchen table skinning peppers and draining aubergines, was too oppressive a presence in my present mood and Tony was halfway through a ceramics project. I watched telly for a bit and headed for Jan's.

'Why didn't you turn up for the carol singing?'

I clapped my hand over my mouth. 'I forgot.'

'We waited fifteen minutes for you – I felt such a fool.'

'I'm sorry. I just . . . it's been a bad week.'

'Just as well we did all right or you'd have got the blame.' She grinned. 'Two hundred quid! People were handing over pound notes like they're out of fashion. We're doing a Christmas Eve special on Monday – promise you'll come.' Glumly I agreed, following her up the stairs past clothes drying over the banisters, downwind of Merle's frying plantains, into the little room which smelled of gas from the old fire that was keeping it warm. 'I've got some Bacardi, d'you want to try it? My mum swapped it for a tenner – I told her I was sick of giving something for nothing.' She laughed. 'Guess who got done – as usual?' She found two old water glasses, mixed the drinks half and half and had a taste. 'It's a bit strong! They should put a warning on the bottle.' She handed

me the lethal cocktail. 'Here's to the death of miserable bastards.'

In the warm, cosy, fume-ridden room, now brightened by
pictures of animals and my old Led Zeppelin poster – a present
– I felt relaxed; almost dizzy. I tried to find the words to tell her
Caroline's part in the puzzle, but they wouldn't come. To let
out that secret was somehow a criticism of both Caroline and
Luxy, and that didn't feel right – as if it reflected on me too.
At the end of the day he was my father, a part of me. Was this
what my mother meant by tainted blood?

'It's good, isn't it? Have some more.'

In my wooziness I hugged Caroline's secret to me, but not
with vicarious pleasure: no, vicarious dread. Please God, there
must be something good about him; his lovely face perhaps;
his ability to charm; his obvious business skills – unless he
took back-handers. *Even* if he took back-handers: wily man.
In my mind I was recasting his characteristics the way I'd seen
Tony recasting pots: remodelling misshapen edges, covering the
cracks, changing the incline, deepening the groove, all the while
turning a disaster into, if not a success, at least something
that was acceptable to the consumer. Here is my father, the
flawed but well-shaped vessel from which I was poured: see
how brightly his glazing shines under artificial light!

'You know, Jan, this Bacardi is great,' I said, before passing
out on her bed.

'You've been with that boy, haven't you? After all those
promises to stay decent!'

'I was at Jan's.'

'If you were at Jan's, why didn't you ring me?'

'Because I fell asleep.'

'You were with that boy, Mala. Don't lie to me.'

'I'm not lying. I went to see Janice, had a drink and fell
asleep.'

'A drink? Janice is giving you alcohol?'

'No, of course she isn't. Well—'

'Because you *weren't* with Janice. How many times I asked
myself if it was the right thing, but you promised. So confidently
you promised not to let me down. Like a fool I believed.'

'I have not slept with Tony.'

'*Chi*! See how your mind is filling with filth.'

'I *have* been at Jan's. I'm sorry I didn't call.'

'It's seven thirty in the morning. You return home skulking, like a woman of the night.'

'I don't have to listen to this, Mum.'

'Already it is rubbing off, isn't it? Only days after finding him, you don't come home. You want to be your father's daughter.'

'Leave it, Mum. You've got him on the brain. You're wrong.'

'This is what the great man does for you. I will not let you see him again!'

'I don't want to see him again. Once was enough.'

'That Tony. I will not let you see *him* again.'

'You can't stop me. I'm a free agent.'

'I forbid it. Free love: you know, Mala, I expected so much more of you. You who mean everything to me.'

I got up and walked to the front door. 'I've heard enough.'

'What do you think, Mala – that you can run to him and he'll welcome you after years of neglect?'

'I'm not chasing after him, Mum – I'm escaping from you.'

'How can you do this to me?'

'I've not done anything to you,' I said, opening the door, 'you've done it to yourself.'

Tony looked pleased to see me. 'Hello – you look a real state.'

'I haven't changed since yesterday.'

'You'd better come in.' He grinned. 'It's all right – Mother Bloodhound's doing last-minute Christmas shopping, Marianna's already gone to school and Dad's at work. I was just having breakfast.' Without asking, he produced a second bowl of Frosties and a cup of tea. 'So where've you been?'

'I got drunk with Janice.'

'Your first time.' We cleared away together. 'No lessons this morning?'

'English at eleven.'

'That gives us an hour to play with.'

'What about your pots?'

'What about them?' He looked at me sheepishly and smiled. 'I could go and slip into something a little more comfortable . . .'

'I'm all smelly and horrible.'

'Have a shower.'

'Would that be all right?'

'Anything's all right.' He put a cautious hand on my shoulder. 'I could soap your back for you. Isn't that what they do in films?'

Inside, my sad heart lurched like the dog that spots the rabbit, but terrible thoughts of my Quasimodo legs and rounded stomach beat my longing into submission. He gave me a towel. 'I'm right here. Call if you want me.'

I didn't call, which was a complete disaster, because it wasn't until I emerged, a vision in flannelette, that we fell into each other's arms, clutching at uncovered mysteries with a reduced working time of forty-five minutes in which to attempt the fumbling, bumbling overtures of making love. Laughing, we rushed at it like Paddington commuters about to miss the Reading train: hang on, driver, I can't get the bloody door open! But eventually we pulled it off and gave a cheer. Oh God, what have I done?

Afterwards, in the few minutes before real life called for the dragging on of clothes and a quick canter down Elgin Avenue to school, Tony said: 'What's the matter? Was I that bad?'

'I'm just thinking this would never have happened if Mum hadn't thought it had.'

'Is that supposed to make sense?'

'Nothing makes sense.' I rolled on to my side, instinctively covering myself with the sheet. 'I'll have to go on the Pill now. I don't want to end up like Flick: eighteen, in the club and alone.'

'I'd never leave you.' He moved the sheet back and slowly ran a finger across my chest. 'God forbid we should have a baby, but it wouldn't change anything.'

I pushed his hand away. 'Don't make promises you can't keep.' He looked confused. I took it back and kissed it. 'The world is full of people breaking promises. You shouldn't make them so easily.'

'Not all men are like your dad, Mala.'

'Is that supposed to make me feel good, or bad?'

Christmas passed in a blur. Tony's mother grudgingly invited me; then was grudging that I couldn't go. Then, somehow, I got him invited to ours for New Year's Day and he was a hit despite my mother's thin-lipped disapproval: could she tell by looking at us? I was at pains to seem aloof, but as he came in I whispered: 'I took my first pill yesterday,' and he squeezed my hand. Ronnie said: 'It's so nice to have another male about,' and they chatted together until all twelve of us, including Jan and Caroline, had found spaces around the room. 'Happy new year!'

As Tony ate his third plate of milk rice and onions and my aunties passed Rohan around for general admiration, Caroline cornered me by the window. 'It's funny to think Luxy was married to a woman like your mother, isn't it?'

'What do you mean by that?'

'Well, you know, he's so . . . sophisticated; a man of the world.'

I looked across the room at my mum grating extra jaggery into a glass bowl. 'He wasn't when he came here. He became one. A bit like *you're* becoming a woman of the world.'

'Jealous, Mala?'

I lowered my voice. 'Just stating facts.'

Caroline said coldly: 'Don't be so babyish.'

I looked away, full of unexpressed rage, suspicion and frustration. 'Cheer up, Mala, it may never happen,' Ronnie shouted across the room, and I saw Jan watching us curiously.

Caroline started rummaging for her coat. 'He's got us two really big money men. Martin's thrilled – with me as much as him. Big bucks, Mala – commission for the firm and me. I'm not talking a pathetic couple of hundred – I mean thousands! Anyway, he sent his regards.'

'Luxy? Sent his regards?' She nodded.

I said nothing: there was nothing to say.

She dug in her bag. 'Here, this is my new business card – what d'you think?'

Caroline Chong, negotiator, Park & Wright, sales and management.

'Nice.'

'Keep it.'

She walked across to my mother and thanked her graciously. I saw her to the door. 'Are you seeing him? Like that, I mean.'

'Don't be ridiculous.' We eyeballed each other. She leaned forward angrily. 'I have not slept with him since that first night. He's asked me to, I've thought about it: sometimes I even want to. But I haven't, okay? Not because he's your dad but because he'd eat me for breakfast and move on to the next girl without even noticing. Does that make you feel better?'

'Yes. It does. It really does.' Suddenly there was light where I'd painted darkness. I said: 'Thank you for being my friend.'

She looked at me crossly. 'It's nothing to do with being your friend – it's common sense.'

'Whatever.' As she started up the steps I asked: 'What's the resolution for 1976?'

'To get rich. To make money and yet more money and move into one of the Welbeck House studios.'

'I bet you'll do it too.'

'Just watch this space,' she said, and was gone so quickly that I was watching a space almost immediately.

# 14 ∫

I'd thought it was all great fun when Jan dragged me carol singing for the homeless, but when she joined women's self-defence classes and threw out the Led Zeppelin poster in favour of Che Guevara I started to get worried. 'Why are you doing this?'

'Al says women should realise their own strength.'

'You're always doing what he says. You've been there four months and he's already got you doing unpaid overtime as his bloody note-taker. Now you're wrestling with a bunch of lesbos on Liverpool Road. It's ridiculous, Janice.'

'I've covered four evening meetings since February, Mala – that's not taking advantage. And I joined the class because it was advertised on our bulletin board. After Ritu did it, she fought off two muggers on York Way.'

'I thought you said she screamed until some man came out of a pub and laid into them?'

'She wouldn't even have done that before the course.'

I stared gloomily into my chocolate shake feeling like King Canute. I'd tried moaning to Caroline but all she said was: 'I thought you agreed with all this trendy leftie crap.'

'It's the way he's got her jumping through hoops. She's like a bloody police dog.'

'She's always been a pushover for bullies.'

I slurped the bottom of the glass: was Al a bully, or someone who genuinely wanted to put the world to rights? He could, after all, be raking it in as a proper lawyer, but had chosen to earn peanuts helping those in need. And Jan, for all my misgivings, now effervesced like a shaken Fanta: so grateful to be freed from the tyranny of typing in triplicate that she willingly did anything and everything he wanted. As a result, she'd become the world expert on all subject matter that appeared in Al's in-tray. Right now, sitting in the Regent, it was nuclear power.

'How does it work, then, Jan?'

'What?'

'Nuclear power. I know it's bad, but you tell me why.'

'I can't explain it.'

'Then how can you oppose it?'

'I read a Friends of the Earth pamphlet about it.'

'But that only gives you one side.'

I held her exasperated gaze until she started laughing. 'Am I going over the top again? I can't help it: everything's new. It takes me ages to switch off in the evenings. I'm just buzzing.'

'I've hit my second commission target already,' Caroline said. 'Martin's sending me on a driving course as a thank-you. I'll get an office car as soon as I pass.' I made a face. 'It's all right, Mala, a car's tax-deductible. It hardly costs the company anything. Rich men's perks.'

'You're so lucky.'

'It'll be you soon – or are you still set on university?'

I shrugged. 'I don't know. I can't get my head round work at the moment. It's like everyone's moving on but I'm still at square one. Jan's doing all these new things; now you're getting a car. When do I get to call the shots?'

'You're just feeling sorry for yourself.'

'No, it's not that. I'm sick of people controlling my life – telling me what to do. Sometimes I just want to walk out of the school gates and never go back.'

'It's *you* who wanted to do it this way.' She examined a chipped nail. 'What's brought this on?'

'I don't know. It's just me.'

Since the beginning of this final term, each of my teachers had taken me aside for private words. 'Your work's so sloppy. You can't afford mistakes this late in the game. You must pull yourself together, Mala.' But I couldn't. The whoopee cushion of school life had been punctured. And central to this muddle was my father's image which, like a character from *Scooby Doo*, kept popping out at me from cupboards and desks when I least expected it. It was like living a lie; or a half-lie, anyway.

'Do you still want to be a journalist or has that changed too?'

'Of course not.'

'There've been running ads for trainee reporters on the Capital jobline. There's obviously work to be had. You'll have your As in a couple of months – then you can go for it.'

Dear Beth,

   I'm sorry I haven't written for eons but it's not as if you reply . . . I've lost my virginity to Tony!! I think my sanity's next . . . I'll end up like Josh Chong mumbling in doorways. Not that he does any more. Jan's having a great time working at a law centre in King's Cross. Her boss is a tyrant. Caroline got her promotion (of course!) and she's learning to drive. She's raking in the commissions and it all gets divvied up at some point . . . You'll never guess what? My dad turned up out of the blue. He's alive!! Don't ask me about it – it's too complicated. I'm trying to pretend it hasn't happened – which isn't hard as he doesn't want contact – ha ha. What was your baby sister's name again? Not that it matters. What else? Exams are looming: boo hoo. I've applied for a reporting job advertised on Capital – just to get a taste of what people expect: forewarned is forearmed as my mum's always saying. (Shame I wasn't forewarned about the family skeleton!) Please write – I need cheering up.

   Mala xxx

'NO. You cannot do this, Mala. All these years I stayed for you to have a British education. In eight weeks you'll sit your exams: then you can do what you like. Don't throw it away like this – it's madness. What about your future? Only this morning you got your acceptance from University College. Please, Mala.' My mother started to cry. 'Please don't do this. A woman these days needs a career. Don't do this to me: don't do it to yourself.'

'This is a proper career, Mother.'

'A job you get from the radio?'

'It's a news agency. They provide stories for the London evening papers, the local papers and all the dailies. It's what I've always wanted, for goodness' sake!'

'You'll be making the tea.'

'I'll be reading stories over the phone to Fleet Street copy-takers. After three months I get put on reporting duties myself.'

'Where is the training, Mala? These fly-by-nights prey on foolish girls like you. Do you think success comes from a packet? You can snigger now, but when you look back and realise how you ruined your own chances it won't be a laughing matter.'

I sighed loudly. 'Why do you always look on the bad side?'

In my mind I reeled through the previous day's events for short-term relief. It had been so exciting in that small, smoky room full of steaming corduroy jackets, ringing phones and a running comedy track of topical banter. Around the edges of the office was a continuous worktop where reporters – old, young, male, female – hunched over ancient typewriters bashing away and shouting into mouthpieces: 'That's m for mother, o, l, y, n for nuts, e, u, x.' Shelves of phone books, back copies of *Who's Who* and a dozen different *Kelly's Street Directories* sagged on the discoloured cream walls. Every time there was a call, little light panels flashed on the desk: 'Hello, Ready News.' On the wall near the 'news desk' was a giant map of Britain. Someone had written in heavy letters on the wallpaper underneath: 'If you can't find it, check the Gazeteer – *No Guessing*.' As I read it, the boss, Keith, said: 'There are at least five Highams, two Hatches and who knows how many Woottons – I can't have a marauding squaddie from Berkshire suddenly being relocated to the Western Isles. You get the point?'

Lists of phone numbers for the Fire Brigade, ambulance and police around the country were haphazardly tacked to the soft plaster. At right angles to the news desk was another executive work area behind which were pasted photos of page-three girls with rude captions across their mammaries. 'This is the picture desk – say hello to Monty. Take no notice of his collection, he's a dirty old man – dream on, boy.' The anteroom in which I'd been interviewed was for overspill on busy days: 'It can get a bit like Euston Station in here.' Heaven! And then there was the photo library – a series of floor-to-ceiling shelves stacked with negatives going back sixty or seventy years. I didn't understand its purpose any more than I understood the workings of the development lab in the basement or the feature writers' office at the top. As for what good it would do me: who knew? There'd been too much to take in and Keith had paid as much attention to my green knee-length boots as he had to my questions, qualifications and ambitions. 'When would you like to start?'

'Next Monday?'

'We'll kick you off at seventeen pounds a week.'

'Is that all?'

'Is that all?' He laughed. 'You've got the right attitude. It goes up after six months. Welcome on board.' Welcome on board! Suddenly the whole enterprise had seemed crazily unreal. It still did. I earned as much working evenings and Saturdays in Boots.

My mother said: 'Was this Tony's idea?'

'He doesn't know yet. I told you first.'

'Because he won't get to university—'

'He's already got a place at St Martin's, Mum.'

'It's those girls: Janice and Caroline. Because they've done it you follow suit – but they're not as clever as you. You'll have a good position one day. I've given up everything for that – not just the clothes off my back – the flesh!'

I shook my head and got up.

'Eight weeks, Mala: eight weeks to your exams.'

I went to the door. 'I could be dead in eight weeks, Mother.'

'It's nothing. Nothing compared to your future.' She wiped her eyes again with the *pallau* of her sari. 'Think about it, Mala. Just because someone offers you something, you don't have to say yes. If jobs are so easy without qualifications, imagine what offers will come with a degree.'

'Why should I imagine,' I said, 'when I can hold it in my hand?'

'Seventeen quid? That's criminal,' Jan said. 'All I do is type and I get thirty. And you'll be exhausted working shifts.'

'It's a rota. News doesn't stop when people sleep.'

'I've never heard of Ready News. I thought a news agency was where they sold newspapers – like Clive's. I think you're crazy. You should go to university.'

'I don't need to.'

'Al says university gave him something to react against.'

'Too much, by the look of it.'

'I'm just trying to be helpful.' She giggled. 'I suppose you're joining the superstructure now – that's what newspapers are. Don't ask me what it means, though.' I groaned. 'It's Marx. Al says I should be politicised. Sounds like a brain operation: my mum should've had one. You know she's going to be done? Like a dog. Her tubes are mangled. Too many kids. Too much booze. She asked me to take Tammy! Where would I put her?' I looked at her blankly, rolled my eyes rudely and sighed.

She said: 'The good thing is you'll only be up the road from me in Farringdon. We can meet up in our lunch breaks, go for walks around Percy Circus. It's so pretty – you can't believe all the pros are only round the corner: of course, I know most of them now from Al and Evie being duty solicitors at the magistrates' court. They come down from the north, y'know, for weekends: take it in turns to look after all the children while the others go on the game. I couldn't do it.'

I feigned death and she stopped. 'What's the matter with you? Honestly, they don't half give us the runaround: they keep changing their names. But it's not fair, is it – that the women get booked and the men who rent them don't?'

Finally, I was overcome with fury. 'Look, Janice,' I exploded, 'I know you've been working for nearly two years and I know you're a global oracle, but for God's sake put a sock in it.'

'There's no need to shout. What's got into you, Mala?'

'I don't know: you haven't stopped long enough for me to consider it.' I shut my eyes and took some deep breaths. 'I just feel so . . . tense. I think what I'm doing is right, but everyone's telling me it isn't and I'm frightened I'll hash up my life.'

'No one's going to hash up your life,' she said confidently. 'You'll do well whatever you do: you and Caroline. It's just your timing. If you're sure it's the right thing, do it.'

'I'm sure,' I said; but I felt I was much further out than I thought, like the man in the Stevie Smith poem: not waving but drowning. Nonetheless I had to go with the flow – there was no other way to take charge of myself. 'Now what about you?' I said to Jan. 'Who'll take Tammy when your mum goes inside?'

She made a face. 'Well, I'll fight it, but if there's no one else . . . Jack's so bloody useless, the only answer is to move back into Westbourne Terrace for a while. They haven't given her a date but it's a big op, Mala – she'll be in St Mary's two weeks and she can't carry weights, not even a full kettle, for another six weeks. I can't be toing and froing all that time.'

'But Jan, that's instant death.'

'Tell me about it,' she said grimly.

'You're crazy to throw it all away, Mala. And wrong.'

'It's the chance of a lifetime.'

'Your lifetime hasn't even begun.'

'You sound like an old man, Tony.'

'You're the one who's old – taking on work and responsibility when you could be having fun; making something of yourself.'

'I will make something of myself.'

'Your boss sounds like a slimeball – looking at your boots all the time. You're not getting the job because you're the best – he fancies you, that's all.'

'I don't care why I've got the job – all that matters is I do well at it. Anyway, I just told you that for a bit of fun.'

'By the time you regret it, you'll have lost your chance to sit your exams – and your university place. Don't come bleating to me that your life's all grey when mine's just taking off!'

'Mine's already taking off and *you're* the one doing the bleating.' He didn't respond. I felt all whiny. 'What does any of this matter as long as we're together?'

'What about the holidays? All those things we were going to do together once exams were over – galleries, lunches, day trips – where will I fit in around your job, Mala?'

'I'll get days off.'

'But not a full six weeks. You're signing your life away for what? Not even money. They're cashing in on you. Don't do it.'

'I've got to do it, Tony. You don't understand—'

'Don't kid yourself, Mala – it's not me who doesn't understand, it's you. Everything we've done together, all the plans we made: you're ditching it on a promise of nothing. Maybe you should have put on your boots and gone tramping round to *The Times* – at least that would have been a job worth boasting about.'

'You sound like my mum.'

'And you're going to end up like her: working your fingers to the bone for sweet Fanny Adams.'

On the eve of my first day at work it seemed to me I didn't have a single friend in the world. There was no gold watch to signify the end of my school years; no timetable of curricular activities to prepare me for the routine of the new. I was barely speaking to my mother or Tony; Janice had spent the weekend at Allie's; and Caroline, who'd whooped with delight at news of my departure, was nowhere to be found when I went and knocked on her door. The sight of Ellie, now chronically overweight, did little to lift my gloom. 'Hello, Mala,' she said sadly; largely. 'Caroline says you're leaving school.'

'Yes, I'm going to be a journalist.'

'I hope it goes well.'

'Thank you.' Desperate for someone with whom to share my burden, I hovered: even Ellie would do. But she was too distracted to pick up the cues. 'Josh is helping his father fit the new till. There's no one here. I was just sleeping.'

'Are you all right, Ellie?'

'Oh, I'm fine – I have these tablets that make me a bit zomboid. And fat! They slow your metabolism. I wanted to keep working but doctor's orders, you know.' She smiled. 'This isn't what you want to hear, is it – on the threshold of your new life?'

'Is that what it is: a new life?'

'Isn't that why you're doing it?'

'Well, yes, but it hasn't gone down well – because of my exams. You know mothers.'

Ellie shrugged. 'Seize the moment, Mala. This is the seventies: you can do whatever you want. You can be whoever you want.'

'That's right, isn't it?'

'That's right,' she said, and absent-mindedly closed the door.

So here I was in a corner of the newsroom being taught by another junior, Giselle: how to use the phone system; how to sell a story to a news desk; the shorthand vocabulary of dictation. I explored the building, locating the graffiti-covered loo next to the coffee machine on the half-landing. Using it later that morning, I bent to read a message near the floor: 'You are now shitting at an angle of eighty degrees.'

Giselle said: 'That's creative genius for you. We've only just had it rebuilt. One of the snappers used to sling his empties into a hole in the wall. The whole thing collapsed one day when the boss was on the bog.'

'What happened to him?'

'Old Charlie? He got a job at the COI – Central Office of Information – they're always desperate for staff.'

'And the boss?'

'You've just been speaking to him, haven't you?'

Mid-morning I learned it was my job to get liver sausage sandwiches and endless cappuccinos from Brirati's, the Italian café on the corner. Mid-afternoon I was left to get on with calls, ringing the London and Home Counties fire, ambulance and police controls to find out if there had been any 'shouts'. I ticked them off my list: East Sussex, West Sussex, Surrey, Surrey North, Essex, Thames Valley, Kent, Berkshire, London North, South and East. Finally a tanker spillage: Giselle took over and was soon cobbling together a line at her typewriter: 'Action stations, Mala. You hit the *Standard*, I'll do the *News*: we should make the briefs.'

I picked up the phone fearfully. '*Standard* news desk? Oh, hello, my name's Mala Fonseka from Ready News – would you like a couple of paras on the oil spillage at the Dartford Tunnel? You would?' I was put through to an officious Scot and read slowly, word for word, while he typed. At the end he said: 'Don't say "full stop" darling, say "point". And it's not "para", it's "par". Otherwise you're doing fine – you've a lovely voice.'

Everyone cheered when I'd finished. I sipped tea from a polystyrene cup, filled with joy. One day it would be me intently typing, correcting and fighting my corner. It would be me despatching the latest junior for coffees while combing the papers for ideas, leads and updates. It would be me ringing in with urgent information from phone boxes in the London area.

The photographers were coming back now to check if films returned earlier by messenger had been developed and despatched. One snapper came in with some negatives that Monty studied at the far window with a magnifying glass. 'Oi, Keith, brilliant shots of Blonde on Blonde.'

'They're overexposed, mate.'

'They fucking are in this picture, I can tell you! Where's Scoby?'

'He's on the slab – take it down, see what he says.'

There was constant movement, argument, chat. 'Hello, who are you? New girl? You'll brighten the place up. Hey, Harry – what happened to the Headingley idea? Bloody *Mirror* – they never take pictures unless they're exclusive. Did anything come up on that Baader Meinhof lead? Giselle, darling, come over here – I need you to do me a little favour . . . Mala, is it? Welcome on board – have you done police calls lately? Good girl – we pay a bloke to tune into their frequency, but he can't be at it all day. It's boring but we do hit gold sometimes. What we need is six dead in a motorway smash and Windsor Castle burning down – then we'll be laughing. Eric! Any news yet on funds for a fisheye? Got to speculate to accumulate.' Caroline's favourite line. Somehow it all felt strangely familiar, and I was buzzing as I headed for Farringdon Station.

On the way home I bought the *Standard* and there it was amongst the briefs on the back page: 'Tunnel Tailback'. Giselle's words but my story! I felt so excited: but who could I share it with? My mother wouldn't see the point and Tony didn't want to. Margaret was swotting round the clock, Jan was out leafleting with Al, and Caroline . . . where *was* Caroline? Instead of getting off at Paddington, I hung on until Bayswater and headed for her place again. Josh opened the door. I said, surprised: 'Are you still here?'

He looked around him. 'I think so. Can you see me? If you can see me, then I am definitely here.'

'I meant . . . Ellie was here yesterday.'

'She too is definitely, defiantly, here. Is it against union rules: no flying relatives allowed through the gates of council estates?'

I felt exasperated. 'I'm looking for Caroline.'

'She's working late – eight or nine, she said.' I turned to go: I could be there in ten minutes. 'Is anything wrong, Mala?'

'No, I just wanted to tell her about my job.'

'I heard you'd left school. I hope it's the right thing.'

I shrugged. 'Too late to hope now.'

'Are you going to her office? I'll walk with you.'

I'd meant to take the bus, but it was nice to have company and he listened with interest to my news. 'Two paragraphs? That's a good start.' Sensing my umbrage, he laughed. 'I'm serious: success takes time – but it'll come.'

'I thought this was it.'

He took my hand and kissed it. 'It's a taste of the future.'

'Like you with programming.'

'That really *is* the future.' He dropped his hold; my hand felt empty. 'But not how I imagined *my* future.' We walked in silence, cutting down Sussex Gardens and turning south towards Marble Arch. It was a nice evening; mellow. At Park and Wright we found Caroline and Jonathan, literally up to their elbows in paperwork, putting together brochures for an overseas mail shot: Hong Kong – a fertile pocket of wealth, waiting to be tickled by the investment prospects of Mayfair summerhouses.

Caroline said: 'Make yourselves useful – you can help by sealing envelopes, Mala. Josh, if you get the roll of address labels from Martin's desk and stick them on, we'll be done in half an hour.' And somehow, even though I had so much to say and he, perhaps, had intended to continue walking, we found ourselves doing as we were told while Jonathan, over a pile of buff, shook his head in disbelief and appreciation.

Afterwards they took us to Trader Vic's at the Park Lane Hilton for cocktails. Mine was blue and tasted of Benylin, but I knew what it cost and savoured each sip. Even Josh, enjoying his sister's confidence, was relaxed. Caroline said: 'Here's to you, Mala – seventeen quid a week for two paragraphs in the *Standard*,' and she laughed, but nicely. 'I'm proud of you. I was beginning to think you were getting dull and boring: now you're in the real world.'

'So that's what this is,' Josh said, extracting the sting, 'the real world.' And he winked conspiratorially at me.

After a second round Jonathan got up: 'I've got a date,' and it was Josh who bought the last drinks as the two colleagues had a final conflab at the door: 'One for the road.' He sat next to me, his arm lying casually along the back of the seat. 'So how's Tony? Shouldn't you be together on this momentous day?' I didn't answer. 'No gypsy violins for love's young dream?'

'He wanted me to stay on.'

'Because?'

'Because I'm buying into the system instead of striking out and trying to create new ways of looking at things.'

'And A-levels pave the path to true consciousness?'

'Not A-levels; university.' I looked at him anxiously. 'Do you think that's true?'

Josh shrugged. 'I'm not the man to ask: my academic history is, to say the least, fractured. But certainly it taught me new ways of approaching things.' He smiled. 'But a lot of people there were just textbook dummies – they'll never use or understand half of what they learned: so who's got it right? You, Mala, will discover what you need for yourself and you'll apply it in your own original style. The strictures of academe may well have extinguished your light.' He stopped and brushed my cheek with his finger. 'What I'm saying is I think you've made the right decision. This is the way forward.'

Without thinking, I took his hand and kissed it as he had earlier kissed mine, and I held it in my lap. He was surprised; pleased. 'What was that for?'

'To say thank you. Because you've just made it right.'

'You mean I've articulated what you couldn't.'

'Probably.' I raised his hand to my mouth and kissed it again.

'It looks like I've returned just in time,' Caroline said, aghast. 'What's going on?'

'Your best friend is expressing gratitude for my erudite absolution in the confessional of life.'

'Meaning what?'

'Meaning we've finished our drinks and if you want us to keep you company while you have yours, you'd better be civil.'

'You're not getting your own back, are you, Mala?' she said huffily. 'That's extremely childish.' And when I looked blank she added: 'Let's keep our families separate, that way everyone's happy. You stick to your own; I'll stick to mine.'

'Have I missed something?' Josh said, keeping his hand firmly on my leg as I hastily, angrily, let go. 'You're surely not jealous of your best friend showing your married brother a little affection, Caroline? Innocent eroticism: there's nothing finer – or is it inappropriate here? You should have said.'

It was nearly ten o'clock. I made my excuses and left. Josh followed me outside. 'Is everything all right? What was that about?'

'Nothing important.'

'Girlie business?' I nodded. He put a hand under my elbow. 'Come on, let's get you to the bus stop while Miss Chong powders her nose and straightens her skirt. I suspect you've got slight double vision.'

He literally ran me across four lanes to the central island; then again across another four lanes of cars hurtling round the bend in the throes of accelerative northbound ecstasy. At the empty request shelter he waited the two minutes it took for the bus to arrive. 'No more of this when Caroline passes her test.'

I jumped on to the platform and he pulled my head down and kissed me softly on the mouth. 'Thanks for tonight, Mala. I needed lifting, and you did it.'

Almost faint with excitement, I entered the bus and the conductor winked. 'First love – eh? Now don't go pretending you're half-fare.' I grinned and sat near the front as he widened his remarks to include two old ladies returning from bingo. 'I'm glad she's still using London Transport,' he said. 'My daughter claims she's walking on air – that explains why she wasn't home till three this morning.' He started whistling jauntily: Brotherhood of Man: 'Save Your Kisses For Me'.

\*     \*     \*

'Mala! Where have you been? I've been ringing your office, your friends. Nobody knew!'

'I've been with Caroline. You rang my office?'

'You said you finished at six. I expected you home by seven.'

'How could you? God, I'm going to die of embarrassment.'

'Why didn't you come home?'

'Because I went out.'

'On your first day?'

'Well, it's not as if you're interested, is it?'

'I made your favourite curry—'

'You've hardly spoken to me since I told you.'

'But it was a special day.'

'A special day! All you've done is put me down and now you've shown me up in front of all my new friends by ringing up like I was some silly little girl—'

'You're only young—'

'I'm eighteen—'

'Next month—'

'I have a job. I earn money. And I decide what I do, including whether or not I go out after work.'

'You are still my daughter – you live under my roof.'

'Would you rather I didn't? Because I won't if you start calling my boss and treating me like an idiot. What did they say?'

'Who?'

'My office.' My office!

'They said you'd left at six.'

'And that's all?'

'That was all I asked.'

Her shoulders sagged. I saw the dishes still being kept warm in the hostess trolley and felt terribly sad for her; for us; for dreams consumed like long-forgotten meals; *her* dreams which somehow had become muddled with, and muddied by, mine. I sat down and took a deep breath. 'If there's still some left, Mum, I wouldn't mind a plate.' And I forced it down, mouthful by mouthful, as she hovered uncertainly on the threshold of my maturity, the rice server like a steel shield in her hand.

# 15 ∫

In the pub Harry said: 'I thought you didn't drink.'

'Well, I didn't till I came here.'

'Isn't it always the way?' He put a little glass of Drambuie in front of me. 'Here you are, miss, as ordered: Dutch courage for the morning, is it? You'll need a clear head on your own between six and eight – make sure you check all the dailies, mark our copy up for invoicing, and do a full round of calls straight away so you catch the shift change. If anything big's happening, the staff numbers are in the top desk and Keith always checks in before leaving home.' He winked. 'Don't oversleep.'

Afterwards I walked down Farringdon Street to the station. It was only six weeks but I felt like I'd been in the job for ever. When Giselle moved to the crown court at Knightsbridge I intended to ask if I could take over her magistrates' court in Battersea. I'd already started typing up bits and pieces I picked up on calls. 'Trying to run before you can walk, Mala?'

I liked all the juniors: Giselle, Keiran, Carla, Baz. It was their job to cover all the main courts, feeding the best stories to the nationals and the run-of-the-mill regular stuff to the locals. The older reporters, the ones that kept the pub in money and had cars, were both working for the agency and moonlighting with shifts on the nationals. They covered the 'real' news, the day-to-day events and excitements; the press conferences, the diary stories, the emergencies. One day! As I met Tony outside the Coronet on Praed Street I was already halfway up the ladder of my own ambition. He looked at me appreciatively but kissed me without passion. 'That's a nice dress. New?'

'Birthday money.'
'Lovely. Shall we go for a walk?'
'Didn't you want to see a film?'
'I've got revision overload – can't concentrate: Chaucer.'
'I'll help you with Chaucer.'
'I don't need help from you.' He frowned. 'Had a good day?'
'I picked up a fire rescue – two injured, turntable ladder, hero neighbour and ruined home. I couldn't believe my luck!'
'Your luck?'
'Keith says if I carry on like this I'll be running the place.'
'Two injured? That's terrible.'
'And one a child! Oh, don't look like that – they'll both survive, and it makes great copy.'
He shook his head. 'What's happening to you, Mala? You've changed – you're so hard.'
'I'm not hard – I'm doing a job. Why do you always read the worst into what I say?'
'I loved you as you were.'
'And you don't love me now?'
He shook his head. 'No, that's not what I'm saying. I do love you – I really do.' He pulled me to him and held me tight. 'But I don't know you any more, and I feel like I'm trailing behind.'
'That's how I used to feel. But it doesn't matter. In a few months' time you'll be at art school and we'll both have new beginnings. We can't be schoolkids for ever.'
'Schoolkids? Is that how you see me?'
'You know it's not.' But somewhere inside me a rebellious little voice mouthed angry words at his childish intransigence. I looked up into his eyes – warm and honeyed like black molasses – and wanted to dissolve into them. I wanted to feel his skin on mine, but we had nowhere to go. I didn't know how to make things better and I was frightened he was right: that I had started thinking differently. That the little crack made by my departure was becoming a fissure. I didn't know how to make things better so I stated the obvious: 'I love you, Tony.'
'And I love you, Mala, always.'
'Then we'll be all right.'

\*     \*     \*

Janice and Al were already inside when Caroline and I arrived at the Toynbee Hall. 'I hope my bloody car's all right here,' she muttered. 'The East End's full of villains.'

In the shadow of the tower blocks she parked the Triumph Toledo under a lamppost. 'If they can see inside, they'll see there's nothing worth taking.' We checked the doors and headed for the entrance of the squat concrete building opposite. 'I hate that bloody car,' she said, 'it's so boxy. Martin's being a real meanie – he says I can't have something sporty because of the insurance. I'd set my heart on a soft-top Vitesse.' She crinkled her nose as we came downwind of the smell on the stairs. 'Why are we here? What's so important about this meeting?'

'We're supporting Jan. She says it's time we put something back into the community.'

'Like what, exactly?'

At the top of the stairs two crop-haired girls in bomber jackets gave us pamphlets: 'Help us in the war against racialism'. Caroline looked at me and raised an eyebrow. I kept a straight face. This was going to be fun.

Inside the hall a little area had been sectioned off and a table set up for four people: a turbanless Sikh, casually handsome in jeans and jumper; a straight-backed white woman in combat fatigues; and a note-taker who was anonymous, metal-rimmed glasses glinting under a mass of dark hair. At the end of the row a small Bengali man in cheap cotton flares and a nylon shirt sat awkwardly, playing with the discoloured skullcap in his hands. About thirty chairs had been put out for the audience, but only ten were occupied. Janice and Al were at the front, smoking, alongside Ritu and the new rights adviser, Syd. We sat behind them. Jan turned round: we'd come – a direct hit. Not that I'd given Caroline the full thrust of her argument . . .

'We're talking about people like you – black people in need of help,' Jan had said when issuing her instructions for attendance. 'You can't ignore what's happening in the East End just because you're all right.'

I wondered what the little Bengali man thought about being called black. Somehow I thought he'd be much like my mum and think it an outrage: an insult added to injury. 'We are not black, Mala, we are Asian. We have our own cultures going back thousands of years: how dare they group us with people whose origins are quite alien to ours? Do they not know that black people victimise Asians too?'

'And vice versa: if we got the chance?'

Jan said: 'Black just means "not white" Mala. It's about power: if you're white, you have a voice; if you're black, you don't.'

'Is that what Al says?'

'Yes: and he's right.'

'All right, I'll come. If nothing else, Royston Bailey did introduce me to the Soledad Brothers.'

'Are they Tamla Motown?'

'No, Janice, not unless they've changed career.'

When I'd mentioned the meeting to Keith he'd yelled: 'Hold the front page!' and started laughing, but as I left that evening he called me back: 'Hey, Mala – your friend's right. It's getting quite ugly out east. If you spot a good line, make a note of it and get some bloody contact numbers – those sparts are like badgers – down a hole before you can catch 'em by the leg.'

There was a rustling of papers. Caroline muttered: 'What the hell are we doing here?' I put a finger to my lips: we were showing solidarity when the chips were down. When the curry and chips were down: I'd seen them on offer in a takeaway on the Whitechapel Road. What kind of moron eats curry and chips? Maybe a racialist moron.

The Sikh man introduced himself as Raj; the woman was Frannie. They launched an attack on the National Front, the British Movement and the police: 'We've recorded several incidents where police called to protect premises have deliberately charged the complainants with attacking the attackers.'

'Like hell,' Caroline whispered, but there seemed to be an awful lot of examples on offer. Behind me two men shouted 'Pigs!' every time the police were maligned. Jan was on the edge of her seat, but I felt self-consciously foreign. Al looked down at her affectionately; his disciple. I wondered if he fancied her.

The woman was setting up an organisation to help Bengalis on the estates: 'In the worst cases, families are literally barricaded into their homes. This man here – Mr Uddin—' She indicated the Bengali, who nodded, '—lives above his shop in Canning Town. Every window in his home is barricaded against fire-bombs. We have witness statements that bottles and bricks are regularly thrown but the cops won't act. They've had two petrol bombs through the letterbox. This man is up all night fearing for his children's safety. If nothing else, we can take over his vigil.'

I looked at the man whose life was a living hell and felt deeply moved. But it was not, as Jan had intimated, like looking at a brother; at a fellow passenger on the journey through life. We had nothing in common: he was as foreign to me as I myself was feeling in that room. I tried to feel his fear, but all I could feel was sorrow: sorrow that his brownness had brought destruction on his head. And anger that nothing was being done. Like my mum, whose experiences made me weep, but were the experiences of an outsider: and I was not an outsider. I was British. I had drunk from the same fount; had learned the same lessons that spawned this ugliness. 'I'm more one of them than I am one of her, Caroline. How can she forgive me?'

'What's to forgive? She's the one who chose this way of life for you: every silver lining has a cloud.'

Afterwards we all went for a curry in Aldgate, in a restaurant on the raised ground floor of a Victorian house, the windows wide open to let out the summer heat. 'The prices are dirt cheap.'

'Because the Health and Safety clearly haven't been round yet.'

Al scowled at Caroline and turned to me. 'So what did you think of the meeting, Mala?' I told him. He said: 'If you lived here, nobody would say "Here comes Mala, she's all right" – they'd say "Here comes an Asian, let's get her". They don't differentiate between those who speak Bengali and those who speak the Queen's English; between those who wear *salwar kameez* and those who're poured into button-front loons.' I winced. 'All that counts for nothing against your colour.'

There was fire in his eyes, but I would not rise to the bait. Was he suggesting my loons were too tight? The men in the office thought they were great. Bloody cheek! His Yorkshire tones became more insistent: 'You must look at the wider issues and lobby for change.'

'I've told her,' Jan said.

I looked across at Caroline; she'd switched off. Her food remained untouched. Honestly, one freebie in Veeraswamy and she was the crown princess of curry. 'They have a turbanned doorman,' she'd boasted. Even Mum had been impressed. Not that she was talking much to me. With the university term about to start, she was back in mourning for what might have been. Next thing, she'd be wearing white saris and making vows for my redemption. How much longer could I stand it?

As Al and Syd argued, I imagined going home to a place of my own: a seed planted by Caroline's imminent move to Welbeck House. 'It'll cost next to nothing because I've agreed to take on caretaking duties – replacing dead light bulbs, that sort of thing.'

'People like you ought to be reporting what's going on.'

Who: me? I looked up and met Syd's eye. 'Those who turn their back to what's happening are as guilty as the perpetrators. You're a reporter, Mala – you should be using your influence to change things.' My influence?

I was suddenly suffused with a warm glow. I'm a reporter. Syd was assuming I had status, influence: and one day maybe I would. In the meantime . . . why shouldn't I do as Keith had said and look for 'a line'. I suddenly saw that my job had a purpose.

'I've only just started covering courts,' I said seriously, 'but I've kept all the stuff from the meeting and I'll pass it on. If I push it hard enough in the office, I'm sure we can get a few lines in the *Standard*. Leave it with me.'

Caroline moved into Welbeck House in mid-autumn. An old lift rattled us up to her third-floor flat. All three rooms were off a dark corridor: on the left a large, square, high-ceilinged studio with a view out on to Seymour Place. On the right a narrow kitchen – no bigger than our kitchenette at home but modern; and a tiny, rectangular bathroom with no bath – just a shower, a sink and a toilet. It even smelled posh. 'It's great,' I said.

'Isn't it? It's such a relief to be away from Hallfield. Ellie's around all the time these days. I think my mother's caught her depression.' She opened a window, letting in the sound of traffic. 'I've got a table and chairs on order and I'll dress up the bed with cushions. It's such a good address: I want it to look good too.'

I checked out the wall of mirrored wardrobes. 'Tony's good at working spaces. He could advise you.'

'It's still going strong, then?'

I shrugged. 'I don't know really. I mean, what I'm doing isn't exactly big-time – but the *Wandsworth Borough News* buys every court story I write. Tony just doesn't understand how important that is. He says I've sold out – but he's the one mixing with weirdos. You should see them. I half expect to find him with a bone through his nose.' I looked out at the world from Caroline's window. 'I don't know what's happening between us.'

'Do you care?'

'I don't know. We've been together over a year now.'

'There's true love for you.' She snorted. 'I'm sorry to bring it up but the best thing I ever did was meet Luxy: I got a proper education without the hassle of arguments and broken hearts.'

I was absolutely still as, across the street, a blanketed young woman was stretchered into an ambulance. A proper education? You don't get that from just one lesson. I felt a tightness across my chest but didn't say anything. What could I say? That she didn't seem to have learned an awful lot about love? Well, of *course* not. Look at her teacher. My birthday had passed without even a card – I was halfway to the next one, for God's sake. How time flies when you're enjoying yourself. Fuck the bastard.

That night I told Tony it was over.

He was genuinely upset. 'I know things haven't been brilliant but we'll weather it. I love you, Mala. Just bear with me – I've got new beginnings too.'

'I don't really see any point,' I said. 'We've been pulling in different directions for a long time. I do love you but we're not exactly an advert for happy ever after.'

'It's been a hell of a year, that's why.'

'That doesn't fill me with hope for the years to come.'
'We'll get there.'
'Get where? When? I'm sorry, Tony, it just doesn't feel right any more.'

Dear Beth,
   I felt like screaming a few words into the ether so I'm writing to you. I've split up with Tony. Don't ask me why because I'm not sure: sob. Anyway, he hasn't exactly been kicking the door down to get me back, so that's it. My job is just brilliant: I'm court reporting. Sometimes the proceedings get a bit boring so I've bought a pocket Solitaire to play during remands, motoring offences and committals! Leaving school was the best thing I ever did!! Have you got a job? Caroline's just moved into a little studio flat off Seymour Place – very swanky. The main room's not much bigger than Jan's, but it looks fantastic: just goes to show what a bit of detail and a wad of dosh can achieve. What else? Jan's become a leftie: true!! There's a solicitor who's taken a fancy to her – a bit like Professor Higgins and Eliza Doolittle. She was out selling *Socialist Worker* last week!! My mum's still having a pop at me about my job: I try to be out most of the time. Then she has a pop at me about that!! Are you still living at home or are my letters sent on to you? If you're in the West End, why don't we have a drink together one evening? I've put my office number at the top.
   Love, Mala xxx

It was nearly two years since I'd visited the Tappett midden. Nothing had changed: except the settee had collapsed on one side and was propped up on an orange box. Just forty-eight hours into her nannying stint, Janice was worn out. 'I can't wait to return to work tomorrow. It's like being in a time warp.' She sighed. 'No jokes, this *is* the Rocky Horror Show, Mala.' She stepped around Tammy, who was colouring pictures on the floor. 'Come on, toodles; teatime.' Tam looked up and grinned, little teeth gleaming in a scrubbed blond face. I laughed. Jan said: 'You're in a good mood.'
   'I've had a good show this week.'

'Lucky you. I phoned in to check all was okay and got bawled out because Al had lost a file. Sometimes I could strangle him.'

'That's one way of getting your hands on his body.' She looked at me quizzically. 'Well, you *do* fancy the pants off him.'

'Do I?' She paused. 'D'you think he fancies me? No, he couldn't. He's so important and I'm just a . . . dogsbody.'

'You haven't got a dog's body, Jan.'

'Piss off.'

'As it is, I do think he fancies you.'

'But he's twenty-seven. And a solicitor.'

'Solicitors think sexy too.' I thought of some of the delicious young lawyers I'd met at South Western Magistrates Court. A couple had asked me for a drink and I'd said no: but I was a free agent now. How exciting!

Jan shook the fish fingers from the grill pan on to a plate: 'I wish he hadn't been so cross with me.'

'He's missing you.'

She emptied a half-tin of beans on top of the fish and gave it to Tammy. 'I can't believe we finally got the old cow in, Mala. After the second time she was booted out for being drunk, I thought they'd end up doing the op in our kitchen.' I laughed. 'Really: it's been a bloody nightmare – on, off, on, off – I just hope she's up and about by December because I don't want to spend Christmas in this hole.'

Tam pushed her plate away after three mouthfuls. Jan sighed. 'I've twisted Jack's arm to wait with her after school. He's bone idle.' She cleared away the leftovers and gave Tammy a bag of crisps. 'I better nip up to the hospital – see if the old cow's all right. She was still a bit groggy this morning.' She nodded towards her half-sister. 'Kids aren't allowed on the ward. D'you think you can cope?'

I looked warily at the deceptively quiet Tam. 'As long as you're not too long. Or we could walk up with you and wait outside?'

Tam said: 'I want to go with Janice.' It was decided.

At the main entrance to the hospital we stopped to buy a spray of carnations at the flower shop and then climbed the

central staircase to the first floor. Tammy and I sat on a vinyl
bench seat and watched the visiting flow while Jan disappeared
to dance attendance on her mother.

'Are you enjoying school, Tam?'

'I suppose.'

'Do you know your alphabet?'

'What's that?'

'ABC, you know.'

She shrugged, head bent in silvery contemplation – like Allie,
but without the roots I'd once mistaken as a vital ingredient in
the recipe for true beauty. She was like an angel, I thought. A
fallen angel. No roots on Allie now, queening it in a four-storey
Hammersmith house with a doting older lover and a burgeoning
jewellery business. 'You ought to do a feature on me, Mala.
They're always using my stuff in fashion shoots.' Harrods
was ordering one-off pieces and selling them on with huge
mark-ups; she'd even had a mention in *Harpers*: 'Her jewellery
can be as eclectic as that of Andrew Logan, but conversely
captures the classic lines of Cartier.'

She, of course, found the whole thing enormously funny.
'Now don't get ideas that this is making me rich, I only sell
one piece a week and each one of them is three days' work.
The rest is the usual tat and I'm working flat out – even
with help.' She yawned lazily. 'I'm giving up on markets –
the girls keep leaving or setting up with gangsters who nick
the takings. I'm negotiating contracts with Swan & Edgar and
Bourne & Hollingsworth. An outlet on Piccadilly and one on
Oxford Street will keep things ticking over very nicely, thank
you. If I can up the supply I've got deals in York and Bath for
the taking – very chi-chi.'

'Has Allie been to see your mum, Tam?'

'Not yet.'

'I haven't seen her for months.'

A shrug.

'Don't you like her?'

'She's nothing to do with me. Her dad's different.'

'But her mum's the same. Like Jan.' No response. 'I bet
you're missing her. You know she's going to be poorly for quite
a while?'

'She's always poorly.'

I gave up and went off to read the fire evacuation notice by the lift. A group of doctors were laughing near by: a private club of self-importance. Nearly eight o'clock: surely Jan didn't have that much to say to her mum? I wondered if I should pop into the ward and see, but I had nothing to say at all. I leaned on the banister rail and watched the people rushing to and fro below me. Ahead, Tammy was still on the seat, picking her nose. Two old men had taken my space and were smoking roll-ups. One didn't have his teeth in. Yuk! I thought about getting some chips on the way back – I'd told my mother, on principle, that I'd be late. If Jack was out I would sit and watch TV with Jan. If not . . . I could sit and drink tea with her. An emergency trolley trundled past the foot of the stairs below and, as I looked down, the woman with the tubes in her mouth and nose looked a bit like Ellie. I wondered if Josh's kiss all those months back had meant anything; and if so, what? Innocent eroticism. How dare Caroline equate that with shagging my father! Out of the corner of my eye I saw Tammy rise. I wandered back: 'What's the matter, Tam?'

'I want to do a wee.'

'Hang on, I'll find out where the loos are.'

'I can't wait.'

'You'll have to.'

The doctors had gone. There was a men's toilet on one side, but no women's. I didn't know what to do. Tammy started hopping from one leg to the other: 'I want to go now. I can't wait.' One of the old men said: 'It's downstairs.' I took her hand and virtually dragged her down the curving steps into the main corridor. A nurse directed me to the opposite end. I trotted, pulling Tammy behind me. 'Half a minute.' There it was. As I got to the door I came face to face with Caroline. Her parents were two steps behind. We stared at each other uncomprehendingly and I said: 'What are you doing here?' She didn't respond. 'You haven't come to see Mrs Tappett?'

'We're here with Ellie.'

'Ellie?'

'She's taken an overdose.' I suddenly remembered how a passing trolley had evoked the gentle warmth of Josh's mouth on mine. It had been her: I felt sick. 'I think she's dead, Mala. They're pumping her stomach.'

'Then she's not dead – she's savable.' But Caroline wasn't really listening and now Mr and Mrs Chong, their faces like the tragic masks of a Greek chorus, pulled away from the magnolia wall and moved into action. Caroline said: 'I'd better go with them to the waiting room.'

'She'll be all right.'

'Do you think it was anything to do with us?'

'You barely speak to her.'

'Exactly.'

'Where's Josh?'

'I don't know. We only found her twenty minutes ago.'

I went to touch her, but even in a crisis Caroline was too controlled to need or appreciate sentimental gestures. I let my own hands drop.

Suddenly, behind us, there was a petrifying wail. Turning, I saw that Tammy Tappett was standing in a steaming well of wetness, hot tears of shame obliterating her perfect little features. 'I told you I couldn't wait,' she screamed, 'but you didn't believe me!'

# 16

Christmas 1976. Deck the tree with boughs of holly, tra-la-la-la-la-la-la-la-la. I draped the lights around the fronds of green plastic: 'There – the first Buddhist Christmas tree,' and switched them on. 'Doesn't it look wonderful?'

'Better than ours,' Jan said. 'It always falls over. Jack said he'd fix it, then he said he'd get a new one, but it's still there, bare branches and all.' She sighed. 'I can't wait to get back to my own place. The old cow's milked this operation for everything she's got. I've warned her: come New Year my goodwill runs out. She can pop her clogs – I won't give a damn.' A slight flush. 'Sorry.' She took the strand of red-and-gold tinsel from her neck. 'I'm a real sucker, aren't I?'

I stuck a paper fairy on to a gold star and Sellotaped the lot to the top of the tree. It was so beautiful I was overcome with sadness. 'It'll be deadly at Hallfield.' I put the tinsel aside. 'Bugger, now I'm at it.' We carried the tree to the windowsill. 'I've asked Caroline to come on Christmas Day.'

'Good.' Jan picked up our coats. 'We'd better go.'

On the bus to Tottenham Court Road I panicked that I'd be a gooseberry at the restaurant, but she said: 'Listen – there's only five of us in the office right now. If we didn't all bring friends it'd be a wake.' She hit her forehead with the flat of her hand. 'I've done it again. You don't realise how much you talk about death until someone dies do you?'

We got off at the Academy cinema and walked up to Charlotte Street. Inside, the Greek restaurant was awash with retsina and revelry. Evie and her husband were already at the corner table alongside Syd and a very pretty girl in dungarees. Al, apparently

alone, was slouched against the opposite wall. He motioned Jan
to sit next to him, looking both amused and appreciative as
she revealed her maroon Crimplene dress with the sweetheart
neckline. Crimplene! They were all wearing it at the Lyceum, she
said. How grown-up she looked, I thought, curved and flawless,
thick hair loose on her shoulders: and then, How grown up we
all are. We are grown-ups now. For God's sake, I'm dating one
of the hottest freelance snappers around; and even the *South
London Press* is ordering my court copy. This is serious big time.
To think that twelve months before I'd just rediscovered my
father and was feeling more childlike than in all the years when I
really was a child! But that was a lifetime ago: a different lifetime.

I sat with Evie as Ritu and her friend Nita came in and
squashed up with Jan. Twenty minutes in and we were on
our third carafe of ouzo. In the big room beyond, cantina music
blasted out of the floor speakers. 'I suppose all this proletarian
hedonism makes you uncomfortable?' Syd's girlfriend said.

By the time the food came it seemed to me that everyone
was drunk. 'Cheer up – it's Christmas,' Evie's husband smiled.
I tried to oblige, teeth inescapably jammed in a fatty piece of
*kleftiko*.

The dark-haired waiter with the tired eyes made me think
of Josh, alone in his flat in Vauxhall. Josh, bent and broken at
the crematorium. Josh, weeping with his wife's parents while
Caroline and the Chongs maintained a glacial serenity behind.
Josh, who, when the coffin slipped through chintz into the
furnace of for ever, cried out like an animal. Poor, poor Josh.
And afterwards the bizarre ritual of reading the wreaths; his
a small circlet of freesias and the one word: Always. Always
what? Always yours? Always and for ever? A code shared by
lovers; a code unknown to me.

And his hair, so thick and straight and black, hanging across
his face like a widow's veil. And poor, poor Ellie, burning in her
box as we stood in the chill November grey making small talk;
Caroline's scarlet lipstick defying both elements and events.

'What did her note say, Caroline?'

'I only scanned it. No light at the end of the tunnel. The usual
stuff. Please forgive me. Love you always.' A pause. 'All I know
is she shouldn't have done it.'

On the way to the service Caroline and I had followed the funeral cars. 'Do you remember when Bethany's uncle came up to London in a hearse and gave us rides?'

She'd replied carelessly: 'Why remember? It's too long ago.'

Perhaps Ellie had lost sight of herself because she too had jettisoned happy memories, thinking they weren't important. Yet she'd held on to the unhappy ones. Were there, I wondered, memories that I'd conveniently lost; or lies in which I'd colluded to blot out memories I didn't want?

At her parents' we had tea with unknown friends and relations who commiserated in oblique language: 'At least the sun shone for her.' 'It's such an unpredictable month.'

I said to Caroline: 'Where's Josh gone?'

'I don't know.' She lowered her voice. 'My stupid mother reminded him that Catholic suicides end up in purgatory – he's probably praying somewhere.' She saw my face. 'Only joking. Anyway, better do my bit.' Picking up a tray of devils-on-horseback, she trotted round the room.

Always. Such passion for someone so round and red-headed. I thought that if I found Josh I'd scoop him into my arms and kiss him till the hurt oozed out, but he hadn't even acknowledged the Chongs that morning, let alone the well-meaning, sex-crazed vulture who now thought of feasting on the bones of misbegotten love. I picked up my bag: 'If you need me to do anything, Caroline, just ring and leave a message.'

She rolled her eyes. 'Leave it a couple of weeks – there's a big mopping-up operation *en famille*.' We walked to the door. 'This is a bloody nightmare, Mala. I've taken so much time off to organise things – my parents haven't a clue and Josh is zomboid. I'll have to work like a loon to get back on track.'

'Come to me for Christmas Day. My mum's still going to Anu's but I'm doing it my way. Jan's coming – Merle probably will too.'

'I'll see.'

But still she hadn't made up her mind and Christmas was a week away. I must push her: apart from anything else, I wanted to tell her about my hunky photographer.

Around me there was a sudden increase in volume. 'Get up,' Ritu shouted. 'You're the only one not on her seat.' I clambered on, laughing as successive groups of drunken office parties took their turn in the dance area, smashing plates against a fake wooden wall and snogging under mistletoe bunches carried on poles by the waiters. Syd's girlfriend was cheering and Evie's husband was Greek-dancing on his seat. I looked down the row for Jan. She was otherwise engaged. Without the help of seasonal greenery she and Al were in an intimate clinch in full view of the world and his uncle.

'Next thing you know she'll be joining the SWP,' Ritu said.

'She already flogs their papers.' I grinned, pretending it was funny, but I thought Jan was making an idiot of herself. This had been coming for months – why not do it discreetly? My stomach clutched with embarrassment on her behalf: it wasn't as if he was Dustin Hoffman or Steve Harley. This was the social equivalent of snogging Neil Sedaka. She'd never live it down.

I set out the food as Jan bought in the Pomagne from outside the front door. 'Lovely and cold.'

'Apple juice,' Caroline said.

'I'm sorry I don't stretch to Moet and Chandon, Caroline.'

'Mo-ay Sh-andon,' Caroline said. 'The t is silent, the ch is soft.'

'Call it what you like. Where are the glasses, Mala?'

I pulled them out. 'You might be a bit previous toasting the chef, Jan – the chilli's too bland and the rice is mushy.'

'Chilli for Christmas?' Merle shook her head. 'Couldn't you stretch to a chicken? I'd have done it for you.'

'I'm not toasting you,' Jan said, 'I'm toasting me.'

Must have slept with Al, I thought morosely: why not if you have the chance? It wasn't as if she had to creep around a sleeping mother at home, armed, as I always was, with a dozen falsehoods prepared for interrogation. But why should I toast Al when he'd pushed Jan into a taxi in Charlotte Street and left me to walk home alone at 2 a.m. humming to stay awake: Showaddywaddy, 'Under The Moon Of Love'.

'Here's to new beginnings,' Jan said. What the hell. 'New beginnings!' What a great drink Pomagne was.

'Well, actually, *my* new beginning. I'm moving in with Al.'

We all stood there stupidly. In my head I did a quick

calculation – from first snog to flat-share in six days: either this was a Burton-Taylor-type sex explosion or she'd gone bonkers. Either was possible.

Caroline said: 'You're not up the duff, are you, Janice?' And Merle, bewildered, asked: 'If you're going, who'll have your room?'

Jan was disarmed. 'What's wrong with you?' She turned to me. 'Mala – you saw I fancied him even before I knew myself.' She shook her head. 'I thought you'd be pleased.'

I searched carefully for the appropriate words. 'Pleased? I think you've gone barking mad. You can't just move in with a man you felt up at the office party! He's about a hundred, anyway. Get real, Janice.'

Caroline elaborately studied the contents of her glass as Jan went a shade of rage. 'Why did I think you'd understand? It's just like Al says: you're totally immature.' She whirled round angrily. 'This is different from other relationships. He's my teacher – I'm his muse.' His muse? 'I'm sorry you can't see that.'

'Why can't you just date like normal people?'

'Because it's too serious for that. Al's been lonely down in London and it's not as if I'm having the time of my life.'

'I thought you'd find someone within the court system, but not a solicitor,' Caroline said. 'Congratulations.'

'If you're saying he's clever and I'm thick, you're wrong, Caroline. Al says I've got a really good brain – that I'm full of ideas. He says exams are a tool to force people to toe the line.'

'Which is why he took so many?'

Jan put down her glass. 'If I'm not welcome here, I'm going.'

'Don't you dare.' I clapped my hands together. 'It's fun time. Merle, any chance of saving the meal?'

Within minutes she'd melted butter into the rice, transforming it into creamy acceptability. She squeezed lemon into the chilli and quick-chopped an onion which she scattered on top.

'What does it say about my life,' Caroline said, 'that I prefer this inedible rubbish to having turkey at home?'

'That you haven't tasted it yet.' Merle handed Caroline her lunch. 'And this,' she said to Jan, 'is for you, Brutus.'

'That's not fair.'

'This affects my future. You should have told me privately.'

I took a mouthful. 'This is a Christmas miracle.'

'Take over Jan's room: then you'll have first refusal on my cooking.'

'I'll miss this,' Jan said. 'Sitting with the girls, being silly. I'll have to be with him most of the time, won't I? That's what living together means.'

'Imprisoned like your mother.'

'I won't let you spoil it, Caroline.'

As I decorated the dessert, Angel Delight, Caroline came alongside. 'She's fucking mad. She just wants a substitute father to lean on.'

'You met her father – if you leaned on him, he fell over.'

She picked up the bowls. 'She's so full of Alspeak, she can't see the wood for the trees. You'll see: he's a bully like her dad – a respectable bully.'

'If we all look for father substitutes, does that mean that you'll shack up with a silent man who's good at stir-frys, Caroline?'

She grinned. 'If he has the same business brain.'

'And I'll get one who runs when the going gets tough.'

Merle peered over our shoulders as I grated plain chocolate into the bowls. 'You couldn't even boil up a Peak Freen pudding?' She shook her head. 'I think you need lessons. Move into Chilworth Street: seriously. It'd be nice to have a familiar face around.'

'Mum, I've decided to leave home.'

'What? Mala!'

'Listen. Jan's found a new place and I'm taking over her room – it's only up the road, and rent-controlled.'

'Rent? Have I asked you for a single penny?'

'It's six pounds a week. If it goes above a third of my salary I get a council grant. Mum: I want to be independent.'

'You're more independent than any other child I know. My friends berate me for the freedom you have. I've trusted you—'

'This isn't to do with trust, it's to do with space. I want to come in from work and put on records—'

'Isn't that exactly what you do now?'

'But I'd like to play them all evening without worrying that you want to sleep. I don't want to creep around you at night-time. I don't want to think of the bill when I pick up the phone. It's crazy that someone my age has to store her books and things under the bed.'

'Someone *your* age? What about me? I've known nothing else. Independence! What independence have I had? *Chi!*'

'That's the whole point, Mum. You're too old to sleep on a sofa and undress in dark corners. You need a life too.'

'I stayed with my parents till the day I married. If I had not married, I would be there still. Let me decide my life. Have I ever complained—'

'*I'm* complaining—'

'Not even boys leave their mothers. For a girl – it is truly a terrible thing, Mala.'

'If it'd make you feel better I could—'

'Better? How can you make the unthinkable better?' She stared solemnly past me, eyes distinctly damp; but I had spent two weeks preparing the ground, writing lists for and against. I'd practised my arguments and tested their validity on Margaret, who always knew the right thing to say. 'Just speak the truth, Mala – it's one thing for a woman and child to live in a rabbit hutch, but two women is impossible.'

'You're so bloody rational, Margaret – why are you here?' I looked around at the other patients – a woman pacing the corridor with menstrual bloodstains on her white hospital nightie; a young man curled on the sofa in the fetal position; an elderly blonde in a two piece suit and straw hat who stared blankly at the TV screen. 'It doesn't make sense.'

'I'm rational about everything but myself. Anyway, I'm doing well now. I was on a closed ward till I put on a stone – that's why I couldn't see you. Another one, and I'm out.'

'By then I'll have learned to cook. I'll make a curry—'

'Please, Mala: it makes me feel sick.'

So I stood my ground. I spent another week slowly wearing my mother down: asking advice; introducing her to Merle; meeting every objection with confidence. Then Caroline piled my stuff in the boot of her car and we drove the quarter-mile to Chilworth Street. Turning the car stereo up, I didn't once look back: the Eagles, there is a New Kid in Town.

But just three weeks later, my mother rang in an agitated state and summoned me to Craven Terrace. As I pulled on my jacket and walked past Queen's Gardens, I felt resentful that, by dint of her drawn face and swollen eyes, she still exerted power over my movements. Perhaps she'd gnawed off her own foot through loneliness? A terrible thought: perhaps she'd seen me walking to Paddington Station that morning, on the arm of my Nikon knight? Please God, no. It was just post-Valentine's madness. She would not stop me doing it again. And again. As I reached the railings, I couldn't decide whether to tough it out or lie. It was my life; my flat; my decision – I shouldn't have come. But I'd arrived. I ran down the steps and stopped at the door. The key was in my pocket, but I rang the bell like the visitor I was.

'Mala: thank God you're here.'

I went in mutinously.

Bethany was laid out on the sofa.

'She turned up half an hour ago,' my mother said. 'She's in trouble, she says. Be careful: she's taken drugs or alcohol.'

'Alcohol!' Bethany shouted. 'I don't do drugs any more. Well – only methadone.'

'Your mother's taken her in?'

'She's on the sofa bed until I get her sorted.'

'You should have thrown her out.'

'But Jan, doesn't she come under disadvantaged women who've had their life choices removed?'

I'd been so pleased to see Bethany – to be reconciled. She hadn't written for over a year and I'd been vaguely uneasy – but that was her way. Now she was back amongst us, but it quickly became clear that the situation wasn't as simple as she'd at first suggested. She wanted her presence kept secret, even from Clive. She had a daily prescription for methadone. She was starting to feel like a liability. But she was my friend and she'd moved my mother's focus from me.

Only Jan, Caroline and my office people knew about her. Keith had been impressed: 'Who'd have thought it – the straightest girl in London putting up a teenage Mariella Novotny. If she's rogered anyone famous, Mala, we might squeeze some money from the *News of the Screws*.' There was an in-built element of bravado involved, but after eight days of smuggling her into Savory Moore for her drugs, the gloss was wearing thin. If she was still addicted, why bother?

'What do you plan to do with yourself, Beth?'

'I don't know.'

'How can we help you if you don't know?'

I wondered if she'd told my mother about the men and the moving from squat to squat. I suspected not.

'I was looking for something to make life normal, Mala, that was all. When I had a hit, the strands all came together.'

'That's why it was all right to shag pushers.' She saw me looking contemptuously at her scragginess and looked away. 'You're getting fed up of me, aren't you?'

I said: 'At least your mother did it to put food on your table.' When she didn't answer, I left.

A couple of days later I was back: 'The last time you came here you tried to hide your drugs; this time you're taking them yourself. It's been a fortnight, Beth, you must sort yourself out.'

'This is the only place I'm safe. I'm home.'

'But it *isn't* your home. Why can't you go to your mum's?'

'I've told you; because I don't want Dingo to find me.'

I listened with ill-humour. She told so many contradictory stories, my milk of human kindness was curdling. First Sam, now Dingo. Everything she said seemed laced with the poison of deceit. Nonetheless I was glad for any wallpaper that covered the cracks of her life, even if it could be easily stripped.

I turned to Jan for the next step.

Jan said: 'If you really want to help her, I'll ask Syd about rehab programmes around London.'

'I just want her out,' I said honestly. 'She still takes methadone and if she's getting any dole we're not seeing it.' I readjusted the cushions in an attempt to get comfortable in the old Lloyd Loom chair. 'Any chance of a coffee?'

I'd hunted out the flat in Battle Bridge Road after work. Al hadn't bothered putting his name on a bell, but I'd instinctively knocked on the first-floor door sporting an Amnesty International poster. The block was one of a series of condemned buildings in an unlit street overlooking the railway sidings at King's Cross. Inside, it was damp and cold, but the rusty red walls made it feel like the kasbah. On a giant noticeboard were circulars from Anti-Apartheid, the Anti-Nazi League and Women Against Violence Against Women. A Trotsky cut-out dominated the hallway and a half-signed CND petition lay on the table: reminders in case Al lost sight of who he was or what he thought.

The windows were covered by raw hessian hung lopsidedly on hand-constructed rails. Jan saw me looking. 'Penny for them?'

'I was thinking Caroline would love this place.' We giggled.

'So Janice is settling with a professional man,' my mum had sighed. 'Now all we need is a wedding. Why can't you find a decent boy, Mala? Did I mention Aunty Prisky's nephew Nihal is back from Sri Lanka? He's a lovely fellow – an engineer. Would you like an introduction?'

'Thanks, but I don't need a man to give me value, Mum.'

I sat now with my friend, who'd given up nights out dancing, eating and flirting, or just sitting up till three mixing snowballs and gossiping, for a bearded Yorkshireman who liked to wipe his plate clean with a slice of bread and butter. In her favour, Al was often thought-provoking and occasionally interesting. He was a man of principle, a defender of our rights, a knight on a plodding piebald mare. But . . . I watched as Jan tidied up. If she preferred the dreary and commonplace, it was not, as Caroline said, because it was her natural inheritance, but because she had no greater expectation. Al was the sea wall guarding her pedestrian life from the moon tides of Westbourne Terrace.

I got up to go. 'If you can come up with something for Bethany, Jan, please do. That girl's been on my turf long enough.'

'Of course he'll be happy to see you,' Caroline said as we drove over Vauxhall Bridge. 'He can't stay in purdah for ever.' She emergency-braked at traffic lights. 'When you think of all the money and effort my parents poured into him – and he loses the plot time and again. I've wupped his arse career-wise: but he's still number-one boy. Why am I part of the conspiracy?'

'Because you've come out tops: and you love him.'

'I used to hate him. It makes me mad sometimes.'

'You've never wanted that type of support, Caroline. Nobody would dare bring you food parcels – you'd throw them back.'

We pulled up outside a flat-fronted Georgian house. Caroline pulled several bags of groceries from the boot. 'Here, take a couple of these, will you: I promised my mother I'd stock his cupboards.' She locked the car, lithe in a close-cut, sleeveless shift dress. 'And don't mention Ellie – let it lie. Let *her* lie. And don't make faces, Mala – it's happened: there's no use pretending.'

She rang the bottom bell and there he was. He looked fantastically well. I'd imagined him emaciated and hunched – a sort of noble, male Bethany – but in the clothes of a young computer executive he looked healthy and clean-cut. The work of Ellie's parents, I thought.

'Hello,' he said blankly. 'Did I order any of this?'

'The folks are worried about you.'

'That's why I've only seen them four times since the funeral, is it?' He opened the door, bemused, and Caroline led us into his flat. 'I see you've brought your trusty packhorse, Mala. Hoping for a grief-relief sideshow: watch while he weeps?'

'Caroline asked me to come. We won't stay long.'

'Nonsense, I can hardly dine alone now.' He watched as Caroline unloaded the bags in the kitchen area of the open-plan sitting room. 'Not a baked bean in sight. Well done, little sister. So, what's brought you here tonight: guilt, curiosity, pity?'

'Duty. And for the record, Josh, I've rung at least twice a week since Ellie died. Mum has called every day – you know they're pushed for time off. You've got to join the real world, bro'.'

He leaned against the wall, arms crossed, as Caroline cleared out his cupboards and put the new food away.

'So how are you, Mala?'

I said coldly: 'Very well. Thank you for asking.'

He looked slightly ashamed. 'I didn't mean to be rude to you. Thanks for the letter, it meant a lot. Ellie liked you very much, though I don't suppose you noticed. Sit down: I'll get you both a drink.' He poured three shots of whisky into squat crystal glasses and we sat at either end of the sofa while Caroline cooked. In front of us was a huge photo montage of Josh and Ellie, mainly in Photo-Me booths: she red and grinning, he cautious but smiling, never showing teeth. 'Neither of us photograph well. How are the old couple, Caroline?'

'Worried sick; you should come over.'

'I can't face it. Blocking things out is my one luxury.'

'She didn't die at the flat, she died in hospital,' Caroline said, crossly. 'Where's the cutlery? I'll lay the table.'

'How are you feeling, Josh?'

'I'm not feeling, Mala: it's much easier that way.'

'Are you busy?'

'I'm always busy even when I'm not – I have the gift of looking constantly pained and contemplative.' He poured himself another drink. 'I hear you've moved into Janice's flat. Mummy must be heartbroken.'

'She's otherwise occupied.' I told him about Beth. 'Thankfully Jan's found a good rehab project that'll take her from the beginning of April. Otherwise she'd have squatting rights.'

'Do I detect a little jealousy?'

'You're joking! She's taken my mum's mind right off me.'

'Precisely.'

I didn't answer. He said: 'Ellie was destroyed by one bad trip. You must save Beth.'

'I'd rather save the whale.'

He laughed. 'You're still angry with her for going?'

'I'm angry with her for returning.'

Caroline said: 'Dinner's ready.'

He pulled me to my feet. 'I'm glad you came. I'm always glad to see you – as you know.'

I smiled at the flutter in my stomach because I was way beyond Josh now. I was a woman who had known love and passion and toil and responsibility and really, I ought to have moved on. I had moved on. So why was I momentarily breathless?

'Do you have a boyfriend, Mala?'

'I've just finished with one: he got a bit too serious.'

'Sensible girl – you don't want to be a widow at twenty-five.' He poured himself another drink and sat at the table. 'Hey, sis, my compliments to the chef.'

# 17

Bethany was painting her toenails on the sofa in one of her focused moments. 'Two days and I'll be gone. Can I take your old clothes with me?' She wiped her nose on the back of her hand. 'My mum's going to die when we do the family therapy.'

'Why did you come back, Beth?'

'Why are you always asking that? So much for the promises we made as kids.'

'You're not the same person; they don't count.'

'Of course I'm the same – I'm just a bit fucked up, that's all.'

Why did she make me so cross? I watched as she sang along with David Soul on *Top of the Pops*: 'Going In With My Eyes Open'. She was almost childlike, as if she'd stopped growing the first day she got stoned: dining out on memories that I'd packed away after taking previous appearances into consideration. I was starting to feel seriously irritated seeing my mother fuss around a junkie while I was starving in a garret.

57 Varieties, they called me in Chilworth Street: a legend in my own lunch-time. Merle would sink her face in her hands at each of my attempts to individualise Heinz sauces with cheese, pineapple chunks or Oxo cubes. 'How much worse can it get?'

The week before, I'd exploded an egg. I was on the loo reading *Cosmo*:

'Are You Hot in the Sack? Do you think the doggie position is a) antisocial, b) anti-feminist, c) good fun?'

Outside the door there was an almighty bang. Dropping everything, I rushed out to see a glob of ectoplasm sail across the landing and dive-bomb into the hair of an Elvis look-alike coming up the stairs.

'Dear God! Fuck, fuck, fuck! What the hell's happening, Mala?'

A waxy drop of yellow goo dripped on to my foot. I looked up and saw my breakfast spattered across the ceiling. Elvis handed me the pan, which had apparently shot over the banisters on to the landing below. 'You idiot! Why can't you have muesli like everyone else?'

As he retreated angrily down the stairs I shouted: 'Hey, Elvis, what's the doggie position?' He ignored me. 'Go on, tell me: what is it?'

A pause. 'On one leg against a lamppost.'

'Man or woman?' Silence. 'Which one's on one leg?'

'Usually the woman: better access. You should try it.'

'Don't worry, I will.'

As he disappeared into the curve of the stairs, he laughed, and I was relieved to be forgiven.

Yet here was Bethany, who was fed on demand, now moaning that my mum had gone to the Commonwealth Institute, leaving me in charge. 'I miss her cooking.'

'You're a bloody drug addict: you're not supposed to eat.'

'She *makes* me. I've got used to it.'

Thinking back to stews and curries and roasts, my heart lurched. Never mind: I'd lost six pounds since leaving home – from beer glass to hourglass. A quiet knock at the door. Beth said quickly: 'Who's that?'

'Probably Jan – I told her I'd be here.'

'But it's ten o'clock.'

I opened the door but barely registered the dark knife-scarred face before I was pushed violently out of the way. 'Where is she?' He ran into the flat. 'Got you, bitch!' I heard rather than saw him launch himself at her. Beth shouted: 'No, Dingo! No!' and then hit the ground with a thud under his bulk. She called out to me to help her, but I was already halfway up the stairs. At the top I stood shivering – shouting out into the empty street. 'For God's sake, someone – anyone – *call the police!*'

\*　　\*　　\*

'It wasn't just for drugs,' Beth said. 'He made me turn tricks for fags; for a drink; for anything. I hated that.'

I shook my head. The drugs, I could live with: there was a certain cachet in joining the ranks of Jim Morrison, Janis Joplin or Jimi Hendrix. Even Mrs Stephens's dilemma I could understand. But to sleep with strangers *just* for money!

Beth winced as the nurse plastered her wrist. I said: 'He'll get put away, you know.'

'No he won't. He's got the Old Bill in his pocket. Wait and see.' She licked her swollen lips. 'I wouldn't give evidence anyway: this is just revenge – it'd be a lot worse if I made him angry.'

I shook my head. 'How did he find you?'

'One of the junkies picking up at the chemist, I suppose. It's a small world. Doesn't matter, I'll be out of it on Saturday.' She became anxious. 'I can't go back to your mum's, Mala, it wouldn't be fair. Will you put me up?'

We rang my mother with a watered-down version of events and arranged to show ourselves the next day. Then, wearily, we walked from St Mary's to Chilworth Street. I gave Bethany the bed. 'That's what friends are for.'

In the pre-dawn cold, I heard her sniffing. 'Don't get all sentimental now, Beth. It's over.'

'I know. I was just thinking how we used to go for walks and things: it was so innocent. Arguing about sweets. You liked anything chocolate—'

'And your favourite were Love Hearts—'

'Remember the day you and Janice had a scrap and she threw your gobstopper down the street and it shattered—'

'And Caroline's salt twist breaking in her mouth, remember?' We both laughed. 'It was all rubbish anyway.'

'Wasn't it just? Mala: thank you.'

I rolled over. 'Let's get some sleep – I've got to be at work in five hours.' Then I rolled back. 'Beth, when you were on the game—'

'That's history.'

'I know. But . . . did you do the doggie position?'

'It was only quick fumbles in cars, you know.'

'Because you'd be caught if you did it in the street.'

'It's illegal to do it in the street.'

'So you never did the doggie position?'

'Well, I did with boyfriends.'

'And was it you who raised your leg against the lamppost?'

'Raised my leg? What are you talking about?'

And only then did the penny drop.

I recollected suddenly, horribly, a conversation over lunch in the London Spa. Keith had been telling the story of a nymphomaniac tabloid columnist. 'Now, boys,' he'd said, 'we mustn't embarrass Mala: she thinks the missionary position's a job in the jungle.' And I, keen to be one of the lads, had retorted to everyone's surprise: 'I've cocked my leg against the odd lamppost, you know.'

Damn and blast that bastard Elvis: may he rot in hell for landing me in Heartbreak Hotel, just because of a stupid exploding egg.

I'd been sitting in the rain for three whole days, nine hours at a time. I knew every knot in the roped police cordon; every window of the block of flats behind Sadlers Wells. Sometimes Alister or Neville or one of the other snappers would slip alongside with some cappuccino from Brivati's, their long-distance lenses protected by plastic covers; often they'd sneak off to the pub with the rest of the press pack. 'It's all right, Mala, Knacker's given us the nod – nothing's happening right now.'

But I stayed: feet aching in four-inch heels, dutifully filing each press update from the phone box at the edge of the estate: the Metropolitan Police today confirmed that officers have made telephone contact with the Islington machete man. The distraught male, who has not been named to protect the identity of the child hostage released on Monday, has been barricaded inside the fourth-floor council flat for four days . . .

So it went every two hours until early afternoon on the Wednesday. The evening-paper guys had poodled off, convinced nothing would happen before their last edition times; the nationals had gone late to lunch after a delayed photocall for the visiting Area Commander. For once, suffering siege fatigue, I'd been tempted by offers of wine and prawn sandwiches, but instinct said the visit hadn't just been duty. Instinct was right.

As the photogs decamped to drop off dull head-and-shoulders shots of a man in uniform, the police support team went into action, smashing down the door of the flat and showing firearms for the first time. There was the sound of fighting. Suddenly, in seconds it seemed, he was there, the machete man, bowed and bloody on the communal balcony in a checked shirt and handcuffs. And – thank you, dear God – he was shouting: he was shouting and I was the only one there with a notebook and pen to transcribe each precious and foul oath! I didn't wait for the phone box: I ran back to the office. Within the hour, my story was in the hands of every newspaper.

'You're right, Mala, you have proved yourself,' Keith said the next day. 'You're dogged, you're fast and you're ambitious. I'll give you one more test. If you pass, you take over the crown court at Knightsbridge: that way you're doing bread-and-butter stuff but you're in central London for a crack at off-diary stories, too. Okay?'

'Brill.'

That afternoon, masquerading as a student, I slipped into the library at Brunel University and cut out a picture from a back copy of their Christian Union magazine.

'Well done, darling, you're a treasure,' Keith said. 'Not much of a looker, is she, but I guess those Mormon boys are grateful for anything.' He called Monty over. 'What d'you think, Monty, can we sharpen this shot up a bit? It's not as good as skiing naked down Everest with a rose between her teeth, but she's almost as crazy; and a tiger between the sheets – so the story has it.'

'Where d'you get this, then?'

'Mala's been out looting and pillaging.'

'Is it going to get us in trouble?'

'Of course not – there were hundreds of kids that year; it could have come from any one of them.'

Monty studied the picture with his magnifying glass. 'We can do it, I reckon. Blow it up and give it a quick shine, it'll be fine.'

The next morning it was on the front page of every newspaper: 'Mormon Sex Case Girl – First Picture!' Keith called me over with a grin. 'Well, you pulled it off, Miss Fonseka

– you'll be working in the shadow of Harrods from Monday.'

Beth:
   A rushed note. I'm so pleased that you're doing well. I've been promoted! I started at the crown court a couple of months ago: you can't imagine how my vocabulary's improved after hours of listening to barristers droning on!! I've been office-based the last couple of weeks because of the summer recess but it's back to business as usual tomorrow. Caroline's passed her commission target. Again. Jan's still with Al . . . Mum's very well – she's starting evening classes. Write soon.
   Love, Mala xx.

'Fab tortilla,' Caroline said. 'Worth the money. Have you seen the latest stuff in Harvey Nichols? I've bought some designer sewing patterns – there's a woman in Kensal Rise who makes them up.'
   'You always look dead posh anyway.'
   'Not posh, stylish. I won't have anyone pointing at me and saying "She comes from a council estate".'
   'Nobody does say it.'
   She blotted her lips. 'Anyway, today's news is I'm buying a flat. I got a builder a good deal on a couple of wrecks near Marylebone Station. I'm getting a two-bedroomed flat at discount.' Wow!
   'Isn't that a bit near the Lisson Green estate?'
   'Mala: one side of the bridge, Shitsville, the other, paradise.'
   'How much?'
   'Eighteen grand. Don't look like that: I'm getting it half-price. It's a bargain. Mind you, he got the site for a song. These out-of-town solicitors get lumbered with probate and they haven't a clue – they guess the prices and sign anything that'll shift it. Double commission for us, though – first the sale to the developer, then the sale of the development: eight flats.' She grinned. 'Martin says he'll retire when he's fifty and give me the company. *If* I stay.'
   'If you stay?'
   'I want to be a partner. I'm bringing in as much as the big

boys but all I get is a small percentage of the commission I make.'

'Caroline: I'm earning twenty-two measly quid a week and you're buying a flat in Marylebone. What more can you want?'

'It's not about money, it's a point of principle: I want my value to be recognised.'

'You'd better see Jan about starting a union.'

'*Please*.' She finished her coffee and I watched her with envious pleasure – two months from twenty and getting her own place. 'What're you thinking, Mala?'

'That you're brilliant and I'm glad you're my friend.'

'Because I'm a bloody terrifying enemy?'

'Don't be stupid.'

'So I'm forgiven my rejection of your good causes?'

'If you mean refusing to drive me down to see Beth in Somerset, yes, you are. I know communes aren't your thing – too much soul-searching and nut cutlets.' I finished my own coffee. 'I'd better get back – court starts in ten minutes. When can I see the flat?'

'We've a drinks thing tonight; tomorrow? I don't suppose you want my studio, do you? It's cheap for what it is.'

I shook my head. 'I've done my room up: it's looking great.'

'Never mind: I'll double the rent and pass it to our lettings arm.' We gathered up our bits and pieces. 'Good case today?'

'It'll make a few pars in the *Express*, maybe the *Torygraph* – a war veteran stealing food.' She feigned a yawn. I laughed humourlessly. 'I feel that way too. It isn't like the fast turnover in the lower courts – here it's taken two days to solve the mystery of the missing marrowfat peas. You know – those horrible things Al eats.'

She opened the door on to the windswept street. 'Not exactly an imprisonable offence.'

Heading back down Hans Crescent, I thought morosely that anyone with Al's habits deserved prison – especially if, like him, they rolled in pissed at midnight and woke their women to make them supper. I checked the afternoon lists for new cases: nothing. I trudged back into Court 1.

'It's not that he's a chauvinist,' Jan said. 'How can a man who fights for equal rights be a chauvinist? It's just that he's useless with a frying pan.'

'So he gets you out of bed to make him steak and chips?'

'I'm often still awake. Don't cast judgment, Mala.'

As I went through the door, I sighed. The usher looked up and gave me a wink. 'It isn't that bad, love, only the summing-up left.'

'So much fuss about mushy peas.'

'My husband's favourite.'

'Because he's a northerner?'

'Because he's lost his teeth.'

Mala,
   Thanks for the tenner. I've decided to stay on here and work with other addicts. Hope you have a good xmas and a brilliant 1978.
   Love, Beth xx

Caroline finally moved in on Valentine's Day: the day of Aunty Prisky's fortieth birthday party. 'You go, Mala. After all the contract problems, all I want to do is get a takeaway and sleep.'

Prisky's little house off Willesden Lane was already buzzing when I arrived. Her English lodgers Vivienne and Nicky had made a huge chocolate cake which dominated a table already laden with cutlets, patties, tiny three-tier sandwiches, kebab sticks and asparagus rolls. Everywhere there were paper chains and streamers. 'Christmas decorations from my school,' Anu said, letting me in. She pulled me close for the official Sri Lankan greeting: the alternate touching, three times, of cheeks, accompanied by a soft blowing sound. 'I've been delegated "greeter".'

I was amused. 'Maybe you've missed your vocation?'

'Careful, young lady, or you'll have to stand in the corner. Has Mummy told you I've applied for the post of deputy head? If they can get past my surname and my sari, I'm the best candidate.'

'You're bound to get it.'

She grimaced. 'Who knows how their minds work. You were brought up here; it may be different for you.' She pinched my cheek. 'You know we only want the best.' Over Anu's shoulder I saw the ancient Mrs Sivanandan bearing down on me with a tray of fruit punch.

Quickly I headed for the kitchen where my mum was spearing silverskin onions and cheddar squares on cocktail sticks. 'Go out and get them started, Mala.' She handed me a bowl of crisps. 'Do your bit.'

Vivienne was checking her tick list. 'Everything done, bang on time.'

I popped a cutlet in my mouth. 'But Sri Lankans are always late.'

A voice at the door. 'Not if they're married to Englishmen.'

Mina, in a black velvet dress, appeared at my side. 'Mala, you look so grown up. I haven't seen you in so long. Every time we visit Mummy I hope you'll be there, but you're always busy.' She saw me note her stomach and looked sheepish. 'I know, after telling everyone I would never do it again, it happened. God only knows how: I think Ronnie must have tricked me when I was too tired to notice. Never have children, Mala. People tell you only the good things. Look at my face: not crow's-feet – the whole bloody bird.'

'You look fine.'

'And down below: every time you sneeze, a leak in the gusset.' She lowered her voice. 'I've told Ronnie that if they use forceps this time, he's to put a gun up there and shoot the child. Or he can shoot me; but I can't suffer more stretching.' She sighed. 'So much work. When I was a baby I had two ayahs. Every day a new dress was made for me to wear. Whatever I needed I got – my father even sent the cook out at midnight to find sweets when I cried. My mother has never washed a dish. But here: you have the children, and you have to raise them too. They expect you to shop, cook, clean. It's very difficult.' She checked we weren't being eavesdropped. 'Perhaps I should have married a boy from home.'

'He wouldn't have liked your miniskirts.'

'They wear mini-saris now.'

'Not moaning again, is she?' Ronnie rolled up, smiling as always. 'Don't tell me – she doesn't know how her Trim

Wheeled stomach inflated like a balloon and her old maternity clothes don't fit because her bottom's gone phut?'

'Ronnie!'

'Don't fret, honeybun, I'll love you even when you're old and fat. How's Fleet Street, Mala? Got your name in the *Guardian* yet?'

'Give me a chance.'

Across the room I saw an apparition. A young man. A young man with a profile like Michelangelo's David. I extricated myself nimbly and approached him slowly. 'Hello, I'm Mala.'

'Nihal.'

'Are you Indra's son?'

'No, I'm Prisky's nephew. The engineer you didn't want to meet when your mother asked.' Ah, yes.

'She said you were over from Sri Lanka.'

'I was. I spent a year there finding my roots. Why, d'you have a problem with Sri Lankan blokes?'

'Not that I know of.' He said nothing. I struggled to fill the gap. 'I just don't like my mother matchmaking.'

'Fair enough,' he said. 'But just for the record: I didn't want to meet you either. I heard you'd flunked school, left home and got a low-paid job; I thought you were probably a talentless slapper.'

'It's because I don't like my mum running my life.'

'It's because he came from Sri Lanka. You're such a coconut you thought that made him second-rate.'

'I chatted him up, didn't I?'

'Only after seeing him. Up to that point you made the racist assumption that someone from your home country was too foreign for your whitened sensibilities.'

'Merle! You've been spending too much time with Janice.'

'And you haven't been spending enough.' We stopped while she did up her jacket. 'So you're seeing him next week?'

'Yes. But I can't sleep with him or he'll say it's true I'm a talentless slapper.'

Laughing, we turned under the bridge into Brick Lane. 'I wish I were anywhere but here,' I said.

'Snap.'

Steeling ourselves, we passed the skinheads selling *Bulldog*. One had a Staffordshire bull terrier that snapped at our heels. 'Hello, girls – adding a bit of *colour* to the proceedings? Why don't you just fuck off back to Bongo Bongo Land?'

From the next block Jan shouted: 'Fuck off, fascist scum.' I shuddered and willed myself on. Syd and another man were selling *Socialist Worker* as she handed us Anti-Nazi League leaflets to give out to shoppers navigating a course between the markets at Petticoat Lane and Columbia Road. 'Tell sympathetic ones there's a form on the back to send off – supporting the cause, you know.'

'Where's Al?'

'He's busy.'

Merle and I exchanged knowing glances and, taking our piles, headed for Wentworth Street. Welcome to Merle and Mala's righteousness way station. I said: 'If we shift these quickly, we can go shopping.'

'We've got five hundred leaflets here, Mala. Let's buy some bagels and do it properly.'

Business was surprisingly brisk. Members of a housing collective at St Katharine's Dock came and chatted with us. A black bus driver from the local depot took a handful of leaflets. 'If we don't fight ourselves, we've no right to ask others.'

Later we all met up and walked to Bethnal Green, to the vegetarian café next to the Florist's Arms. Jan rubbed her eyes. 'I'm exhausted. Marie turned up at the flat last night – she's run away from the home.'

'She must be thirteen.'

'Fourteen and a half going on forty.' She shook her head. 'I don't know – she was in a right state – saying all manner of wild things about the house father. She says he's been messing about with her, but it doesn't make sense: he's a social worker, not a dirty old man.' She sighed. 'I don't know what to do with her. She won't go back. What if it's all true?'

'Is she still there?'

'Yeah. I left a note for Al asking him to call Allie when he got up – not that she can do much with two sick babies newly home.' She groaned. 'I can't bear the thought of getting back and having to sort it all out. Where do I start?'

Merle said: 'You should be glad she came to you instead of just running off.'

'I suppose so,' Jan said, 'but when something goes wrong in our family, why's it always me who carries the can?'

'Hello, Mala,' Luxy said. 'You're looking very elegant.' He glanced admiringly around Caroline's sitting room. 'Your friend's done well for herself.'

'It's a beautiful flat.'

'It certainly is. I hear you're a top-flight journalist now.'

'I'm still learning the ropes.'

'You'll be a great success, I'm sure.' I didn't respond. He smiled. 'I think you've inherited my ambition.' I stiffened. 'You had to get something useful from my side: not just your looks.'

'You're wrong,' I answered. 'It's not ambition, it's perseverance, and I get that from my mum. All I've inherited from you is the ability to walk away.' And as he made to reply, I turned and headed into the kitchen, where Mr and Mrs Chong were arranging short eats on silver trays.

Alone in the corner I danced, as they erected a spring roll pyramid with deft hand movements. Abba: 'Knowing Me, Knowing You'.

Keith was jubilant. 'We've done it. Mala, you're a genius. It's taken eight long weeks but we've pulled it off.'

'We've nailed Trevor Edwards?'

'Dirty bastard. Sharon's tracked down two teenage girls who he molested in care. They're at Bindmans now, signing affidavits. I've got Bob Smith doorstepping him in Sunbury. John's got snatch shots of the old bugger going in and out, so to speak. Social Services are going fucking mad! They've been denying it for weeks: let's see how that slimy PR Johnson slithers out of this one. The *Mirror*'s gagging for it: we've got that arsehole bang to rights.' He gave me a hug. 'I've had your interview with Marie Connors lawyered: well done. The big man wants to see you about a rise.'

Thirty quid a week and senior reporter status, even though I stayed at Knightsbridge: not exactly big time but better than a kick up the bum. Never mind, tonight someone else was paying: Peter and Allie were taking us out for dinner. Something about an announcement, Allie had hinted. Probably to do with the twins, I thought, and all the pernickety little setbacks that had accompanied their premature birth. 'My miracle boys,' Allie had said in the story I sold to the *West London Observer*: 'Fighters like their mum.' Even now, at five months, they were being monitored weekly, but the future looked good. And the whole Marie crisis had been a blessing in disguise. Mrs Tappett, who appeared to have forgotten all about her, had agreed to her return if she looked after Tam. Given the circumstances, as Jan pointed out, what choice did Social Services have?

'And Sean?'

'He doesn't want to come back: he's in the football team. You know what boys are like: why swap his mates for that hell-hole?' Jan sighed. 'Poor Marie: the latest in a long line of Connors girls to do hard labour in the old cow's nursery. I'd rather have some dirty scuzzbag sticking his hand up my skirt once a month.'

We laughed until we cried.

And now we were outside Hammersmith station waiting for Allie and Peter to pick us up.

'No Al?'

'They don't rub along very well.'

The bottle-green Range Rover pulled up. Allie shouted: 'All aboard.' We scrambled into the back. 'We're going to the White Elephant on the river. Caroline's meeting us there. No Al?'

'He got an emergency immigration case.'

Peter said: 'I hope it's not on Legal Aid I don't pay supertax for any old Tom, Dick or Ali Baba to waltz in demanding free services.'

Jan mouthed: 'See what I mean?'

At the restaurant Caroline was waiting in a clipped dog's-tooth jacket and black knee-length skirt. 'I've ordered a glass of Piersporter, if that's all right.'

'Subscribing to the hock explosion, Caroline? Well, if nothing else, it's the best of an overrated bunch.' Peter shook out his napkin. 'Alison only drank Blue Nun when we first met.'

'Don't be such a snob, Peter.'

'As I do mind about these things, is it all right if I take over the ordering?' Within minutes champagne was being served.

'What are we celebrating?' I asked.

'I'll let my wife tell you.'

'Your *wife*?'

Allie started to giggle. 'Peter and I wanted you to be the first to know. We married at Chelsea Town Hall last week.'

'Congratulations!' I started to sing the old Eurovision hit but Allie said: 'Don't start caterwauling.' Seeing her sister's long face, her tone softened. 'Don't look like that, Jan, we didn't tell a soul. We got witnesses off the street. It didn't feel right to make a fuss while the boys were poorly.'

'That's all right,' Jan said grudgingly, and I thought Allie must have been very distracted not to tell her first.

Our champagne flutes refilled, Peter cleared his throat. 'The other thing we wanted to tell you is that I've sold Milverton Holdings. I am no longer a businessman – at least, not a London-based businessman. I've – we've – just bought five hundred acres in Ireland. I'm going into horse-breeding.'

'Horse-breeding?'

'It's his big love,' Allie said. 'We've got two racehorses already.'

Peter grinned: 'We'll be breeding Arabs in an established stud. We're inheriting orders and staff. Jon and Beccy are champing at the bit, if you'll pardon the pun, and the clean air will benefit Rory and Eliot.'

'It's the back end of bloody nowhere but—'

'It's back to your roots, Alison. It's not that far from your father's home town. Who knows, now he's back there we may run into him—'

'Don't spoil it, Peter! The point is, the main house is enormous – and there's a guest cottage – though Guy gets first refusal at weekends.' She made a face and then laughed. 'You can all stay. We're converting the barn into a workshop for me – the builders start next month. I'm snowed under with orders. The babies slowed everything down. You know the Galerie Lafayette is making enquiries? I'll have a full-time staff.'

'But Ireland—'

'It's just across the sea, Jan. I'll send you air tickets. As for you, Mala – get Miss Fancypants Chong here to take time off and drive over – it's beautiful.'

'I'd die in the countryside,' Caroline said.

'I used to say the same thing: but people change. I'm a mother of four turning over a hundred and fifty thousand pounds a year – I don't have time to enjoy London.' A hundred and fifty thousand a year – it was more than I could imagine. Allie started laughing again. 'Now who'd have thought I'd end up in a stately pile?'

# 18 ∫

The last place I expected to meet Josh was at a Saturday matinée of *A Chorus Line*. Margaret and I were coming down the side stairs of the Drury Lane Theatre humming 'Tits And Arse' when I saw him at the bottom, reading the programme.

'Josh, what are you doing here?'

'Standing.' He made a face. 'I thought I should see it before it closed. A mistake.'

'I loved it: this is my second time.'

I introduced Margaret and we wandered together across the main square in Covent Garden where the lovely old fruit hall was under tarpaulins for redevelopment. 'I can still remember coming up here in the holidays, can't you? The pavements were covered in fruit and veg boxes and there was always a beggar outside the church, like in *My Fair Lady*. You could smell the fruit as you turned into Long Acre.'

'I'm sure that's true,' Josh said, 'but I don't think I ever saw it.'

'My granny used to bring me here,' Margaret said. 'We'd have lunch at Simpson's on the Strand and walk back this way to buy peaches or clementines to take home for tea. It's so sad seeing it all boarded up.'

'Progress,' Josh said as we stopped to admire a mural on the makeshift builders' barricades: The Covent Garden Association – New Life in the City. 'New life. In a few years' time, we won't know the place. Another generation of memories turns to dust.'

'They say the best thing is to always look forward. If you tell yourself that each day is a new beginning, it's much easier.'

Josh looked at Margaret with interest. 'Who says that?'

'My shrink.' She laughed anxiously. He said nothing. 'It's called anorexia nervosa: a very grand term for self-starvation. If you think I look bad now, you should have seen me a year ago.'

'I don't think you look bad.'

I looked from one to the other suspiciously, but if Josh was moved by Margaret's bony Audrey Hepburn-ness, he was keeping his impulses firmly earthed. I felt distinct relief. 'Let's hope the station isn't shut for work today. Sometimes it feels like the whole of London is under wraps.'

'Hidden promise: a bit like you, Mala. Now, are you girls following an itinerary, or do you fancy walking down to Chinatown and trying out a new restaurant?'

Margaret frowned. 'Try it,' Josh said gently. 'If it makes you uncomfortable, we'll leave. One day at a time, remember?'

She was fine until the shredded seaweed arrived. 'There's a lot of oil in it, isn't there? You can see it on each strand.' She pushed her unused plate away. 'It's a risk. As it is, I'm feeling fine about myself. Would you mind if I went home? I'm stronger around boiled vegetables.'

I said: 'She's just started at South Bank Poly, so she's a bit jumpy. She had a place at Edinburgh, but she says the word "university" makes her break out in hives.'

We talked about work and Caroline's flat, which she'd recently had painted citrus and pink. 'It's like being sucked into an ice cream,' Josh said, 'comforting but cold.' He picked up a chilli prawn with his chopsticks and popped it in my mouth. 'Try this.'

'Is that my reward for balancing a ball on my nose?'

'It's an *incentive* to balance a ball on your nose.' I went red.

Afterwards we walked off some of the excess in Leicester Square, where a man was dancing to a portable gramophone: Yvonne Elliman, 'If I Can't Have You'. In Athena I splashed out on some Mucha posters. 'You're well and truly into the spirit of bed-sit land, aren't you?' Josh said. 'Do you have a bubble lamp as well?'

'Why don't you come and see?'

'Okay. Let's get a cab.'

My heart was in my mouth as we got into the taxi, but he placed a distance between us, looking at me with a thoughtful intensity as I plugged the gap with idle chitchat. I could feel heat, but didn't know if it was his or mine. As we entered the house I felt his breath on my neck and it was like a hundred volts shot through me, transforming the slightest contact into a charged sensate thrill. But he didn't touch me until I opened the door to my room. And when he did, it was like an explosion of energy filled the air with blue light. A sexual poltergeist, cupping my breasts from behind and pushing me on to the bed; tearing off clothes with a frenetic urgency and coming at me, it seemed, from all directions so that all I could do was lie there and feel with every inch of my being. A happy starfish pentacled out.

Afterwards, exhausted, he rolled over and lay next to me and I covered every inch of his pale body in kisses until he pulled me back up and held me tightly. 'You have the healing touch, Mala.'

'I love you.'

'And I love you.'

We lay there breathing in tandem for a long while; and I filed away each precious detail of those moments with an instinctive certainty they would never be repeated. Heaven must be like this.

Much later, Josh said gently: 'This can't happen again: you're like a sister to me. It would stop feeling right.'

'I know.'

Slowly we started to caress each other and the second time we made love, it really was that: something I'd never experienced in my whole life. When we were one, I wanted to stay like that always, but even then another part of me said: Let go.

So, at midnight, as he pulled on his clothes, I held him against me fiercely, but kissed him chastely.

'That was my first time, you know, since—'

'I know.' I put my finger against his lips, not wanting to hear her name.

He rested his head on my shoulder. 'You are very precious to me, Mala. A very special woman.' A woman . . .

As he started down the stairs I called: 'Josh: wait a minute.' I wrote down Margaret's phone number. 'If you're at a loose end, take her out and cheer her up – she needs an understanding friend.'

He looked amused. 'Perhaps I will.'

'Penny for the guy, missus?' Missus? I gave him just a penny for that! Going down the steps on to Waterloo Road I located my mum. 'What exactly do you want to buy, Mother?'

She sighed. 'I don't know. There are so many children and two weddings: expense, expense, expense.'

We walked down to The Cut where patch-leather handbags were a fiver and a flared black skirt with a frilled petticoat edging was just eight quid. 'But no one in Sri Lanka wears this nonsense, Mala. For you? Why not: a Christmas present *in absentia*.'

Two hours later there was something for everyone in her shopping trolley: clothes, chocolate, fabrics, Dinky toys. 'Let's hope the children are mainly boys.'

'We can work it out over lunch.'

As we went through the Waterloo underpass, she said: 'I wish you were coming with me, Mala.'

'I'll come next time, I promise, but I'm on news desk duty over Christmas. If I get it right, I might get off courts altogether.'

'You could have joined the Civil Service and been an executive officer if you'd completed your A-levels.'

I shook my head. 'Thanks, but I'm happy as I am.'

We took the exit for Upper Ground. 'You don't see Nihal now?' my mother asked casually.

'He's a Tory, he doesn't drink and he bought the *Grease* soundtrack. We've nothing in common.'

'Life is about compromise, Mala, not daydreams.'

Perhaps, I thought, but only when it has to be. Nihal was certainly drop-dead gorgeous, but that wasn't enough. I reeled through my night with Josh, knowing it had coloured everything for me: had proved that the impossible can happen. And while we had no future – how could we, when he was still so bowed by the past and my eyes were forever on fast forward – he had renewed my belief in fate. My belief in what my mother called karma.

We carried the trolley up the steps to the Royal Festival Hall entrance, our hair blown into our faces by the strong river wind. 'It'll be nice to be somewhere warm,' my mother said, 'though truly, after coming here, I can't stand the heat for any length of time.'

In the restaurant we got baked potatoes and coffees and found a table overlooking the Thames. 'In six weeks' time you'll be off, Mum. Do you remember when I stayed with Anu? She really made me work.'

'Always she had the makings of a headmistress.'

'I wish she'd let me write up that row.'

'You mustn't be capitalising on people's misfortune, Mala.'

'But she won. It's about beating the odds, Mum – like Allie; like Marie. I've written up Caroline for this week's *Paddington Mercury* – she's Park & Wright's youngest ever office manager – she's going to run the new Mayfair outlet.' I grinned. 'That's what's paying for our lunch.' She was unamused. I said: 'If you run off with a vicar, Mother, I promise not to sell the story.'

'*Chi*! You know I'm not interested in that sort of thing.'

'You're only forty-three: look at Elizabeth Taylor.'

'Once bitten, twice shy.'

'That was a lifetime ago.'

'A shark bite, child, is fatal.'


Dear Beth,

If you stay in Somerset any longer you'll turn into a Smurf! At least find yourself a rich farmer to marry. Otherwise come back and join the real world. We're all very well at this end. My grandad's died, but it's good timing because my mum's over there anyway. Caroline's driving around town in a BMW!! Al and Jan are still jogging along – she gave me a good NF story from the Ocean Estate the other week. The law centre's having a funding crisis. Merle and I have had a rent rise, but the landlord's doing up the bathroom and kitchen areas, so it's worth it. That's all, really. Happy Christmas.

Love, Mala.

'It's just lemon and sugar: traditional,' Merle said.

'Looks fantastic.' I took a bite. 'Delicious.'

'I got the batter just perfect. The secret is to chill it first.'

'God bless Shrove Tuesday.'

She took out a warming plate of pancakes from the oven. 'I'm going to fill these with an apple strudel mix – but you're only allowed one because the rest are for my guest.' I pricked up my ears. 'My *lady* guest.'

'And I thought you were finally bringing home a man.'

'Well, I am, sort of.'

'A drag queen?'

'A lesbian.' Oh. 'Like me.' No. 'I met her at an exhibition at the ICA: she was wearing foetus jewellery and we got talking.' Foetus jewellery? 'I've embarrassed you, Mala.'

'It's just that I—'

'It never occurred to you, did it?'

'No.'

'If you're worried, rest assured you're not my type.' I was both relieved and offended. She took my plate and loaded on the strudel pancake. 'I think free-range eggs produce better pancakes.' I nodded. 'They're creamier and lighter – though you need a sensitive palate to spot it.' I kept eating. 'What's wrong with you, Mala? Have you never come across a lesbian before?' I shook my head. 'Well, it's taken me a while to admit it, but why should I live a lie?' Why indeed: I made an appropriate face. 'For God's sake say something.'

I looked around, struggling for inspiration. Then saw it on the worktop. 'I'm just embarrassed, Merle, that's all. I should have noticed before that you like to keep all your eggs in the one basket.'

'When's your mum back from Sri Lanka?' Caroline said.

'Next week – it's taken three months to sort out her dad's land.'

'Is it arable or building land?'

'I didn't ask: I'm only interested if it's in Paddington.'

In the back, Jan and Al laughed.

'Does she see your father's people over there?'

'Why should she?'

'No reason at all.' Caroline nosed the sleek black saloon into Jermyn Street. 'You were wise to keep a distance, Mala. Martin was questioned by inspectors from the DTI last week

– they're investigating Luxy's backers.' She raised an eyebrow. 'The money may not have come from the sources he suggested.' She parked outside L'Ecu de France. 'Don't ever tell Martin I've told you – he wasn't exactly co-operative in case it prejudiced any transactions.'

'So you don't hear from Luxy any more?'

'The office line, which is also true, is that he stopped calling.'

'The story of his life. Here one day, not calling the next.'

I congratulated myself on my far-sightedness. Well done, Mala: let's hope he drowns in the spume from his own off-course rotor. And yet, inexplicably, part of me felt sorry for him.

As we got out of the car, Jan said: 'Why don't you write it up?'

'My dad?'

'You'd be playing with fire,' Caroline said.

'But you love all that, don't you, Mala?'

'Not when it's me that's going to need the plastic surgery.'

We walked down to 55. The guy at the door knew Caroline and let us in for free. Inside was a huge room with a long bar at one end and a dance-floor in the middle. We sat at a small round table and ordered cocktails. Al looked round unappreciatively. 'The white stiletto brigade.'

'Slightly more West End, Al: the Louis Vuitton handbag hags.'

'I wouldn't know.'

'Of course you wouldn't.' Caroline turned to me, her exotic features accentuated by a new elfin haircut. 'Franco should be here soon.'

'He must be pretty special if we're allowed to meet him.'

'What does he do?' Al asked.

'He sells personalised number plates.'

'You mean he makes them to order?'

'You can't make them to order – they're issued by the vehicle licensing centre. He buys cars with distinctive plates and arranges their transfer once they're sold.'

'And this makes money?'

'Ask him yourself.'

A gorgeous dark-haired man in a white silk shirt and expensive cords kissed her on the mouth and drew up a chair. 'I just

got the mother of all numbers: ten grand in an afternoon!'
He noticed us watching with interest. 'Hi.' Turning back to
Caroline, he said: 'How d'you fancy the Caribbean, Caro?'
Car-o? Another flip and he was facing the bar. 'Hey, Lou,
same again for everyone – and a Tab on the rocks for me.' He
spun back, grinning. 'Gotta keep my licence – I'm handling top
marques.' He paused for breath, catching us by surprise. 'Well,
aren't you going to ask me?'

'Ask you what, darling?' Darling!

'What kept me.'

'You said you'd got a great plate.'

'Yes, Caro, but what is it?'

Al said: 'A3? M1? 3D? B52? UB40? LIVERPOOL 8?'

Franco was unamused.

Caroline said: 'Give us a clue, Franco: is it a postcode, a set
of initials, what?'

'It's a body part.'

Al tried again: '2-W-I-N-G-S?'

'The human body.'

'4-I-S-E'

'Why don't you tell us, darling?'

'Okay – you'd never get near anyway. Listen to this: it's
P-E-N-1-5. Get it? P-E-N-1-5: penis!' Franco slapped the table
and roared. 'I told you it was the mother of all numbers!'

'Surely,' Al said, 'you mean it's the father.'

'All he can talk about is money, cars and holidays.'

'But he's young, rich, handsome: just what she always wanted.'

'You missed out a vital ingredient there, Beth: intelligent.'

'He can't be totally stupid. He must have something—'

'Sex. That's what he's got. She's finally been turned on. I just
hope she realises that's all it is: she's not one for being told.'

'I'm dying to see her. Does she think I let the side down?'

'You didn't let the side down: you let yourself down.'

'I worry that I don't fit in with Jan and Caroline any more.'

'Well, you'll find out soon enough; but don't forget it was
Jan who moved the earth to get you into rehab, and Caroline
*did* send you half her old wardrobe.'

As she sat on my mother's sofa, the only pointer to Beth's

past was her waxy skin and a slight nervous tic in her cheek. A friend had hennaed her hair and it tumbled redly down her back as she curled into a foetal ball. 'It's so strange being in charge of myself, Mala. First I had Dingo, then Geoff at the project. Now it's just me. I miss having someone to lean on.'

'Stop leaning: that was the point of the last two years.'

'Do you have a perfect man?'

'Yes: Bryan Ferry.' I stood up and touched my toes. 'If he asks me out, I don't want to say no because I've tied myself down to some idiot man. You're only young once, Beth.'

'But I feel ancient.'

'Become a Buddhist – then you get a second bite.'

'Don't let your mum hear you say that.' She watched as I straightened and stretched my arms into the air. 'It's ever so good of her to put me up again; I know she's busy making offerings for her father and all that.' Getting up, she rooted through the fridge. 'I should have sorted out a place of my own by the end of the month.' Out came the cheese. 'Maybe this job is my second bite. I know it doesn't sound exciting but there's a real rhythm to basketwork and it's a good thing for disabled people to earn their own money.' She popped a piece into her mouth. 'I think I'm quite good at teaching – even the hard stuff like chair seats.' She looked up crossly as I did an inner thigh stretch. 'Don't laugh, Mala. If it wasn't for this project I'd be back on the streets. Drugs give you a sort of momentum, you know; things happen without you having to think about it. But here I am with my own momentum.'

'You've done really well.' I watched as she systematically worked her way through the half-pound block of Cheddar. 'You'd better watch those calories.'

She laughed. 'I don't care. The more I fill out, the more normal I feel. When did you last see a fat drug addict?'

'I can't take this, Mum.'

'I want you to have it. It was left to me by my father.' Proudly, she opened the brown jewellery box and held it up so the extravagant decoration caught the light. 'This piece has been in the family for three generations. His mother was given it as a wedding present when she married the present Prime

Minister's great-grandfather's third cousin on the mother's side. This year is your coming of age, Mala. You're an adult now. You must reflect it in your tastes and behaviour.'

'You're making me feel old.'

I looked at the exquisite watch which reflected neither my taste nor my behaviour and said with honesty: 'I'll look after it properly, Mum. I'll keep it somewhere safe.' So I never have to wear it!

'At last you're learning the value of things. You're a good girl.'

'Am I?'

She gazed at me fondly. 'I told everybody at home how well you're doing. I showed them every cutting you sent. You are headstrong and impulsive, but you have a good heart and a sense of purpose that will see you successfully through life.'

'Like you?'

'I wish I could write like *you*. Even my diary is dull.'

'So's mine, but I'll turn it into something good one day.' She laughed. 'You're glad I'm not a pen-pusher for BT, Mum?'

'You're still a pen-pusher, Mala, but in a different way.'


'Is it strange being labelled the new Sex Pistols?'

'Who said anything about the Sex Pistols?'

'Your record company.'

'That's crap.'

'So you're not?'

'Not what, darlin'?'

'Not the new Sex Pistols.'

'Bollocks!'

'Never mind the bollocks – are you or aren't you?'

'We fucking hated the bastards.'

'So you're not?'

'Fuck off!'

'Is that because your music's better?'

'What is this, a CSE paper?'

'Do you?'

'Do we what?'

'Think your music's better?'

'Darlin', why don't you open your legs and do something

you're good at? Sex Pistols! Fuck off – they were fucking crap. Crap! Orright?'

'So how would you describe yourselves?'

'How would you describe us?'

'Punks.'

'She'd describe us as punks! Punks! Fuck off, you silly cunt! Punks! We're post-punk, orright? Fucking Sid Vicious – he fucked himself, didn't he? Punks! Silly fucking bitch! Why's she here?'

'I think maybe we'll call it a day,' said the lady from Chrysalis.

'Maybe I should have brought a bunch of bananas.'

At this, one of the band, possibly the drummer, jumped up and charged at me, apparently with the intention of blowing his nose in my hair. Ed, the agency photog, ran at him and was punched in the face for his pains. 'Fucking scum!' Around me the room erupted in chaos. A muscular roadie in a black T-shirt put his arms around my head and hustled me out. The PR lady came running behind. 'You know how it is; they've been spoiled by the trade press. All this Pistols stuff is a bit touchy.'

'But that's the line *you* sold us.' I looked up as Ed emerged rubbing his chin. 'Shall we get back?'

At the front door, the roadie caught up with us. 'Look, I'm really sorry about what happened there – can I buy you a drink?'

'Maybe later.'

We got into Ed's car. 'What a bloody waste of a morning.'

'Oh, it wasn't that bad, Mala. I got a couple of cracking close-ups when you upset them – plus a full frontal of that idiot coming at me. Write them up as a bunch of thugs, and we'll slip it into a diary somewhere.'

That evening I met the roadie for a drink at the Zanzibar. 'I'm sorry about this afternoon,' he said. 'They're a bunch of shits. I'll tell you whatever you want to know: they deserve it.'

Four hours later we were still there and he asked me out for the following Friday. I declined. 'It's my twenty-first birthday and I'm spending it with my three best friends in the whole world.'

\*　　\*　　\*

'You should have invited him,' Jan said, slowly dribbling spoon-fuls of warm Rocky Road ice cream into her mouth.

'I'm not interested.' I grinned. 'But I'm going to keep him guessing till he's back on the road with Roxy Music.'

'To help him hump amplifiers?'

'Of course not, Caroline. I'm hoping he'll help me hump Bryan Ferry.'

We all got the giggles. Bethany said: 'This is the best night I've had for years. I feel almost normal.' She took another After Eight. 'I'm rediscovering chocolate.'

'So what happened to Franco, Caroline?'

'Thank you for asking, Janice. We're no longer an item.'

'Why not?'

'He wanted to borrow money from me. I refused. He took this to mean I no longer wished to continue the friendship.'

I stopped mid-choc-nut-sundae. 'What did he need money for?'

'He's been having cash flow problems. He saw a plate that he thought could turn the company round.'

'But vagina's too long for a number plate.'

'Very funny, Mala.'

'What was it, then?' Jan said. 'Fanny?'

'I believe it was P-O-O-1-E.'

'Pooey? Who'd put that on their car?'

'My argument precisely.'

Now we laughed till the tears ran down our faces.

Janice suddenly sobered. 'My tub's empty. What else is there?'

I went out on to the landing and returned with chocolate éclairs, custard Danish, a dozen Penguins and another bottle of Tia Maria. 'I thought it might be a long night.'

Bethany bit into an éclair and it oozed down her front.

'That's my old Aquascutum sweater,' Caroline said. 'Have some respect for it.'

I passed across a white cotton hanky with lace insets. 'Use this.'

Bethany stopped, fingering it lovingly. 'It's beautiful.'

'A birthday present from my mum.'

'That's a bit old-fashioned, isn't it?' Jan said.

'Family tradition: the start of my bottom drawer.'

'This brings back memories.' Beth pressed it to her face. 'Remember how we used to spend sixpences in the linen shop?'

I nodded. 'This one will always remind me of tonight. I'll have to knot the corners – one for each of us.'

She handed it back. 'Don't spoil it. I'll get a cloth.'

I put it away and took out the ornate silver watch. 'My mum gave me this as my main present: for my coming of age. She says I'm an adult now.'

'She's noticed, then?' Jan put it on her wrist and turned it to the light. 'It's midnight! I promised Al I'd be home by now. He needs some notes typed up for the morning.'

'Are they urgent?'

'Not really, but I promised.'

'Bugger Al,' Caroline said. 'Let him read his own handwriting. Be your own woman, Janice.'

'Yes: bugger Al,' Jan said, pouring a second glass of liqueur. 'I was up at six making his breakfast – I deserve a night off.'

I sank my head despairingly into my hands.

Caroline snapped: 'What's the matter with you, Mala?'

'I am weeping for womankind.'

'You mean Janice?' And somehow this was terribly funny and we all, including Jan, roared.

Later, when we were all prone on various pieces of furniture, Jan asked: 'Has it been a good year for you?'

'Yes. The best.'

'For all of us, I think,' Caroline said, stretching elegantly. 'I'm thinking of starting my own agency: I've found this area called West Hampstead – it's full of dying refugees from the Second World War: huge houses – you could get at least four flats from each. The commission possibilities are endless.'

'Don't you think about anything but money?'

'Forgive me for finding it slightly more exciting than cane footstools, Bethany.'

'Take no notice,' I said, keeping a straight face. '*I* think you're brilliant. One day I'll do a story about you: Reformed Heroin Addict Makes Good.'

'Thousands don't.'

'In that case you'll have us to answer to: I don't want any needles near my old lambswool sweaters.'

'And I love you too, Caroline,' Beth said gently.

'Put the coffee on.'

I went out and pulled some cups together. It was three o'clock in the morning and I felt brilliant: I was twenty-one. Twenty-one! The previous morning, my story and Ed's snaps of the Industrial Savages had made three front pages. That afternoon, one of our old reporters had called to ask if I'd like freelance shifts on one of the tabloids. I am a pig in shit, I thought, spooning out the Nescafé.

Balancing the mugs on a dinner plate, I went back into the room. Bethany was asleep in the middle of the floor and Jan had put on a record; Gonzalez: 'Haven't Stopped Dancing Yet'.

Caroline uncurled herself and took the drinks from me. 'This has really been a brilliant evening,' she said.

I laughed. 'I know. Isn't life great?'